WHERE THE JASMINE BLOOMS

a novel

WHERE THE JASMINE BLOOMS

a novel

by ZEINA SLEIMAN

Roseway Publishing
an imprint of Fernwood Publishing
Halifax & Winnipeg

Copyright © 2025 Zeina Sleiman
All rights reserved. No part of this book may be reproduced or transmitted in any form by any means without permission in writing from the publisher, except by a reviewer, who may quote brief passages in a review.

Development editing: Fazeela Jiwa
Copyediting: Amber Riaz
Cover design: Ruth Ormiston
Text design: Lauren Jeanneau
Printed and bound in the UK

Published by Roseway Publishing
an imprint of Fernwood Publishing
Halifax and Winnipeg
2970 Oxford Street, Halifax, Nova Scotia, B3L 2W4
www.fernwoodpublishing.ca/roseway

Fernwood Publishing Company Limited gratefully acknowledges the financial support of the Government of Canada through the Canada Book Fund and the Canada Council for the Arts. We acknowledge the Province of Manitoba for support through the Manitoba Publishers Marketing Assistance Program and the Book Publishing Tax Credit. We acknowledge the Nova Scotia Department of Communities, Culture and Heritage for support through the Publishers Assistance Fund.

Library and Archives Canada Cataloguing in Publication
Title: Where the jasmine blooms : a novel / by Zeina Sleiman.
Names: Sleiman, Zeina, author.
Identifiers: Canadiana 20240504992 | ISBN 9781773637204 (softcover)
Subjects: LCGFT: Novels.
Classification: LCC PS8637.L465 W44 2025 | DDC C813/.6—dc23

*To Jeddo and Teta, Mama and Baba,
and all my ancestors who suffered at the hands of colonial oppression.
May we bear witness to the liberation of Palestinians wherever we may be.*

CHAPTER 01

April 2006

I have this fixed image of my mother. She's sitting in a stained armchair with a threaded needle in one hand, her clothes stacked on a table next to her. She sips coffee from a tiny cup and begins repairing her clothes, always at the neckline because that's where she liked to start ripping. When Mama got angry, she'd grip her shirt there and, with her strength alone, she would would tear the very fabric through the middle. The last time she threatened to do this, we were at the local grocery store in Montreal. I had asked her about going back to Lebanon for a visit.

"Who put that idea in your head?" she responded.

It was my friend Samar, who recounted enchanting stories from her summer in Soor. She ate fresh figs, swam in the open sea, and spent nights playing board games with her cousins. "I want to meet our family, Mama," I insisted.

She took a deep breath and placed a bag of tomatoes in her basket, then leaned down in front of me and looked into my eyes with a glare that said these would be her final words on the matter. "Yasmine. There is nothing but 'araf in Lebanon. It will suck you dry of happiness and any sense of belonging."

I was ten at the time, with a burgeoning sense of control over my life, and her answer wasn't sufficient. I stomped my feet and yelled back. "I want to go next summer!"

She dumped the groceries on top of the stack of avocados, the milk carton falling to the floor and making a splatter. Gushing liquid leaked onto my new sandals. She grabbed my wrist and I tugged it away.

"No! Not until you promise!"

All eyes were on us.

"Wallahi Yasmine, if you keep this up, I'm going to rip my clothes right here and everyone will look at you like you're the daughter of a crazy person." Her hands gripped the top of her shirt — a threat.

I understood, then, that I had lost the battle, and we never spoke of Lebanon again.

Since then, I have learned that there are two types of Arab women. The quiet ones who observe the oppression around them, who take orders and nod, believing they exist solely to serve yet quietly making plans to escape to where they might breathe, where they might let their lungs propel oxygen into every nook of their limbs so they may experience the relief that comes from nurturing their neglected bodies — the same bodies that house their cracked hearts and their tears, perceived by no one. Then there are the angry ones, like my mother, who can no longer contain the frustration of servitude and of witnessing their loved ones suffer due to war and displacement. These women's hearts splinter and there is no one around to hold them.

Now, I picture Mama shaking her head as I stand in front of the Beirut-Rafic Hariri airport. At twenty-seven, a grown woman, I am still afraid of disappointing my dead mother. The people here remind me of her. Everyone moves with a quiet rage, like the world merely functioning is inconveniencing them.

I close my eyes for a moment, breathing in the scent of humidity and petrol and try to quiet the chaos outside. The sound of my cousin's sweet voice shakes me out of my thoughts. In so many ways, Reem reminds me of Mama, or what Mama might have been like had she had a chance to live longer and experience happiness. She moves through life propelled by her resistance to rules, demanding all that's rightfully hers, insisting that rights exist for people like her. She has hope.

I walk past the slew of cars and cross the street, falling into her thick arms. I hold on to her hand for a moment, admiring her brown eyes and plump lips, noting their resemblance to mine. I put a thumb on her cheek and gently rub her face.

She takes my hand off.

"It's nice to finally be here," I tell her.

She pulls me into a hug. "You're skinnier and shorter than I thought, and your skin ... You'll have to show me how you get that smoothness." We speak in comfortable Arabic as she packs my suitcase into the trunk of the car.

I clip my seatbelt on, and she asks about my flight. I tell her that I spent two dollars buying ketchup at a restaurant in Austria during my connection and that I panicked as the plane landed in Beirut because I couldn't see the land from my window. It looked like we were going to be crashing into the water.

"Did Yousef finally accept that you'd be coming on this trip?" Her car speeds across a ramp and moves onto the highway.

"He doesn't have a choice. Plus, his mind has been on his wedding lately."

"What about Tariq? Did you tell him you were coming?"

I shake my head and run my finger across my bottom lip. I haven't spoken to Tariq in six months, not since we'd announced our intention to divorce to his parents, or rather my intention.

I rest my elbow on the window. On my left, the Mediterranean Sea flows in its vastness. Mama used to say that the ocean scared her. It was too big, with too many unknown creatures living below the surface, lurking in the darkness: "The water could just suck you away, and you wouldn't know what hit you."

To my right, the ground expands upward with hills towering over more hills. Flat-roofed homes, churches, and mosques line the curvature of the earth surrounded by overflowing greenery, punctured by narrow gravel paths that lead up toward the magnitude of the open sky. When I was a kid, my Lebanese friends all referred to this place as "the Switzerland of the Middle East," and I could see now how their love for the natural landscape and its people could make them desperate to believe in what their home country had the potential to be — a country where diverse people flourished under the burning sun, through the generosity of the earth and the immensity of the open sea, if only it wasn't haunted by the impacts of colonialism, perpetual corruption, and the consequences of a fifteen-year civil war.

"This is going to be a good summer; it's been a peaceful year." Reem speaks to me as if we are sisters, like we've known each other our entire lives. She had reached out to me three years ago through Facebook, and our connection was instant. She has everything I want: knowledge of our family history and a grounding in our heritage. And I think I give her an opening to a possible future in Canada. During our earlier conversations, she asked me about school programs, scholarships, and visa applications, and I passed on information willingly, enamoured by the prospect of having family nearby. At first, our relationship was transactional, and then our conversations became an escape from the upheaval of my life in Toronto.

"InshAllah," I say.

Palm trees and large billboards line the highway advertising everything from perfumes to an upcoming Wael Kfoury concert and Abu Arab's bread pies. We pass Arabized versions of familiar fast-food chains. I wonder what drives people to desire Burger King or Dunkin' Donuts when there are local restaurants selling all sorts of delicacies native to this part of the world.

"Can we get some shawarma?"

She side-eyes me. "Like, right now?"

"No, I'm not hungry, but eventually. I want to taste the real thing."

She laughs. "Do they not have real chicken in Canada?"

"They do, but there are no good shawarma places in Toronto. They all mince the meat into tiny shreds and the garlic sauce is just watered down with yogourt and potato starch."

She wrinkles her nose. "Maybe we'll go tomorrow. There's this place near my work."

Once in town, she speeds past red lights, assuring me that people don't follow traffic signs here and that stopping would cause an accident. She rolls down her window and yells at someone who cuts her off. "Ya ibn il kalb, kiss ikhtak sharmouta!" Vulgar words I haven't heard since Mama died. Words she once used on the phone in conversation with people she never introduced to us.

I ask Reem to stop, discomforted by the prospect of a stranger following us to get revenge. "Let him try to come, then I'll really teach him a lesson." She smiles mischievously and the car stops in front of a three-storey brick building with a red-tiled roof: the place that's going to be my home for the next six months. A jasmine bush with tiny white flowers running along the edge of the entrance covers arched windows.

We get out of the car and she helps me with my bags until we get to the door. "Are you going to be okay? You can still stay with us, you know."

I hesitate for a moment with my fingers on my suitcase. "I'll be fine." I force a smile, hoping that my face masks the unease brewing inside of me. What might come of living alone for the very first time? This is going to be it, my attempt to — as my therapist suggested — embrace the unknown.

She says okay, and we say our goodbyes.

The heels of my shoes clap against the uneven stone floors as I walk past the thin hallway leading me into an open courtyard. The sweet scent of jasmine is intoxicating, and I gasp at the beauty masked by the structure's outer walls. The building is an old Syrian-style home renovated into a series of small bachelor apartments and long-term hotel rooms. Blue and green tiles embossed with red tulips cover the only walls that aren't canopied by vines. A large fountain made of ceramic tiles and surrounded by herb plants ornaments the centre of the courtyard.

An older, tall woman in a blue hijab and long grey abaya greets me in English from behind a reception desk with a warm smile.

"Welcome to Athar Suites. I am Intissar, the owner of this hotel. Did you already book?"

"Yes, I called to book a few months ago," I respond in Arabic.

Her face glows and she switches to Arabic. "Oh, you're Lebanese. We get a lot of people who study at the institute nearby and they all think they can speak the language before they know anything," she chuckles. "But between you and me, I'm not sure what language they think they are speaking. I can't understand a word they say. Where are you from habibti?"

"I'm from Canada, but my parents are originally from Trablous."

She writes something down on a piece of paper. "Are you staying at this hotel alone? Why are you not staying with your family?"

I fiddle with my hoop earring. "I don't have a lot of family and my parents are gone."

"Oh, I'm so sorry, Allah yirḥamon." She raises an eyebrow. "What about a husband?"

"No, it's just me. I am doing some work for my PhD."

Her eyes fill with pity. "A beautiful girl like you, you shouldn't have trouble finding someone." She puts a set of keys on the counter. "Come down in the morning and I'll make sure you have a good meal." She leans over the counter and whispers. "Oh, also, Yasmine. Don't let anyone know that you're here alone. Come to me if you need anything." She hands me a sheet of paper with her number on it and I place it in my bag before turning away.

I roll my suitcase down to the single elevator. A man with thick dark hair stands with his back to me. Tariq had hair like that. It was one of my favourite things about him. Especially when he'd let me run my hands through it, creating a rare moment of harmony between us. Truth is, there wasn't much beyond those rare moments of peace with him. I remember the week after he passed the bar exam when his life was absent of the stressors that brought out his rage. He was happy, and whenever that happened, he was generous with his love. I held onto those moments like a raft in a hurricane for as long as I could, until it wasn't viable anymore.

The elevator pings and the man opens the door, gesturing for me to go in first. I avoid eye contact and walk toward the far end, resting my back against the cold wall. It makes a large rumbling noise and shakes as we move up.

A few seconds into the ride, the lights flicker for a moment and then everything goes dark. The elevator halts to an abrupt stop. I widen my eyes to see better, but it's useless.

"You okay?" The man asks in Arabic.

I rummage through my purse and find my phone along with the paper that Intissar handed me, dialling it with trembling hands. "Khalto, the elevator stopped working. Please, can you help? I'm stuck inside and I can't see anything. What should we do?"

"Oh, don't worry habibti, it's because the power went out. I forgot to tell you that we lose power every day. We have a generator, but it's being fixed right now. Can you wait a little bit?"

"No, Khalto! Please, get me out of here now."

The stranger puts his hand on my shoulder and I shrug it off.

"Okay, okay, I will get some people and come and get you out. Don't worry, this happens all the time. You will be fine."

I take deep breaths, pacing around the small space, counting the steps from one end to the other. My head spins. I'm exhausted from the trip.

The man clears his throat. "Mashi, mashi. We're fine; this happens all the time."

We are not fine. I am not fine, but he can't possibly understand that and I am not going to explain myself to a stranger who thinks he can tell me how to feel or what to do. I say nothing. He whispers incoherent things to himself, and we stay like this for a few minutes until a crack of light appears from above.

"Can you climb up?" A man looks down at me, kneeling next to the half-visible door, a crowbar in his hand.

I take a deep breath. "I'll try."

"Here, I'll prop you up." The stranger in the elevator bends down on one knee, making a step by interlacing his fingers. I regret my previous assumptions about him.

I put one foot on his hands and leap up, reach the floor, and crawl onto solid ground. My companion follows me. He propels his body up with nothing but the strength of his arms.

"My suitcase!" I yell.

Intissar steps forward. "I'll get it for you when the power comes back."

The stranger and Intissar eye me with disconcerted pity. It is the same way people looked at Mama in that grocery store. They see that you need help but are afraid of what you're holding. It's also the look Tariq's parents gave me when I told them what he'd done to me. They knew it was true, but they couldn't bear to live in a world where that knowledge was made public.

"I'm so sorry for making you all come here," I say.

"Oh, don't worry about it habibti. It's okay. It can be scary if you're not used to it." She rubs my arm. My heart slows, and blood begins to flow to my limbs.

"Do you need help getting to your room?" The man from the elevator asks.

I shake my head and thank him before he walks away.

Intissar follows me to my room and lingers at my door, watching me struggle with the key. I turn it clockwise and then counter clockwise before she grabs it from me and opens the door herself.

She steps to the side and hands me the keys. "Are you going to be okay?"

"Yes, I'll be fine as soon as I can get my suitcase. Thank you."

"I'll have a few snacks and some tea brought to you. It might calm your nerves."

I thank her and she walks away. I close the door behind her and turn the large metal lock, securing myself in the little apartment. There's a single bed near a window with a white crochet blanket laid on top of a thicker leopard-print flannel. A blue armchair is nestled by a sliding door that opens out onto a balcony. I step outside and lean my hands on the black metal railing, absorbing the view of the sun setting over the Mediterranean. Waves crash against rough edges of earth, splattering the grass between my new building and the shoreline. Car horns and bird songs vibrate from behind the building.

I take my socks off and lie back on a green plastic chair at the corner of the balcony. I stay there until the sun disappears beyond the horizon and only a glimmer of light remains. The wind brushes the soles of my feet, dust swirling across the floor. I tell myself I'm going to be okay, nestled in this little room.

I stay that way until someone knocks on the door. I open it to find no one there, but I see my bright pink suitcase with a large manila envelope resting on top of it. I lean closer to read the words written in Arabic: "Deliver to Yasmine Hassan."

A tingling sensation runs across the back of my neck. I gingerly grab the package and put it on the table near the kitchenette. For a second, my mind explores the possibility of poisonous powders hiding in the envelope. The writing is unfamiliar. Nobody besides Reem and my faculty adviser knows where I'm staying. I wonder if Tariq tracked me down and is threatening me with something. No, he's not that evil.

A forceful wind blows in from the balcony.

I take a fork and crack open the envelope. Inside are little papers and notebooks. I grab a spatula to pull out a sheet. It's a note written in Arabic: "Yasmine, your father left these in my care. Some of them are letters he wrote to your mother after you went to Canada, letters he never sent. Others are things from his research. I hope you can benefit from them."

It's not signed, but that isn't the most jarring thing about it. What shakes me is that my father left all this behind, that he had been alive after we had moved to Canada. I had always been under the impression that he disappeared during the war, right before we left.

I swallow the lump in my throat. The voices in my head grow louder, telling me I'm foolish. Mama's voice rings clear, warning me not to go digging into our past to undo all the work she had done to forget her pain, to forget the hardships she had endured and the misfortunes that had come with losing her family and having to resettle in a country across the oceans, sans any familiar comforts — alone.

No, I don't want to forget and pretend like things are okay.

I close my eyes and picture Baba alive, remembering his last day with us spent by the jasmine bush in our yard and the worn edges of his brown leather suitcase. He had stopped by the old Mercedes and called out to Yusuf and me for hugs. We had run to him and he had smothered both of our faces with his wet kisses before disappearing from our lives forever. That's how I remember it. That's how I like to remember it. But now I don't know if his last hug was longer than usual or if his briefcase was actually a suitcase.

My body feels drained, and I huddle in the bed's corner. A heaviness weighs down my limbs and my heart fills with a longing for everything I know I want but don't understand.

CHAPTER 02

After dropping Yasmine off at her hotel, I drive down to Beirut to celebrate with friends for our upcoming graduation. I have often wondered what I might have become had I grown up in a different place, under different circumstances. Yasmine is as close as I'll ever get to seeing it, like that spam mail that tells you they'll predict your future or what your kids might look like if you pass on the email to ten other people. Only, she's real.

Surprisingly, she's not as foreign as I thought, and this perplexes me. How does someone hold onto a language when they are surrounded by foreign voices? How and why had she held onto her faith when she had been surrounded by temptations of ease and comfort? These are questions I've asked her in the past, but her answers have left me unsatisfied. She doesn't understand the premise of them, how strange it is for someone like me who's never left Lebanon. My goal this summer is to give her a taste of life here, both the good and the bad, so she can understand my questions.

For now, there's a week left until the end of term, and this may be the last time I see my friends. When I get to the Bay Rock Café, I see a familiar figure standing by the arched entryway. Only, I hadn't expected to see Hamza tonight. He's still, eyeing passing cars with hands in his pocket like he's waiting for someone. His hair is gelled back and there are no obvious scars on his face.

I haven't seen him since we broke up a few days before the incident. I rub my sweaty palms against my thighs and wait for him to move. But he just surveys the area with his wandering eyes. His narrow shoulders are stiff.

I step out of the car, careful not to trip with the heels I'm unaccustomed to wearing, and I hear his footsteps rushing toward me.

"Reem!"

"Hi, Hamza. It's so good to see you." I plaster on a smile and keep walking toward the restaurant.

"Wait. How are you?" We stop on the narrow path leading to the entrance. The music is loud and people squeeze around us to get through.

"I'm okay. You look like you're doing good."

"Yeah, I just ... I thought you'd call or come see me in the hospital." He rubs the back of his neck.

"I've just been busy." I turn and walk into the restaurant. He's by my side, our hands an inch away from each other. Sarah, Maysaa, and Omar are sitting at a large table by the edge of the patio overlooking the Beirut cliff. I settle into the brown leather chair and breathe in the ocean spring. The latest Haifa Wehbe song plays overhead. Twinkly lights and candles light up the space as the sun sets.

Maysaa and Sarah offer me a puff from the argileh they share. I take it. Omar eventually lifts his eyes from his cellphone and greets Hamza with a hug.

"Your leg is finally healed." He taps him on the back as Hamza launches into an explanation.

Sarah nudges me and softly asks, "Are you guys back together?"

"No, we just arrived at the same time."

"Look at him, he's so sad and traumatized. Just marry him already."

I twist my lips and straighten my hijab.

I would have married him. Hamza and I were together for four months. He made me laugh and feel safe. He'd been unusually drawn to my loud-natured temperament and, over time, I pictured the possibility of waking up next to him, then drinking a coffee that he'd lay out for me. I'd pictured him coming home to me and then cuddling and watching Syrian dramas until we fell asleep. I dreamt of a life that was easier, where I didn't have to worry about money, because he would work at his family's bank and I — well, I'd spend my days at home, cooking and cleaning because I couldn't become a lawyer like

I wanted to. Palestinians cannot hold positions of power or jobs that might give us influence.

Eventually I had asked if he'd consider moving away with me to another country. "This is where I belong," he had said. That was our last day together, because I knew then that I had no future with him. I couldn't spend my days idling over housework, waiting for someone to come home. That space I had carved out in my heart for that easier life would fill with resentment, and neither of us deserved that. So, I took those fantasies of partnership and sealed them away into the back of my mind.

I hear Omar asking Hamza about his plans for the year, if he was going to graduate with us. He tells us that he's going to stay behind for another year to make up for lost time.

I can't help but interrupt. "You should get the government to pay for that semester. In other countries, you would get compensated if something like that happened to you." I quickly look down at the menu, even though I can't afford anything beyond the fruit cocktail.

Omar laughs. "Yes, well in other countries, people don't get assassinated on a regular basis and you don't need to be afraid of an old Mercedes parked on the road."

Hamza tilts his head toward me. "My parents are paying for it and honestly, I don't want to think about it. I just want to forget about everything."

"Did you go see a psychologist?" Maysaa asks.

"I'm fine. I don't need a therapist. I just needed time to realize that this event was just a freak coincidence and the odds of it happening again are slim."

It's a lie. The trauma is written all over his face, in the way his leg shakes and his eyes dart from one corner to another. Nobody gets over something like that. I don't care how many times people act like these explosions are normal. My heart reverberates with unease every single time a blast is announced, every time the earth shakes, signalling destruction. I don't want to be desensitized to it, because that's how it all begins. That's how corruption and greed take root, when the consequences no longer send shivers up your spine and it all becomes normal. This can't be my life.

"Does this make you change your mind about staying in Lebanon?" Sarah asks Hamza.

His eyes meet mine. "A part of me wants to stay here even more. Like there's more of a need, like maybe I can make a difference and stop these things from happening again."

I scoff. "What are you going to do? Singlehandedly stop the Syrians or the Israelis from interfering in our country? Right. If only Hariri had hired you before he got blown up, then maybe we'd all be saved." I have a sudden image of us all in class, the walls shaking. We all heard the explosion that killed the prime minister. We didn't know then that it would be one of many assassinations in this country.

No one speaks, but Sarah shakes her head and I receive the message loud and clear: I've gone too far. Hamza's passion is admirable. I just wish it didn't cost me my dream of access to a better life. He should have never made me choose between him and my future.

"Sorry, it's actually none of my business." I drink from my cocktail.

The conversation shifts to our summer plans. Sarah and Omar are going back to Dubai to live with their family. Maysaa has a job at the airport. I'm still looking, but I have a stable backup teaching gig at the Arabic Institute. I don't tell them about my plans to move next year, once I get accepted into a graduate program abroad. My grades, my efforts are going to be my ticket out of this country. We finish our food a few hours later and agree to meet next week and say our goodbyes.

'Ammo Faisal is sitting outside his café in the dark when I get home. His shop is more of a nook really, with its slanted roof and no real walls, nestled between two buildings. Baba helped him build a small kitchen in the back before he died, the same way he helped a lot of people upgrade their homes in the camp. He installed doors, fixed windows, put in bathrooms, and repaired leaking roofs. When my grandparents first came here in 1948, they lived in a tent. Over time, the prospect of returning home to Palestine dominated stories more than reality, and the tents slowly transformed. They built shacks to shield themselves from the cold winter months and, as years turned into decades, the tin roofs and makeshift cloth walls were upgraded to cement. Bathrooms and kitchens were installed for those who could afford them. Generations of families grew up here, and the buildings grew too — upward, because there was nowhere else. The Lebanese government wasn't going to expand the walls of our encampment and continued to keep us isolated from the rest of the population.

A group of men shout amicably at each other over a game of tarnib from inside the café. 'Ammo Faisal's eyes are low and I wonder if he's sleeping, his arms folded and his green plastic slippers swinging above the gravel.

"Assalamu 'alaykum 'Ammo," I say.

He looks up and shines a toothless grin. "What are you doing out so late Reem? People will see you."

I shrug. "Let them see me. What are they going to do?"

"Nobody can contain you, ya Reem." He stands up. His back is hunched over and the soles of his slippers scrape against the ground. "Wait here. I have something for your mom."

I stand across from the parking lot. The light of the full moon reflects off the metal of cars. During the day, this is the only place where you can feel the sun's rays unobstructed by crowded structures. At night, it's where the cats come to sleep — in the cracks between the walls.

"Here, my kids came to visit me last week and they brought me some medicine. It's too much for me, so give it to your mom." He hands me a green plastic bag filled with bottles of Tylenol, Advil, and Tums. 'Ammo Faisal's two children live overseas and constantly distribute bottles of painkillers and antacids like candy. I thank him and he tells me to go home before anyone sees me.

I move through the narrow alleyway toward the edge of the camp. The homes are all attached to each other and only doors decipher the line between dwellings. A new painting adorns the wall next door to our house. Moussa, the neighbour's kid, is a skilled but secret artist. Most people don't know that he's the one who painted the large olive tree in the centre of the wall by 'Ammo Faisal's shop. This new artwork on the wall next door looks like a white bird with clipped wings hovering over a large apple tree. It isn't finished, but I admire the way Moussa uses imperfections from the cracks in the walls to create a feathered texture for the bird.

Mama whispers from above while I'm staring at Moussa's artwork. "Reem, where have you been? Stop lingering outside and come in."

I don't respond to her but walk inside the house quietly, careful not to awaken my little sister Fatme. I trade my shoes for my slippers in the entryway. All the lights are off and I make my way upstairs. In my room, I remove my hijab, run my fingers across my long curls, and sit on my bed with a blanket covering my feet. I pull out my instructor binder and lay out the student profiles for the new semester. A light breeze through my window rustles the stained curtains.

There are five students in my Arabic language class this term. Saroise is from the United States, here to study Arabic for her Masters degree as is Eric from Yale and Adar from NYU. Another student is from Montreal doing the same, but the fifth one's origins and purpose are unclear. His name is Minjoon Haddad, a common Lebanese family name. But he looks Asian and has a degree from the University of Toronto. He graduated seven years ago. His profile doesn't include a current address or an occupation.

I lean back against my pillow and scratch my chin. The school typically requires that kind of information upon registration; it helps the instructors tailor their lesson plans. When it's not there, it means they either omitted it for my files at Minjoon's request, or it was never provided and they made an exception. There are only two reasons why the school would do this. The student may have connections in high places, potentially a child of someone important or a diplomat. The other possible explanation is that he is a criminal, wanted by someone. Maybe he's that one student I've been waiting for. The absence of information gives me space to fantasize about him having connections that might provide a pathway to a life overseas. Someone who might be enamoured by my charismatic personality and my grades; someone who might make my exit from this country easier. I've been waiting for it to happen ever since I started teaching, but so far, I've had students with no real power who just ask about my life as a refugee to make themselves feel better in their pity for me. I never fully understood privileged people's obsession with dwelling on other people's misery.

The door to my room creaks and Mama walks in. "Where were you?" she whispers.

"I was out with school friends. I told you." I stack the pages and stuff them into the folder.

"You said you were going to pick up Yasmine." She rubs her hands together. "Who are these friends you were with? What will people say if they see you coming home at this hour?"

"Here." I hand her the medicine. "'Ammo Faisal wanted me to give you these."

"Ah, Allah bless his hands." She peeks inside and forgets about her scolding. "What about the doctor? Are we still going tomorrow?"

I sigh. "Mama, we went to see the doctor last week, and he said you're fine." She does that a lot, forgets that something happened or imagines things that didn't. It all began after Baba died in that car accident eight years ago. Last week she came home frantic, declaring that she had seen my brother Ahmad at the souq. She said he looked at her and when she called out to him, he ran. "It was different this time," she said, trying to convince me that her sighting was real.

"What about Ahmad? Did you go ask the shopkeeper if he saw him? Did you show him the picture I gave you?"

I didn't. My brother went to Syria three years ago in an attempt to find work. He sent money back occasionally, and then about a year ago, the money stopped coming and he couldn't be reached. My aunt said that he went to Homs for a better job, but nobody was able to locate him and we haven't heard from him since. I'd always assumed that he bolted, trying to make a living on his own and be free from the constraints of supporting a family at such a young age. Or maybe he just died.

I put a hand on her shoulder. "Mama, it wasn't Ahmad that you saw last week."

"Are you sure? Did you show him the picture?"

"Mama, I'm telling you it wasn't him."

"Ya Reem. It was him, I know it. Go tomorrow and check please."

"Okay." I rub her back and walk her to her room. Mama lives a life preoccupied with fixing the past, regretting the choices she'd made as if she could bring our loved ones back through her remorse. She even regretted mundane things, like the shoes she bought or what she made for dinner, constantly caught in this loop of imagining what her life might have been like if she took different steps, if she made different choices. I would have thought that she would have conceded at some point and learned to let go of the things that she couldn't control. Learned that none of it was her fault. But no, Ahmad's disappearance and Baba's death made it worse. She tightened her grasp on the future, circling through possibilities of an alternate life.

I'm not going to live stuck in the past. My teaching, work, and grades are going to form openings for me inshAllah. I'm going to live in the reality of my life.

CHAPTER 03

The next morning, I open my eyes and stare at the envelope lying on top of the wooden dresser. I blink once, twice, then run my fingers along the quilted fabric of my blanket. A rooster crows and cars honk outside.

The letters. They're staring back at me, threatening to expose all of Mama's secrets. She never did explicitly say that Baba died. I rarely asked her about him, but the few times I did her eyes swelled with tears and she shrugged off the question with something about the past being out of our control. "He loved you and that's all you need to know." Only the dead were referred to in the past tense.

I walk across the bedroom and lay them out on the table. There's a notebook and five letters written in black ink. The blue on the outside of the notebook is faded like the summer sky. Inside, it's filled with Baba's writing.

November 2, 1972. S. meets with Suleiman Frangieh's aid. Gives him money.

October 3, 1973. S. purchases land in Aramoun, a druze town.

December, 1974. C. takes family and hides in North Beirut, during B bombing.

February 1977. S. interacts with Jumblatt's aids.

March 1977. Kamal Jumblatt. Murdered.

Pages and pages of names and events that mean nothing to me. Encrypted messages of murders, land purchased, money exchanged, people who went missing, and random locations. Was he collecting information for reporting? Was he documenting something for a greater purpose? Why was this notebook passed on to me? I recognize a few of these politicians' names but mostly, the words are foreign.

I rub my temples, pull my knees up to my chest, and lean closer to the paper.

Baba stretched out the space between the circle and the line in his م, he connected the two dots of the ت and formed a straight line. His fingers had once touched these papers and his breath had hovered over this ink. I hold the notebook against my chest, a treasure trove of remembrance, and I close my eyes.

A few minutes later, someone knocks on the door. I zip my sweater up and put the letters inside a drawer before opening the door.

"Good, you're awake. Come downstairs. I made foul this morning." Instissar places a hand on the door frame.

"Thanks, Khalto, but I'm not that hungry."

Her eyebrows gather and she folds her arms. "Nonsense. Come and eat. Once you've tried this foul, you'll never want to eat anything else." She raises an eyebrow and turns around. "Yallah, I'm waiting for you downstairs. Don't make me come back up here."

A few minutes later, I'm downstairs looking for a table in the crowded courtyard when someone by an arched window catches my eye. The brown window edges match the frames of his glasses. His eyes are focused on a book on the round metal table. His straight black hair is a little longer than I remember it and his long fingers wrap around a glass tea cup. He looks up, like he senses that I'm staring, and our eyes meet. A relaxed smile crosses his face and I lose a breath. He walks over.

"Yasmine?" His eyes are kind, and I hold onto the familiarity in that gaze.

Surely, it can't be him, halfway across the world from where we met.

He takes a step forward. "Yasmine, it's Ziyad. From undergrad." His hand rests on his chest, as if trying to convince me. The man who hasn't left my mind in seven years. And here he is, looking at me with the same eyes that once made me feel like the world was filled with infinite possibilities.

"Oh my god, Ziyad, what are you doing here?" It already feels strange to speak in English.

"I'm studying Arabic, taking a little break from life." He laces his hand through his hair and gestures toward his table. "Come sit with me."

I follow him across the fountain, away from the prying eyes of Intissar's guests.

He pushes the seat back for me. "This is so crazy." He breathes deeply, his eyes searching mine. "Yasmine." We stare at one another like we're both convincing each other that this moment is real. "What are you doing here?" he asks.

"I'm doing research for my PhD."

Intissar walks over and puts on our table a plate of foul, a loaf of bread, and a tray of vegetables: tomatoes, parsley, olives, and pickled turnips. "You know each other?" she says in English.

"We're old friends," he says.

"Tayyeb, fill up and enjoy." She walks away slowly.

I rub the back of my ear. "You're taking a break from what?"

"Life en générale, work, lots of things I guess." There's a sadness in his eyes. A part of me wants to know more, hold that sadness for him. Another part regrets asking him. He's always been an open book. It's something I admire but it makes me uncomfortable, alluding to a proximity between us — one I'm not sure I want.

"Shall we?" He hands me a slice of bread. I layer the foul with parsley and mint before placing it in my mouth. The mushed fava beans and chickpeas coat my mouth with a warm layer of softness, and I settle deeper into my chair.

"It's good, right?" he smiles.

I nod and savour every hint of garlic, lemon, cumin, of love that went into preparing the meal.

"Aside from being busy becoming a doctor, what have you been up to?"

I shrug. "Not much, just school." I wipe the side of my mouth.

"What about you? Do you still write?"

"No, I'm taking a break from work right now." A pained look overcomes his face, and he pauses. "My wife died about a year ago, so life's been a little shitty lately and I'm trying to eat, pray, love here. You know … like the book? Or at least, I'm hoping to. Maybe not as much love though, but like the spiritual kind of love, not the sexual kind." He blushes and shakes his hands like he's trying to wring the embarrassment out of his body.

"Oh Ziyad, I'm so sorry, I had no idea."

His presses his hands into the edge of the table. His wrist is wrapped in a string of little wooden beads. A misbaha? I wonder if he has transitioned his beliefs over our time apart.

"So why are you studying Arabic now?"

"Well, I became Muslim about six months ago and I figured it's about time."

I suck in a quick breath. "What about family? Do you have any relatives here?"

"None that I want to know." He looks up as if startled. "Sorry, I don't mean that. It's just, I'm not sure if I'm ready to meet any of them. I have a weird relationship with my dad's side."

Ziyad is the son of a Korean mother and a Lebanese Christian man. He's one of those rare mixed-race Arabs. I'd always been curious about his family, about what it was like growing up between two households across continents, but our friendship had been one forged in the present. We had rarely spoken about personal things and preferred spending our time thinking about the future.

"Why here? Why not go to Beirut?"

"It's quieter here, and the school is smaller."

I think about his wife dying and something crawls on the edge of my stomach. I run my fingers along the white petals of the jasmine plant next to me, careful not to disturb the delicate flowers. "So, how are you enjoying Lebanon so far?"

"I haven't seen much of it, but so far, it's been stressful." He leans closer. "Between you and me, I've been pretty uncomfortable. When I first got here, it took like an hour to get my bags at the airport because the spinny thing that brings them out was broken and then, right after I checked in here, I went to take a shower and there was no hot water, and then this power outage thing." He shakes his head. "I don't know, I guess I'm feeling a little selfish and ungrateful, like I might be a snob."

I smile, emboldened by his honesty. "You're not a snob. Well, you weren't seven years ago so I don't think you are now. Unless, somehow, you became rich and famous in those years and turned into some sort of diva."

He shifts in his seat. "I don't know. I guess you'll have to wait and see how long I can survive without my silk bed sheets and caviar." His mouth curves into a fuller smile when he looks at me.

Intissar comes over with a tray of drinks. "How was the food?" She winks as she picks up the dirty dishes.

"It was amazing," Ziyad says.

"Good, come and eat here every morning." She winks at me again and walks away.

Ziyad takes a sip of his Arabic coffee and grimaces.

"Is it too strong?"

"I'm still getting used to the coffee here."

"I think you can ask for an American coffee."

"I did, a few days ago. It's basically instant with condensed milk. It was surprisingly good, but not coffee good." He laughs.

I put a cube of sugar into my tea, stirring, watching the little particles fade away in the swirls at the bottom of my cup.

He looks behind me in reminiscence. "Is the Columbian still around?"

That coffee shop hosted most of our hang outs. "Yeah, it is, and I go there whenever I feel like I can afford a five-dollar cup of coffee." We look up at each other and waves of memories cross between us. "Have you been back to Toronto lately?"

He shakes his head. "Not really. I was there for work a few years ago, but that was the only time. Been mostly in Seoul." He leans over the table. "You're right though. I should try to get used to this or find something else that will do the trick." He plops a cube of sugar into the cup and stirs it.

A moment of silence passes; he returns to his book and I sip my tea, taking in the rest of the courtyard. Two other men adorn the space, talking loudly in a Syrian dialect as if arguing with each other, and Intissar laughs with someone behind the desk.

"I should get back upstairs and finish unpacking. I have a lot to plan for my research."

A light frown crosses his face. "Are you sure?"

"Yeah, but I'm happy to have a familiar face around here."

He brushes his hair back. "Same goes for me. Maybe we can do this again and you can tell me about your research. I came alone, so I'll take the company where I can get it. I'm in room 303 if you need anything."

"InshAllah, I'll come around sometimes."

Later in the afternoon, Reem comes to pick me up for dinner at their home in the refugee camp. I'd read about the lives of Palestinians in books and articles for my studies, but nothing could have fully prepared me for what Mama had kept from me. It feels like a betrayal, this act of hiding away this entire life of hers.

On the outside, the camp looks like a large open-air rectangle encapsulated by darkening mud walls. Inside, a maze of buildings is occasionally punctured by a parking lot or makeshift playground. Cafés and shops line the alleyways and kids play soccer in a field shaded by the surrounding buildings. Most of the camp is designed to be navigated by foot. I wonder if that is strategic, to keep the military tanks out. When I ask Reem about this, she reminds me of the massacres in 1982. The Lebanese forces, under the protection and support of Israelis, had had no trouble getting in.

We scramble through the narrow pathways, keeping an eye on the ground, avoiding the sloped centre where sewage water pools just underneath electric wires that were exposed and running between buildings. I picture one of them snapping and electrocuting me while I stand in the water before shaking the thought away.

Reem stops in front of a black metal door and pulls it open. We take off our shoes. I reach for what are clearly guest slippers next to Reem's. My aunt Fawzia, Mama's twin sister, walks out of the kitchen. She's carrying a large silver tray of food. My body freezes at the sight of those brown eyes, pallid cheeks that shouldn't be familiar, but her faint smile has Mama written all over it. I take a step closer and try to get a whiff of her. She holds still, like she's studying me from a distance. This woman is not Mama, but she may be the last thing connecting us.

"Ahlan, Yasmine." She greets me in Arabic. Her face is a mix of sorrow, anger, and longing. I can't tell which dominates.

"Marhaba, Khalto."

"How's the hotel?" She asks, her tone laced with accusation.

I smile with my lips closed. "Alḥamdulillah, it's good."

"You must feel like you're too classy to stay with us in the camp. Did your mother never tell you she lived here in this home? Did she never tell you where she came from?"

"Sorry Khalto." My voice is shaky, and I'm embarrassed by the offence I unknowingly committed. "I just didn't want to burden you for so long because I have work and research to do. I didn't mean anything by it; it would have been an honour to stay here."

"Wallaw, we're family, this is your home." We walk upstairs and she puts the tray down on the living room floor before going back down. Reem and I wait in silence. When she returns, Khalto Fawzia sets a bowl of cucumber yogourt sauce on the floor and sits down. "Aren't you hungry? Sit down and eat." I oblige and fill my plate with ma'lubi.

"Bismillah," I whisper under my breath ushering in the meal. I close my eyes and let the flavours of the food take me back to a time when my mother existed. When I was younger, I used to pick the pieces of eggplant and cauliflower out. Now I let the fried vegetables coat my tongue and cheek, sending an explosion of nostalgic flavours across my pallet.

We eat silently at first. Then they ask me about my life in Canada and I recount stories of my childhood, describing our tiny apartment, the schools I went to, and all the Arab friends I made living between Montreal and Toronto. Fatme, Reem's younger sister, comes home from school and joins us. She asks if I play hockey. I laugh and tell her that I can't even skate. The equipment was always too expensive.

We finish eating. I gather the empty plates and go back downstairs to the kitchen after lunch. Reem joins me. "Don't worry about what Mama said about the hotel; she's just looking out for you." She soaks a sponge with water. "Maybe you're not used to it because I think people in Canada are different. But you're always family here and they are just worried about you staying alone."

"What about you? Do you think I should be staying here?"

She twists her lips. "I think you should do whatever you want."

"Yeah, but do you think that I'm being rude?"

She dries her hands with a tea towel and drops it by the sink. "I know that things were rough with Tariq and that you need this time alone. I can talk to Mama if you want me to."

"Don't tell her about Tariq though, that we're divorcing I mean. I just need to live on my own and feel like I can fully breathe without being afraid to upset anyone or cause controversy."

"Of course, I won't say anything about that."

"I have spent all of my life living under the control of someone else and I don't know how to explain it, but I need to experience life on my own terms for once. I want my own space; I want to go and come as I please."

There's a kindness in her eyes.

Later, when it's time for me to leave, I call out to Khalto Fawzia.

She waves at me from the hallway. "You're always welcome back here, Yasmine." Her words say one thing, but a deep sense of rejection laces her tone. It makes me wonder what else Mama kept from me.

CHAPTER 04

Our families are filled with secrets that harbour the pain of our displacement. Mama's generation tells us stories from their youth. They joke about the noise that tin roofs made when it rained in the winter months, about drumming pots and pans in the underground bunkers while they waited for Israel's raining bombs to end. I myself have spent countless nights in those bunkers, wondering what might happen if the building above us succumbed to the explosives. Would I be buried alive? What might happen to my body after I'm gone?

But our family will not speak about the dead or the emotions that linger below that laughter. They don't share the details of what this has meant for them, of the lives they lived before they became travellers without a clear destination. My brother Ahmad is one of those secrets we don't discuss, ever since he went missing. Yasmine and her brother are another. Their mother, my aunt, was an enigma — the one who made it out.

The camp is filled with families whose daughters married an Arab man in Australia, Canada, the United States, England. Or with those whose sons were smart enough to get an education or a job elsewhere. They came back to visit. They brought medicine and herbs and sometimes fancier things like cell phones and laptops. They left with boxes of baklawa and petit four, a little taste of home to keep them sustained in foreign lands.

But we never saw our family abroad. I wasn't even aware that my cousins existed until I was sixteen. 'Ammo Ashraf had been sitting in the living room with Mama when he told her that Yasmine got married. He had pictures and there was something about the way that Mama looked at them, like she was staring at her own child.

"Who's Yasmine?" I had asked from the corner of my room.

Mama cleared her throat and put the pictures away. "No one you know."

I had gone on the hunt for a Yasmine Hassan shortly after that. And, when the internet became more accessible and when relatives started connecting with each other through Facebook, I found her.

She had the life I dreamt about. Her mother had achieved what so many of us wanted: to give her children a passport, a clear identity, opportunities. I used to lay in bed and picture my cousins living in a house that resembled the one from the American movie *Home Alone*, with the big green luscious lawn. I daydreamed about playing with them, running around with nothing but the breeze flowing through my hair and eating pizza on a large wooden dining table. As I got older, that fantasy became overshadowed by the understanding that Yasmine likely grew up poor in an apartment building with very little grass to run around on. But still, I envied the freedom that she had, the potential of eventually living in a home with a lawn and the ability to travel anywhere. We barely had any sunlight in the camp, let alone grass.

The day after her visit, I go to Yasmine's hotel. She greets me in sweatpants, a t-shirt and fuzzy flippers. We sit on the balcony with a view of the sea. There's a tray with a pot and cups on a folding table in the middle.

"I think Baba was alive after we left." Steam escapes from her tea cup, while she pours more into another.

The sun shines its warm rays on my face and I look up toward the sky. Birds sing as they dance between the clouds. I'm not sure I understand what she's referring to.

She grabs a notebook from the room and shows me. "These were delivered to me. I think they were Baba's. There was a note that said that some of these were written after we left."

"Who dropped it off?"

"I don't know. It was left at my door."

I don't know much about what happened after her father disappeared; all I have are rumours from a time when neither of us existed.

"I don't think he was around, Yasmine. Mama always said that your mom left after your Baba disappeared." I rub my chin. "I don't think anyone has heard from him since."

She frowns and tugs at her ear. "So, you think these are not real?"

"I didn't say that."

"I just don't understand. Why would someone play this sort of sick joke? And if they are real, why would someone leave them here? How did they even know I was here? Intissar said that someone had dropped it off a week ago to give to me when I arrived."

I shake my head. "What's in them? I don't know if there would be a way to prove their authenticity."

"So far, it's just been pages describing stories from the war, but there's a list. A list of names and dates that I don't understand." Her large thick curls drape across the glowing skin of her face. "Maybe we can bring them to someone who could tell me if the writing looks like his? Do you know anyone who knew him? Who would remember his writing?" She raises her voice and snaps her fingers. "Or, better yet, maybe your mom or someone else still has something with his writing on it. We could compare it."

Yasmine appears to be constantly hungry for information, ever since I met her. It is a compulsion. I once asked her about the MA program at the University of Toronto and she sent me a 20-page document that detailed everything, from admission and tuition to the program requirements. She even spoke to a few students currently enrolled and included quotes from them. It's part of what makes her a good researcher, but it consumes her in an unhealthy way.

"'Ammo Ashraf knew both your parents. Maybe we can show them the letters and he can tell us if he recognizes the writing."

She nods. "Who is that? Can we see him today?"

"He's my uncle, my dad's brother. He's been around to help us since Baba died. He knew your parents even before they got married. They go way back." I grab my bag. "But I think you need to calm down. What about your work and your research? We have all summer."

I have to pick up some things for Mama and head back home. Maybe I'll come by tomorrow after teaching."

She looks deflated and I put my hand on her shoulder. "Try to get some rest, habibi. You still seem a little jetlagged. I'll call you when I'm done, okay?"

She walks me to the door. We hug and I rub her back reassuringly.

It's past ten when I get home carrying bags of groceries and household supplies. I set everything down on the cold floor. Mama spends most of her days scrubbing the house, but today the sink is filled with dirty pots and cutlery. A strange orange liquid oozes from the side of the cabinet and shoes are splayed all over the entryway. I trip on an unfamiliar old pair of men's shoes. I hear noises coming from upstairs — laughter. I pick up a knife from the kitchen and walk up the steps on tiptoe.

"Reem?" Mama calls out. "Come see who's here."

Nobody. There should be nobody at this hour. I climb faster, loosening my grip on the knife. Mama is sitting next to a strange, young-looking man. Her head is uncovered, her eyes glistening with tears. My eyes widen, mouth agape.

"Marhaba?" I say.

"Reem, habibte." Mama places her hand on his leg. "Ahmad is back. What did I tell you?"

My brows draw together and I stop breathing for a moment. I look at him again, studying the circles around his eyes. Heat rushes from my hands and into my head. "Ahmad?" He looks to be in his mid to late twenties, with a small build and roughly my height, judging by the way his feet dangle off the couch. When his large brown eyes meet mine, all my doubt about his existence evaporate. My brother. Staring at his face and then back at Mama, I stand still, unable to move or react.

Fire rises through my chest, remembering all the times I shouldered the responsibility of caring for the family for the last three years.

We thought he was dead; I had adapted to a life that didn't include him. "Why are you back?"

"Don't be rude to your brother Reem. Why don't you go make us some tea."

My voice rises. "This brother? Who abandoned us all when we needed him the most? You don't deserve the ground that you walk on."

Mama tries to say something, but Ahmad puts his hand up to quiet her. "It's okay. Reem, why don't we talk in the morning? I'll explain everything, I promise." His voice is raspy.

"I'm not going to wait until tomorrow. Explain it now."

He rubs his head, takes a deep breath, and speaks in a low tone. "I'm sorry. I never meant to abandon you. It wasn't my fault."

I cut him off, my feet tapping the ground. "Whose fault was it then? Do you know what life has been like for us? You don't get to just come back and pretend like nothing happened."

"'Azā." Mama stands between us. "Reem, what's with you?"

His eyes meet mine. "I didn't willfully abandon you."

"Then what is it? Because I just assumed you were dead. The other option is you're a coward who can't be bothered to check in on your family. Yet here you are, in the flesh."

"That's enough, Reem," Mama pushes me back. "He was in jail!"

Prison. There were times when I'd wondered if that's where he had ended up. I had searched, asked everyone who knew him. I had even succumbed to asking Yasmine's Uncle Saleem to use his connections and tell me if they had any information. He had told me he couldn't find anything. That liar! I should have gone to Syria. I should have searched for him more.

Ahmad takes a deep breath and covers his face. I see the shame scrunching his body, making him smaller. I want to tell him it's okay, that it probably wasn't his fault.

"I don't understand. Why?"

"Because they are sons of dogs who don't fear their lord!" Mama shouts, cursing the Syrian government and its prisons while rubbing her legs.

Softly I say, "Mama, khalas, why don't you go and get some sleep? I'll take care of Ahmad."

I help her to her room and when I come back, Ahmad is still in the same anguished position. The flesh on his arms is scarred, telling a story of torture both fresh and old. I sit next to him.

"Who are they?"

"The people I was working for."

"How long were you in prison?"

He turns to face me. "For as long as you haven't heard from me."

"Did you deserve it?" I know he didn't, but a part of me needs the affirmation that he's the same brother who once held my hand and scolded me for stealing the chocolate bar from the dukani but never told Mama. I need to know everything to help him.

His bottom lip quivers, and I regret asking. "Reem…"

I raise my hands in surrender. "Okay, okay. Never mind. You're probably tired; I'll go make you a bed in your old bedroom and we can talk more tomorrow." I get up and make sure there are adequate blankets in the spare room. Mama comes out of her room and follows me.

"Reem." She leans over, her mouth against my ear. "The stuff that Ahmad just told you, keep that to yourself okay?"

"Why?"

"Nobody needs to know what happened. Don't tell anyone he was in jail."

"Mama, people go to jail for stuff they didn't do all the time. It doesn't mean they're guilty. It doesn't mean anything."

She smacks one hand over the other. "What will people say? How will you find a husband if rumour spreads that your brother is a criminal?"

"But he's probably innocent."

"Yes, but the world doesn't know that."

She is right. What the world does know is that people like us, refugees, are prone to falling into messed up shit. They like to brand us as desperate for an escape and that gives those on the outside the opportunity to take advantage. They think our lives are worth less than the lives of people outside of the walls.

That's why the rumours and secrets stay in the camp.

Baba used to say that lies are easier to believe, especially when it comes to Palestinians. No one wants to acknowledge the reality of what happened to us — what they condoned — for, if they did, none of them could bear to live with the shame. Instead, their ignorance rots their hearts slowly.

I look at my mother and reassure her, "Okay. I'll make something up about why he was gone and we'll use it to explain his return."

CHAPTER 05

Intissar laughs when I ask her about getting a Wi-Fi connection in the hotel. We're standing near the reception desk and the courtyard is filled this morning. The clank of cutlery scraping plates punctuates the murmur of conversations.

"We don't have internet but you can go to the internet café. It's down the road, past Nadira's bakery." She sets down a notebook and walks over to one of the tables. I follow her.

"Is there any way I could get internet here? I'll pay for it."

She asks a couple at a table if they'd like more tea, then turns to face me. "No, I don't think so, but don't you want to eat first habibti?"

"Shukran Khalto, but I ate upstairs. Tomorrow, I'll have breakfast here inshAllah, I promise."

"Ok, take care of yourself, habibti. I'm here if you need anything." She looks at me with her wide, plump smile and walks away, into the kitchen.

Feeling defeated, I walk upstairs to my room and put on a maxi dress. I pack my notebook and some of Baba's writings into a cross-shoulder bag and head to the café. Outside, I wander south along Al-Shat road with the open sea to my right. Families and couples sit along the sand with coolers by their side. Cars honk and speed past me on the bustling street. I wrap my fingers around the strap of my brown leather bag and the cool air blows my curls into my face. A few minutes later, I spot the café on the opposite side of the street, next to a bakery.

There are cars zipping by and no crosswalk in sight. A motorcycle carrying three people whizzes past. A woman appears next to me. "You just have to go and trust that they won't run you over. They usually don't." She smiles and takes a step forward. Her foot hovers above the ground. "Ready?"

An incoming black Honda slows down and we run across. My legs move swiftly as I jump onto the edge of the sidewalk. "Shurkan," I thank her. She goes into the bakery without another word, as if I don't exist.

Contrary to the title, there is no coffee or food in this internet "café." Two younger looking men sit behind a wooden desk by the metal-framed door.

"Marhaba." The one with a baseball cap smiles at me. Everyone greets me in Arabic here and I'm relieved.

I return his greeting. "I need to use one of the computers for an hour or two."

He nods and gestures toward the row of desks that populate the space, each with an individual computer. "It's ten thousand liras an hour." He writes my name and the time on a piece of paper. "You'll pay when you leave."

"Thank you." I give him a small, curt smile and he leans over his counter. "You have a beautiful smile by the way. If you keep smiling that way, I might let you use the computers for free. Do you live around here?"

"I'm sorry, I just need to use the computer and I'll be out of your way. I'll pay."

He raises his hands in surrender. "Suit yourself. Tfaḍali."

I walk to the back of the café to find an empty desk far away from the entrance. I pause before sitting, though — Ziyad is here, typing like he's in a competition.

I settle on the desk next to him and glance sideways to keep track of the two men at the entrance. My heart quietens when I turn the other way to look at Ziyad in a pair of dark jeans and a white shirt with the sleeves rolled up to his elbows. His black hair is parted to the left. Ziyad must have gotten most of his looks from his Korean mother because there isn't much about him that looks Arab except for his dusky skin that matches mine.

I click on the internet icon and watch the line on the screen move back and forth while it connects. I lean over the desk with my chin resting in the palm of my hand and tap the desk with a pen.

His eyes widen as he turns to me, and then I get a wide smile that displays a half dimple on his left cheek. "Yasmine! Sorry I didn't see you. How long have you been there?" He removes his headphones as he speaks.

"I just got here. What are you up to?"

"Just emails and stuff. I have to deal with some things back home."

"What kind of stuff? Like, for work?"

"Sort of, yeah."

I nod and then look back at my screen. "Great, my connection is finally up. I need to do some research. Catch you when you're done?"

He smiles again, puts his headphones back on, and returns to his work.

I start searching libraries and archives that I'll need to visit over the summer. Then I work on a schedule to plan out trips to other cities. I search Beirut, locate hotels and museums. Next is Saida, and I note a soap museum that might be fun to visit. I send out emails to local not-for-profits and reach out to my contact at the UNRWA office to confirm our scheduled meetings. I'm hoping they'll connect me with others who lead initiatives that support victims of the civil war.

But not long into my list-making, my memories return to Baba. So, I look up articles that covered stories of missing people from the era. There isn't much online, and I make a note to dig this up at the library. I know there will be thousands of names, all collateral damage from a fifteen-year war — mostly men, taken from their homes in the middle of the night or during raids and massacres, never to be seen or heard from again. My chest grows heavy as I read the testimony of a woman who witnessed the execution of all her male relatives in the Shatila camp.

I close the web page and make a silent du'a for those that have passed.

Then, I put Baba's name in the search engine. This isn't the first time I have done this, and as usual, there are articles that link him to the pan-Arab movements of the 1970s and 1980s. Others declare his associations with the PLO.

I pull out a sheet of paper with the names from the list left at my door, and I start with the first one: Gamal El-Tayyeb. The browser is flooded with articles. He is a journalist who once worked with Baba. More significantly, I learn that he's still alive, living here in Lebanon. There was an assassination attempt against the Lebanese president in the 1990s and he was accused of masterminding it. He's spending a life sentence in the Roumieh prison. I note all of this down, pack up my things, and turn off the computer. My movements cause the men at the front to glance at me more frequently.

My research is going to have to wait. The trail of Baba's disappearance is becoming clearer; the letters were given to me for a reason. I need to find out if he is still alive. What if he's going by a different identity? What if he's waiting for me?

I pull my bag around my shoulder and Ziyad leans over. "Hey, want to grab lunch?"

I look at the two men at the front, and my stomach grumbles. I agree.

We walk to a nearby restaurant called Al-Safari. We sit at a table in the middle of the black tiled patio. The place is empty, save for a small family sitting closer to the entrance. A waiter puts a large bottle of water on the table and hands us the menus.

Ziyad leans back and folds his hands behind his head. "So, tell me about your research."

"You don't have to pretend like you care about my work. Most people don't." That was true for the most part, unless they were fellow academics.

His brows furrow and he leans forward with his elbows on the table. "I've always been interested in your work and you know that."

"We haven't talked in years; how would you know what I do?"

He takes a moment before responding. "I like the way your mind works, or at least the way it used to. I liked having access to your knowledge. But yeah, it's been a while — and whose fault is that, really?" His tone is accusatory.

Just then, the waiter comes by and asks if we were ready to order. I tell him we need a few more minutes, then turn back to Ziyad. "Are you claiming that it's my fault we grew apart?"

"Well, you're the one that decided to ghost me for no reason. I spent a lot of time wondering if I'd done something."

"I didn't ghost you. Things just happened, Ziyad."

He looks at me speculatively, then turns his face to the metal fence draped in grape vines. "Sure."

"I honestly didn't think you would care or notice much." Ziyad had been a bit of an enigma in undergrad. At the outset, he had given strong frat boy energy. He had been very popular: editor-in-chief of the student newspaper, in a band that occasionally performed at local parties, and always bumping into people he knew wherever we went.

I first met him in a creative writing course. He sat next to me for most of the semester and we were paired up for a group project tasked with writing a short story together. We quickly learned that he was a skilled writer and I was bad at structuring narratives. Ziyad had a way with words. He knew how to use them to capture light in darkness and speckles of harmony in chaos. In turn, I gave him ideas for content. He wanted to learn about Arab customs, Arab histories, and Arabic linguistics. He was mesmerized and fascinated by the things I assumed were mundane. It shocked him that I knew how to make a good mlokhiah, or that I interacted with the Lebanese shop owners in fluent Arabic. He craved the knowledge I had, and together we were able to craft a beautiful story. When the class ended, we continued to meet weekly, sometimes daily, over coffee. Our conversations always stayed with school related things, and we rarely talked about families, our pasts, or our futures. I always understood that I gained more from the relationship than he did.

The waiter returns and I ask for a shrimp salad. Ziyad orders grilled fish.

When the waiter leaves, Ziyad doesn't look at me. But he says, "You were one of my best friends back then and it meant a lot to me."

"How?"

He fiddles with his fork. "Yasmine," he pauses, "the time we spent together was like the only time I ever felt fully like myself. I confided some stuff that I didn't tell anyone else because I felt like we had trust. More than trust."

I know he's referring to the invisible pull between us. The one I never wanted to acknowledge. The one that made my heart race with a willingness to shed my walls and tell him everything. Tariq and I had been together then, but he never made me feel the way Ziyad did and that had riddled me with guilt.

"I'm sorry Ziyad."

He waves his hand in the air. "It's fine, water under the bridge now, I guess. But will you at least tell me what I did? Why did you cut me off?"

I had long hoped that Ziyad would have assumed our friendship just fizzled out, but the truth is I had cut him off intentionally because I'd caught myself developing feelings for him. One night, in undergrad, I was in a mild car accident and ended up in the hospital. Without thinking, I called him before anyone else. And like a knight in shining armour, he escaped one of his dad's fundraisers and showed up in a tuxedo. He waited six hours with me as my arm was put into a cast and he then drove me home at midnight. On the way, he'd asked me why I called him over anyone else. I had lied and mumbled something about no one else answering my calls. I knew that if I'd called Tariq, he would have found a way to blame me for the accident, and Yusuf would have gone into a frenzied panic. Things were simple with Ziyad: no complications, no resentment, no anxiety, no worry, no shame.

A few weeks after the accident, we were at a coffee shop discussing the Jordanian poet Amjad Nasser. I'd lost track of time and forgotten an important meeting with Tariq. Our relationship was serious enough then to warrant gathering with his parents, and Yusuf had told me that he'd asked him for permission to propose.

After a deep conversation, Ziyad excused himself to the bathroom and I pulled my phone out of my bag. I saw the missed calls. Panic began to rush through my limbs.

When he returned, I had my bag and jacket. "I'm so sorry Ziyad, I have to go," I said.

"Is everything okay?"

My voice shook. "Yeah, yeah. I just forgot I was supposed to meet someone."

I picked up my things and ran as fast as I could to the law school where Tariq was still waiting for me. His face was red, his jaw hardened. "Where were you?" he had said.

"Sorry, I was with a classmate and time just flew."

We walked to his car but he didn't speak. My steps moved urgently to keep up with his pace.

In the car, he set the keys down and gripped the steering wheel.

"I'm sorry Tariq, I just lost track of time."

"Who were you with?"

"A classmate, I told you."

"What was so important that you missed my calls?"

"I'm sorry, I just … it was on silent and in my bag. We'll explain it to your parents, I'm sure they'll understand."

He slammed his hands against the dashboard. I flinched. "It's not about that. It's disrespectful Yasmine. When you say you are going to be somewhere, you show up. And who's this classmate? Is it the same guy again?" He was shouting. I looked for an explanation, something that could help me make sense of his anger.

"Did something happen at work?"

"Nothing happened."

I didn't know what to do. How was I supposed to calm him? Should I have placed my hand on his? Given him a hug? Stopped talking? He exhaled a long breath and I watched his chest rise and fall. "I'm sorry I yelled. It's just ... I don't know how I feel about you going around meeting that guy out in coffee shops. Like, what if someone saw you? That can't happen when we get engaged and after. What would people say?"

Tariq had alluded to wanting to take things a step further, but he hadn't asked me formally.

"Yasmine, I want us to get married. I think it's time. I spoke to your brother yesterday and he gave me his blessings." He turned to face me. "I'm sorry I yelled. Maybe I was just nervous about tonight."

And that's how it happened. He announced our engagement to our families that night. There was never a question asked, nor one answered. I couldn't find a reason to say no to him. After all, he was giving me a way into stability, and he came with a beautiful family. A child of four with aunts and uncles and cousins. I spent every other weekend at someone's home filled with fresh meals and barbecues layered with love and care.

I avoided Ziyad after that incident, engulfed by the guilt of having gotten lost in his company. I told myself that it's not what good women do. They behave modestly. Their hearts don't skip beats for strange men in cafés, time slipping into late afternoons. I kept telling myself that desiring his company had meant nothing. The friendship we had would have never lasted as a romantic one. A year later, I heard that he had moved back to Korea and over the next six years, I let him slip into my mind only occasionally.

Now, Ziyad is waiting patiently for an explanation I can't give him without exposing my embarrassment.

"I don't know. It was complicated. I was going through a weird phase." I bite the inside of my cheek. "You didn't do anything wrong. It was me, and I'm sorry."

He nods. The waiter arrives with our food. He tells me about his trips to Beirut and Soor and the rest of his plans for the summer. Then he asks, "Have you met much of your family here?"

"Some. It's kind of weird though. I feel like an outsider, like I'm constantly being judged. People keep asking me weird questions about my lifestyle back home."

"Why do you think I don't want to meet any of mine?"

"Aren't you even curious though?"

"There's a lot of drama with my dad and I didn't come here to be questioned about my life and justify my decisions, you know?"

"I get that. It's just your confidence about it all is intriguing."

"Is there anything else you find intriguing about me?" He stabs a slice of fish with his fork.

My fingers tingle. "Do you find anything intriguing about me?"

He chews slowly and a smile dances on his lips. "Pretty much everything about you intrigues me, Yasmine. I'd be lying if I said I didn't look you up a few times."

"No, you didn't."

"I did. To my disappointment though, because you're a mystery."

"Yeah, that's intentional. I like my privacy."

We finish our meal with tea and baklawa in a quiet ease. He pays for lunch and we take a taxi back to the hotel. On the steps of the third floor, we say our goodbyes and I don't turn around to see if he's still there.

I didn't think it was possible back then — and I still doubt it now — to find someone who could support you — love you wholly and not just need you all the time. With Tariq, I was constantly drained and broken. He sucked the energy out of me, and I had to find other things to sustain my body. I thought back then that that's what relationships were like, that the more I did, the more love would blossom. But I learned slowly that it didn't work that way.

I don't know now what to make of Ziyad's renewed presence in my life. It feels possible that an alternative version of love, the mutual kind that could be filled with mercy, could exist. I can't comprehend it, but I contemplate the prospect of it, taking joy in the way it makes my heart flutter. I need something exciting to hang onto.

CHAPTER 06

A few days after Ahmad shows up, I leave early to teach, before anyone is awake. It's our first day of spring classes and there's a lot of pressure to set the right tone. This is when students decide if they like you, if they think you're worth their money and time. The session goes as predicted and we spend most of the time introducing each other. I let them go a little early, with homework to think about the places they'd like to visit in Lebanon. Two students make their way out thanking me for an engaging and lively session. Earlier, I had made a joke about Minjoon's name. That's the student with the strange profile. I told him that his name sounded like *from June*. I regretted it as soon as I had said it, so I stop him on his way out, and apologize for turning his name into a lesson.

His smile puts me at ease. "It's okay, but thank you for apologizing. It was a really good first class."

"Are you also here to study for your degree?"

"No, I finished school a long time ago. I just need to learn Arabic."

"Long time ago? But you look so young. When did you graduate? When you were twelve?!" I laugh at my own joke.

He returns my laugh, though I suspect it's directed *at* me. "Well, I'm twenty-eight. But I'm not in school anymore ... haven't been for a while now."

"What about your last name, Haddad? Are you Lebanese or adopted or something?"

The question seems to catch him off guard. "Uh yeah, sort of I guess."

"Sort of you're Lebanese or sort of you're adopted?"

"I'm half."

My eyebrows squish together. "What's the other half?"

"My mom is Korean. They met in Abu Dhabi."

"And you don't speak Arabic? Did your dad not teach you?"

He looks at his watch. "Sorry, I have to go, but no, he didn't teach me."

"Okay, well, see you tomorrow Minjoon." I throw the rest of my things into my bag, and my mystery student makes his way out.

Ahmad is waiting in the lobby, wearing khaki pants that are too short for him and a wrinkled blue button-up shirt. I pity his inability to dress. The day after he came back, we all sat down in the living room and laid down some ground rules. He told us about the circumstances around his disappearance. Syria had turned out to be a dead end for him. The jobs had been menial, oppressive, and hardly worth the loneliness he lived through. The Syrian people were kind to him whenever they found out he was Palestinian, but it didn't prevent the privileged ones from taking advantage of his desperation. I promised to help him settle in with a portion of my savings. We didn't talk about what got him in jail. I asked, but he refused to give me details and Mama and I weren't certain if we needed the details.

"Let's go to the souq," I say to him now.

"What for?"

"I need to get some things and you obviously need new clothes. How do you expect to find a wife looking like that?"

"I don't need new clothes or a wife. I need a job."

"Well maybe we can find one there."

I grab his hand and walk him to my car. I take him to the new mall in town, the one that's like the ABC in Beirut. This one's been around for almost a year.

"This place looks expensive, Reem." His eyes wander from one department store to another, widening at the shiny floors and the lights above store entrances.

"The prices are the same as in the souq, but some of the quality is better and there's more variety. You just can't haggle. Sometimes the stuff is cheaper, the made-in-China kind."

He fiddles with his hands.

"Don't worry Ahmad, you know I've been working and I make good money." I lie, but I'm so desperate for him to think we're okay.

We stop by one of the two men's shops in the mall. Across the row of suit jackets and pants are button-up shirts displayed against the wall. I pick up a light pink one and another one in forest green, to bring out the hazel in his eyes. "Here, try these on."

"What about this Reem?" He holds a pair of brown pants with weird bears doing all sorts of stuff on the fabric. It hurts to look at it and I yank it out of his hand and throw it across the row.

"Stop picking out stuff just because it costs less, Ahmad. Go try these on and I'll come back with more."

The salesperson is about to kick us out by the time we settle on a few outfits. She rolls her eyes when Ahmad tries to convince her to give him a deal on the price.

I apologize for him. "Sorry. My brother, he's not from here and it's his first time shopping at the mall."

"Right." She rolls her eyes again and takes my money with a limp hand, as if our poverty is contagious.

While we're walking around the mall, Ahmad starts acting weird. He keeps looking over his shoulder, asking me if I see someone looking at us. His eyes shift quickly from one side to another. His pace speeds up one moment, only to slow down the next. He stands behind a pillar or suddenly walks into a random store. I put my hand on his back and he jumps at my touch. He was never like this before, and now I'm making a list of mental illnesses to research when I get home.

Then I remember the only thing he told me about being in prison. They put him in an isolated room for over a month, where there was no light and no one to talk to. He told me that his mind stopped working, like he couldn't form sentences. He'd lost the sense of feeling, words and pictures broken into shards of glass floating in his body.

There was a kid I knew, one of the neighbours, who ended up in jail one time. He was sixteen and stole money from a store with a couple of friends. They were all quickly convicted and sent to prison. He ended up getting hooked on cocaine during his six-month stint. One of the older inmates had a business smuggling it in and selling it to others. It was difficult, surviving those spaces. They were dirty; people were starved and tortured. He had been a good kid, but last I heard, he had gone missing.

We stop at the food court and order burgers. While we're waiting for the food, I look at Ahmad again, gauging whether he had gotten addicted, which might explain his behaviour. He's in his own world and doesn't even notice that I'm staring. I pick up our tray and we find a seat nearby.

"So, what do you plan to do now that you are back?" I bite into a fry.

His eyes wander around the building, looking for something or watching for someone. They eventually meet mine and he takes a sip of his drink. "I'm not sure, but I think I need to get out of Lebanon."

I laugh. "How do you plan to do that? And where are you going to go? Back to Syria?"

His face hardens. "Definitely not Syria, but I've been thinking about Africa. I know some people who went to Ghana and I think I might be able to get my hands on a fake Ghanaian passport."

"What are you going to do with a Ghanaian passport?"

"Get out of here. Maybe get a job and live there. At least I'll be a nobody there. At least then I'll have a passport. I don't think anyone is going to give me a job here."

"'Ammo Ashraf has a construction company now; you should talk to him and see if he'll get you some work." He can dream of going to another country, but I also need help, in the immediate sense. Help that I've needed for a long time and desperately want to find in him.

"Yeah, inshAllah, I can talk to him. For now, that will be something."

"Ahmad. I also want to get out of here, but I at least have a plan." He raises his eyebrows and smiles for the first time since he came back. "Go on."

I tell him about the money I've been saving from the different jobs I've held over the years. He asks me about my grades and I proudly tell him that I've held onto a 3.8 GPA.

"At the AUB?" he asks.

"Yes, and you know where people go when they graduate from the AUB? They get into graduate programs abroad. They can go to Canada, Australia, the US."

This even amazes me sometimes, how I've managed to get it all done, but the truth is, I did it on three to four hours of sleep a night, cramming in schoolwork before going to sleep. I've noticed the growing bags under my eyes that make me look ten years older.

"I'm going to get into graduate school. I'm not picky about where I go, as long as I can afford it and it's in a country that can eventually give me some sort of permanent home."

Ahmad looks at me with a familiar gaze. "You've grown so much from the little girl you used to be. May all your dreams come true and inshAllah you can get us all visas to get out of here."

"That's the plan."

"I hope you get to do all that you dream of." He looks down with a sadness that darkens his tone. His earlier smile has diminished.

I've learned today that there are questions I never want to ask. Details of things that would only generate openings for confusion and pain. I don't ask Ahmad again about the details of why he'd been sent to jail. I don't want to know the source of this tension that moves through his body. This moment with him is enough to steal my memories of a happier, hopeful version of him. We finish our food in silence.

On our way out, he asks me about Yasmine, if I like her, how we connected, and how long she plans to be in the country.

"Yasmine is really sweet and close to the heart. But she's picked up some things from living in Canada. She doesn't have our customs, but I like her."

"Make sure to tell her to stay away from her dad's family."

I stop in my tracks. "Why would I tell her that, Ahmad?"

He looks at me with a knowing glare. His eyes pierce mine and his thin lips tighten. I recognize this from when we were children — it means he's about to say something serious. "Reem, you know her family is no good and you know what I'm talking about. Do you think Khalto took them away to Canada for no reason? It wasn't just for an easier life."

I'm aware of the rumours about Yasmine's family. Someone once said that her uncle collaborated with the Phalange, sold them secrets in exchange for money and protection. Her other uncle, Saleem, is a minister in the current government — the same government that likes to steal money from people.

"I don't know if she knows about her family. I don't think her mom ever told her."

"Do you think she could get us a visa? Maybe she could sponsor us or Mama to Canada," he asks.

"I don't think she can; that's not how it works. I looked into it. She can only sponsor a husband or parents or something."

He rubs his scruffy chin. "Does she have money? Can she help us with money? What about her brother Yusuf, what does he do?"

I can't deny that I've thought about this. But I never found the courage to ask her. I like our relationship the way it is. Still, a part of me can't help but wonder how she can afford to stay at a hotel all summer. That money could have been put to better use.

"Yasmine's had a tough life. I'm sure she would help if she could Ahmad, but everyone has their own problems. I've been dealing on my own for a long time, and I can continue to deal on my own."

We are silent on the way home.

Back at the camp, I pull into the parking lot in my usual spot next to the broken-down white Lincoln with the missing tires.

Sand fills my sandals, rubbing against the soles of my feet like an exfoliator.

"Is this new?" Ahmad points to a vegetable cart parked in front of the olive tree graffiti.

I nod. "'Ammo Omar started bringing in produce from his aunt's farm." We walk into an alley on the left. I stop in front of Ammar's café when I realize Ahmad is no longer walking next to me.

I turn and see that he's a few steps back. "What is it Ahmad?" His body is still and his face has lost its colour.

He shakes his head, slowly taking a step back.

"This again? Ahmad, there's nobody following us or looking at you." I start walking back toward him; I reach for his arm, and he brushes it away. His eyes fixate on something or someone walking past my car.

"Go home, Reem," he says.

"What about you? Where are you going?" I squint and look behind me toward where Ahmad's eyes are fixed.

That's when I see it. Someone is staring at him. He has a cigarette in his mouth, his right hand wrapped around something by his waist. He looks at my brother with threatening eyes. "Do you know him?"

"Go home, Reem," he mumbles through clenched teeth.

"What the hell is going on Ahmad?"

"Go home, Reem. I have to take care of some things." He turns and runs back the same way we came. The sound of his shoes scrunch against the ground until he turns a corner and I lose sight of him.

"Ahmad!" I shout.

When I turn in the other direction, I can't find the strange man. He's gone too. I rub my face with open palms and whisper his name again. There were days and nights when I fantasized about him coming back. He'd bring gifts and hug us all before telling me that he would take care of us now. That's the Ahmad I wanted back. Not this one that's filled with paranoia, bringing danger into our lives. I want my memories back.

I pick up the bag of stuff we bought and blow out a series of short breaths at the unexpected ache that rises in my heart.

The next afternoon, I pick up Yasmine from the hotel and bring her back to my house to meet 'Ammo Ashraf. In the car, I tell her about what happened with Ahmad. About him coming back, about him disappearing again. It spills out of me and Yasmine quietly listens, nodding, tracing the edge of her bottom lip. I wonder if she thinks we're chaotic, if she regrets her ties to me.

"It's worse now, you know?" I say. "We adapted to a different life, then he's back. He gave me hope and now he's gone again, leaving behind a whole bunch of unanswered questions and shit. Mama and I are now even more worried than we were before because we know he's alive. What am I supposed to do with that?"

She puts her hand on my shoulder. "I don't know what to do either, but that sucks Reem, and I'm sorry."

I give her sideways glance. "What do you mean?"

"I mean it sucks, and of course you're angry."

Those words hit me like a brick. I'm expecting her to tell me to calm down, to give me solutions, actions, suggestions, to tell me to be patient. This doesn't give me any of that. Am I supposed to be angry? I look at her again with my eyes wide, my hands holding tightly to the steering wheel. "What do you mean I'm angry?"

"Of course you have the right to be angry and sad, Reem. Who wouldn't be? It's awful. I don't have a solution for you. I'm sorry."

I've been living in grief for so long. I've lived with this anger for as long as I can remember. That's how women in our communities lose their minds; they bottle it up until it explodes. You hear rumours of women like this. Mama's aunt supposedly lost the ability to speak after her son died in front of her. Her husband sent her away to an asylum and married another woman when they lost hope of her recovering.

As if she can read my mind, Yasmine says, "I'm not telling you to bottle it, Reem. I'm telling you to do the opposite. Be angry, scream, cry, so that you don't get stuck in misery forever."

"What, like right now?"

She shrugs. "Sure, if it helps."

So I do, as loud as I can.

I picture Ahmad running away and me sitting alone in my room. I picture the days to come, filled with questions and work and exhaustion that dries up my bones. Pedestrians turn their heads when they hear my screaming and crying, and I pause to roll up my window. Someone shouts from a nearby car. Yasmine begins to laugh, and so do I.

"Is this how you got over your ex?" I say.

"I didn't need to get over him; I'm pretty sure I started hating him a year into our relationship."

"Do you think there was a reason for that part of your life? Like do you think there was some good in it?"

She purses her lips. "I'm sure there was. I don't know what it is though. There are a lot of days I wonder what my life would have been like if I had made different choices, but this is the life I've been given. Mama always used to say that the devil's favourite word is regret." She laughs again.

"Mama says the same thing, but it's ironic because she regrets everything. Just doesn't call it that."

"It's as if they're sisters."

"I don't know why Mama didn't talk about Khalto Samira. Something happened between them. I just don't know what."

"What have you heard?" Yasmine is suddenly serious.

"I heard Mama once saying she turned her back on the family. She didn't come visit and she never sent anything. I know she was mad about her leaving, but I think there's more, stuff that has to do with your dad and the war and his family. Maybe 'Ammo Ashraf will know."

I park the car in my usual spot and I feel noticeably lighter. Maybe the screaming and the laughter did work. I turn the ignition off. Yasmine laces a loose string from her shirt around her index finger. "Tariq, my ex, was the heart of his community. People loved him, and when I told him I wanted to separate, he began spreading rumours that I cheated on him. And you know what that means in our community? It was awful. I lost friends. I often wonder what made him the way he is; I think about his dad and his upbringing, like, did they teach him empathy? Or did he just never see how his actions affected me? I don't know." She turns to face me. "I don't know what happened with Ahmad and I'm sorry Reem. I can't imagine what you're going through. It's a lot, and it's really hard, and you shouldn't feel guilty for having those feelings. Don't let anyone tell you that you're crazy or whiny or ungrateful because you experience things, Ramroum."

I swallow tears. The validation makes me want to scream and cry some more. She's saying the words that I need to hear, words I thought only existed in my head. "Thank you." We hug and make our way to my house. Underneath a clog of electrical wires in a narrow corner, she stops me.

"Reem, do you remember what you said to me after I told you about Tariq?" She says.

"I remember saying a lot of things."

"You said that I should stand up for myself, and the more women like us stood up and cared for ourselves, the less we would become reliant on the men who continue to fail us."

I raise an eyebrow. "What does that have anything to do with this? Are you asking me to stand up for myself against Ahmad?"

"No, but taking care of yourself is a part of that. And sometimes, we care for ourselves by carving out the space to feel the pain safely."

I nod. I understand what she's saying, but living it is another story. She laces her arm through mine, kisses my forehead, and we walk through the red door that marks my home. The air smells of garlic and tomatoes. Mama made qusa, one of Ahmad's favourite dishes, as if she's hoping he'll naturally gravitate toward the smell and come home.

'Ammo Ashraf walks out of the kitchen with plates in his hands. Yasmine greets him and he looks at her with a familiar smile. "I heard that Yasmine Hassan was in town."

"Yallah tfadalo." My mom invites us to sit and eat in the living room upstairs.

Yasmine looks like one of those stray cats in the streets, salivating at the sight of the spread, like she'd never seen a display of food like this. "Can you teach me how to make this? I don't know very many recipes. Mama didn't teach me."

Mama eyes her curiously. "That would require you to come here more often." She grabs a spoon from the tray and starts dishing it out.

'Ammo Ashraf says, "Yasmine, I was good friends with your parents. We grew up together." He places his hand on his chest.

"It's really nice to meet you, 'Ammo."

Ashraf's eyes wander around the room. "I heard that Ahmad was also back."

"He's gone again," I say.

"What do you mean, gone again? Where?"

I shrug. "I don't know 'Ammo, he just left and didn't say anything. We went shopping yesterday and then he just ran away before we got home. There was a man staring at him near the parking lot. I think. Maybe he got involved in some stuff in Syria and people are after him now."

Ashraf rubs his beard. "Hasbunallahu wa ni'malwakil ... tsk tsk tsk. Allah keep him safe and bring him back."

"Ameen, ya Ashraf. Ameen. But please see if you can ask around and find out where he went," Mama says.

He nods, then fills his plate with food. Yasmine compliments Mama on her cooking and says it reminds her of her mom.

"Good, at least your mom continued to cook our food in Canada."

"How was your mother? Were you happy in Canada?" Ashraf says in his deep and commanding voice. His eyes shine blue.

Mama smirks. "Of course Samira was happy. Too happy to come and visit or ask about us." She turns to face Yasmine directly. "Your mother should have kept in touch more. She didn't need to stay away for as long as she did; she could have come back when the war ended."

'Ammo Ashraf interjects, "It wasn't that simple, ya Fawzia, and you know it. She couldn't come back."

"Why not?" Yasmine asks.

"There were some issues, she thought some people maybe were after her, and I helped her. I helped her get some money and I told her to go see Imam Amin after your father disappeared. There were too many uncertainties. It was a different time back then."

Yasmine pulls out a pen and paper. "This Imam Amin, is he still alive? Is he still in town?"

Ashraf nods. "Yes, of course, he's the imam at the Suleiman masjid by the marina. He was very close with your father before he disappeared."

"How did you know my parents?"

"Your mom and I, we went to school together and I met Akram when he started hanging out with her. We became close friends after they got married. Your father loved your mother very much, maybe too much. And then of course my brother ended up marrying Samira's sister. I'm the one who introduced them." He takes a bite of the rice-stuffed zucchini. "Akram supported the Palestinian cause."

"How?"

He chuckles. "Well, he didn't fight with us or anything, but he wrote in the newspapers. Your father spoke English, too, so he would send this to people in Britain and elsewhere, I don't know. He was among the few sympathetic voices that sometimes got published in the West. He was always writing things. He had one of those black-and-white cameras that someone brought him from England, and he snapped pictures wherever we went with that heavy thing wrapped around his neck." He wipes his mouth with a piece of bread. "Your father was a good man, but I think he started noticing some things about our resistance leaders, and it made him uncomfortable. That's when he started getting involved in things he shouldn't have. Allah forgive him."

"Like what kinds of things?" Yasmine asks.

"It doesn't matter anymore. He's gone now and that stuff is in the past."

"Do you know anything about a man called Gamal El-Tayyeb? I think he was maybe friends with Baba. He's in prison and I was hoping to go visit."

Ashraf looks aggravated. "Gamal is long gone, Yasmine, and I don't recommend you visit the prison. It's a hell hole and it's not safe for a girl like you."

"What do you mean he's gone? I think he's still alive."

"Alive yes, but mentally, he's gone. He's been gone for a long time." He shakes his head and puts a spoonful of food in his mouth. "Yasmine, you are young, healthy, and beautiful. Why do you care about all this stuff? Just focus on what you have, on your blessings."

We eat the rest of the meal in relative silence, but I'm now just as curious as Yasmine. I'd never heard this level of detail about Samira and Akram.

Yasmine and I clear the dishes. When we return, she immediately presents one of the letters from her bag to 'Ammo Ashraf.

"'Ammo, someone left some letters for me at the hotel. They are claiming that Baba wrote them, but I don't know if I should believe that." Her voice is shaky.

He pulls out his glasses and opens the letter with the tip of his fingers. He rubs his beard as he reads, his eyebrows lifting just before he sets it back down on the table. "I don't know. This is strange. This looks like some of his writing, or something he would have put together."

"Do you recognize the writing?" She asks, speaking a little faster. "Do you have any old letters from him, or something that he wrote on that you can maybe check?"

He nods. "Yes, I'm sure I might have some old pictures with his writing on the back. Can I take this?"

Yasmine hesitates.

"I'll bring it back to you, I promise."

"Okay, thank you 'Ammo. I really appreciate it. Can you let me know as soon as possible?"

"Yes, yes. I'll check tonight inshAllah when I get home." He takes a sip of his tea and Yasmine's face glows in victory.

I wish that I could draw from some of her hope. Even if we could determine that the letters were in fact her dad's, it doesn't mean anything.

"If they are real, how might that change anything?" I can't help but ask. What is her plan?

She shrugs. "I need to know that these are true. I need some evidence to prove to me that Baba was alive when we left. Maybe he's still alive. Not knowing all of this haunts me."

Mama gets up from the floor cushion. She rests a hand on Yasmine's shoulder and parts her lips like she's about to reveal something, but then closes them and rubs her back. "Leave the past in the past habibti." Yasmine doesn't say anything in response.

I don't tell my cousin that her father is likely dead, just like all the other men from the war. And even if he is alive, he might as well be dead to them, neglecting his family all these years. I can't see anything beyond pain in her future, but I let her relish in her hope, trying to draw happiness from it for the both of us.

CHAPTER 07

It takes a day to confirm with 'Ammo Ashraf that the writing on the letters resembles Baba's. Over the phone, he asks to see more, so I tell him that I'll pass them on to Reem that night. We're supposed to meet at her school for their quarterly student social and she insists I join her.

By now, I've read most of the letters. They document events, names, thoughts. There's very little that could point to an overall coherent narrative, with the exception of a few full letters, written to others. If they are real, they were written after we left so he would have been alive when Mama took us across the seas. It was always a possibility, I suppose, that he was kidnapped and maybe found a way to escape later. But, why wouldn't he look for us? Why wouldn't he come for us? For a brief moment, I wonder if nothing happened to him at all, that he just decided to leave us. That thought is amplified by this one letter that haunts me. It's an apology to my mother.

> *Samira, habibti, 'omri. I am sorry for leaving you all behind. I hope that you will find it in your heart to forgive me, but I had to save you and the children. Amin tells me that you have left for Cyprus. Maybe one day I'll find a way to come back to you all in another country. Please give my salams to the children and kiss them from me, every day.*

Underneath the initial text, there are scribbles in red, like he had been scolding himself:

> *You're never going to send this, you're talking to yourself, let them forget you.*

I run my fingers over the ink, trying to picture him writing it. Why didn't he take us with him? I read it again, looking for clues in the shape of the letters. I try to look for links to the contents of the notebook, but my mind doesn't work that way. I don't see codes and secrets, only words sitting in an ocean of meaning. A paper is just a paper until it holds the key to finding my father. I hold it still until my eyes burn.

The clock strikes seven and it's time for me to leave.

I braid my hair, pick up my bag, and open the door. A paper bag falls on my feet and I wince. I look down the hallway; there's no one there. I peek inside the bag and see a brown leather notebook with a flower design stitched into the cover. A post-it note on top reads:

Recently bought myself a few and thought you might like this one, Z.

Aside from the book, there are a few chocolate bars. I unwrap one and put it in my mouth, locking the door behind me.

I walk out of the front building. A black cat rubs against my leg. I lean down to pet it and it rolls over, exposing its belly. I stroke its head and it purrs, demanding more attention. I rummage through my bag for something to feed it, but all I have are a few crackers that it doesn't seem interested in consuming.

Two young men that can't be more than fifteen whistle at me from across the street. "What's a pretty girl like you doing out on a night like this?"

"Who needs the moon when we have your beautiful face?" The other one chuckles.

I straighten my skirt, ignore them, and walk in the direction of the school by the marina. My steps are rushed and my heels clap against the cement. I make a fist with my hand and place a series of keys in between my knuckles, the way Yusuf taught me a few years ago. The two young men don't follow me and soon, I'm walking alone. I walk faster, keeping my eye on the road, looking back once to make sure. Reem had told me about the cat-calling. "It's annoying. You gotta threaten to punch one of them, and they'll let you be." I try to remember that.

The school building sits along the coast, a three-storey stucco. I walk past the vacant reception desk and take the steps to the third floor where I'm welcomed into a large hall. There are tables lining the walls with platters of food: samosas, stuffed grape leaves, hummus, fruit trays, chips, cheese, and two different types of bread.

Reem steps into the hallway and shouts my name. It echoes across the walls. "Come help, I need someone to carry this last table from the storage room."

Soon, more guests and students begin to arrive and the hall fills with chatter. Reem stands on a white chair. She clears her throat and speaks to the crowd. She starts with an introduction, what they hope students will gain from the term, then tells them to socialize. "Eat lots of food and don't ask me too many questions tonight. I'm not working, so just have fun." She smiles wide. Her big brown eyes and electric charisma light up the room.

She steps down from the chair and comes toward me. "Want to meet my more interesting students?" She pauses, then continues, "If it gets too boring or stressful, you can go up to the roof; it's nice up there." She points at a door behind the food.

Back when Tariq and I separated, Reem was constantly advising me to go out to restaurants, join student clubs, and make as many friends as I could. "It'll help you recover," she'd say. "Who knows, you might even meet someone cute and make Tariq feel bad about the way he treated you."

But I couldn't. I couldn't see anyone during that time. I found healing in solitude. I spent many of my days recovering from the divorce in Yusuf's basement, waiting out my 'iddah, finding wisdom in that isolation period. Sometimes, I wondered if that phase had altered my ability to be with others in large crowds. I explained this to her on a number of occasions and eventually, she understood that social interaction with people I don't know drains me, unlike her, whose soul is fed through laughter and interactions with others.

I look around at the crowd of students wondering what had brought them all here to learn Arabic at a time when so much of the world had developed a deep hatred for the people who spoke it.

Reem introduces me to a couple from Australia who travel to different parts of the world and spend time learning the language from those countries. Then, there's Faisal, an Arab American doing his PhD in Islamic Studies at Harvard. He's genuine and we spend a bit of time talking about our graduate life experience. He does most of the talking though and doesn't ask me much about my work. Ten minutes into our conversation, I start eyeing the door to the staircase. He pauses to take a breath after telling me he lived in Toronto, and I tell him it's where I live.

"What are you studying?"

"History."

"Oh." His brown eyes widen. "Hey, wait, what's your last name?"

"Hassan."

"Wait. This is going to sound crazy, but I think you know my cousin Tariq."

He can't be talking about my Tariq. What are the odds?

"I'm sorry, I heard about the divorce. We don't talk much, but I heard he's planning on visiting this summer." His words are clouded by a buzzing in my ear. "I think he's supposed to be coming toward the beginning of July, and we might connect." He pauses and cups my elbow with his hand. "Are you okay?"

I search for a way out of the conversation. "Hey, I see someone I need to talk to, but I would love to connect again." I start to step away, and he asks for my number.

"Um, yeah, sure." I plug it into his phone as fast as I can, then run out of the room and up the hidden stairway. As I'm walking away, I berate myself for not giving him a fake number.

Up on the roof, it feels like the stars have fallen to illuminate my path. Twinkle lights line the edges of everything. A cool breeze blows and goosebumps rise on my arms. I wrap my shawl around my body and sit in a plastic chair facing the waterfront. The evening sun casts its shadow and I watch as it descends behind the water's edge.

There's an ashtray on a folded table next to me. A cigarette butt looks fresh and I wonder who else knows about this place, how long I'll have it to myself. I take out the stack of books from my bag and prepare to spend the rest of the evening reading up here. Then, I hear a thudding sound and I look around, feeling mildly irritated. In the opposite corner, I see the shape of someone flowing in prostration. My shoulders relax at the sight of a body connecting with the divine in a moment of tranquility. I squint my eyes to get a better look, and it takes me a minute to realize it's Ziyad.

He finishes praying and sits still on the mat, unaware of my presence. He wipes his face and chest and turns to face me. That's when I realize I've been staring, so I look away. His footsteps become louder as he nears.

"I swear I'm not following you around," he says. His thick hair is styled and parted to the right.

"I didn't assume you were." I return his smile. "My cousin teaches at the school here."

"Do you mind if I sit here?" He points to the other chair and I catch the faint smell of eucalyptus.

I tell him it's fine and ask if the cigarette butt is his.

He mumbles something to himself before saying no, then asks about the books stacked next to me.

"Different things. Spirituality, Arabic literature, history," I say.

"What's *Keetab el-ilm*?" He gestures toward Imam Abu Hamid Al-Ghazali's *Book of Knowledge*.

"You can read Arabic?" I ask, surprised.

"Kind of. I'm learning. It's the vocabulary that I struggle with more than the reading." He opens the napkin in his hand and offers me a petit four.

I take a chocolate one. "It's a famous work of literature by an ancient Sufi scholar. This book is the first of a series of forty. I studied a lot of his work during my MA. Some of it brings me comfort when I'm feeling a little lost."

He lifts an eyebrow and gives me a curious glance. "What's this one about?"

"This is the foundation for his ihya' series. It's focused on knowledge, the purpose, its power over all the things that we see and don't see. It's the basis for everything really: how we practice, how we live, how we believe, how we know ourselves and our place in the world." I grab it and hold it on my lap. "There's a group of scholars working on a translation of the text for some of the books. I think one of them may be out, the one on reliance and divine providence."

"But you can read it in Arabic."

"Yes," I respond as a matter of fact. Learning Arabic had taken effort for me. Mama used it with us at home, but I couldn't read or write until I took classes in university. I wanted to feel tied to Lebanon, to Palestine and my family. Learning the language made me feel like I was connected to a deeper part of me that I had lost, that migration had stripped from me. My love for it continues to flourish and I have mastered the ability to read traditional texts.

"Can you read out loud and translate for me?" He seems embarrassed by the request, stuttering at "read."

I'm a little taken aback by his desire for what I contain, because people are rarely interested in this.

At my hesitation, he says, "How about this? How about you read a couple of pages, translate for me, and I'll pay you back by telling you a story."

"What kind of story?" I had once been enamoured by the vastness of his imagination. It had given me an escape into worlds I never dreamt of visiting.

"Anything. I can do fiction and I can do reality and maybe you can guess which one it is in the end, but I promise that most of my stories are good. Did I tell you about that time I was chased by a camel?"

I laugh. "What? No!"

"Great, I'll tell you all about it after you read the chapter." He takes a bite out of the cookie.

"Okay." I begin reading from the *Book of Knowledge*, pausing after each paragraph to explain the Arabic text in English.

His quiet is occasionally punctuated by a question relating to a concept and how it may relate to his understanding of worship. I relish the opportunity to share my knowledge with someone. Reading is nice, but being able to talk about it with someone tickles my intellect. This feels like food for my soul.

We finish the chapter and sit in silence until he asks about my research progress.

"I'm not sure. I'm actually thinking of switching my focus to create a profile of missing men from the civil war, maybe create a historical map of some sort. Document it, find trends and maybe clues as to where their bodies might be or what happened to them. I want to create a narrative of the forgotten. There's some local organizations that are trying to match DNA and stuff, but I want to work on the narrative piece." I pause, considering my words. "I think a lot can be learned from difficulties and struggles, from history, but you have to take the opportunity to look at what happened and understand it to make sure it doesn't happen again. I feel like this country is living through a sort of amnesia."

He nods in agreement, contemplative.

"When the civil war ended, there was a collective amnesty for everyone involved. No charges were laid against perpetrators and some of those war criminals are still in power now." I take a deep breath. "I wonder sometimes what my family was involved in, whose side they were on, what'd they have to do to survive? Do you ever talk to your dad about it?"

He shrugs. "I'm not very well connected to my Lebanese side. I spent a lot of time in Korea after my parents divorced. And my dad … I just … we don't talk a lot." He wipes his hand clean from the crumbs. "But back to what you said about difficulties and stuff. Do you think that good things come from remembering difficulties and struggles? I kind of get it if the people just want to forget, but

I also get it if people want to remember because that's how they get better. Who was it that said 'what doesn't kill you will make you stronger'?"

"It was Nietzsche, and people often misuse that quote because that's not how he meant it. Also, he lived a pretty miserable life so I'm not sure I'd be taking his advice on it." His question feels loaded with something. "But I think there's a lot to be learned from struggles. One of my teachers once told me that God enters the heart through the cracks."

He doesn't say anything for a moment. He's looking up at the horizon and I wonder if he's trying to hide the glistening of his eyes.

"How did she die?" I say.

"It was really random and quick. She got tetanus."

"Wow. I'm so sorry Ziyad. How long were you married?"

"Just a year, but…." His voice is shaky. "It was a bit of a complicated marriage, so her death just generated a lot of other issues."

"Have you been coping okay? We don't have to talk about this, by the way."

"No, it's okay; it sort of helps. Have I been coping? I honestly don't know. I think I'm going through some sort of existential drift, wondering what the rest of my life is going to look like." He turns to face me. "I like having you here. You remind me of home and I like this, talking about books and spirituality with you again. It makes me feel like I'm on some sort of stable grounding."

I don't tell him that I feel the same. I stroke the pages of my book. I want to ask him so many questions about his life. I want to be there for him. I want to lean into him. But that is dangerous territory because I don't like the way I feel looking at him, with his eyes filled with sorrow and loss.

Before either of us says anything else, the door to the rooftop opens and Reem walks in. "Where have you been?"

"Sorry, I was just here talking to —"

Reem interjects, "Minjoon, hi! He's one of my students."

"Oh, um ... what time is it? I forgot my watch," I stutter.

"Habibti, it's almost midnight. I was about to go home. I'll drive you."

I'm shocked when I realize how long we've been up here. I pick up my books and look at Ziyad. "Thanks for the notebook, by the way. I'll see you around; you still owe me a story."

In the car, I'm lost in my thoughts, wondering what to do with this tingling in my heart. I play back our conversation and smile unconsciously until Reem snaps me out of it.

"So how do you know my student?"

"He's an old friend from undergrad."

"An old *friend*, eh?"

I nod. She laughs and I'm relieved that she doesn't ask anything else.

When I'm back at the hotel, the electricity is on and I take a long, hot shower. This place — I don't know what it's doing to me. I'm filled with anxiety and questions about my past and future and yet at the same time, I've never felt so free. Or maybe this is just what happens when you're finally away from the will and demands of someone else. I remember what Tariq's cousin said to me earlier that night, and I wonder if he somehow found out that I'm here. He means less to me here, where I have family and my worth isn't defined by how he values me. I pray that I'll have the strength to walk away from him if I see him, to resist his sweet words and empty promises.

CHAPTER 08

Going to the Roumieh prison is not something I ever imagined I'd do, but Yasmine has a way with words and she managed to convince me to take her by adding an overnight trip to the Bekaa valley. Spending a full day with her, just us girls drifting across the Lebanese mountains and valleys, seemed like a solid way to escape my reality and enjoy what this country has to offer.

The Roumieh prison is the only institution in Lebanon that's built for long-term detention. It houses some of the country's most notorious criminals. But it's also a place of drug addiction, corruption, and overall unsanitary and inhumane conditions. People can be here for a spectrum of reasons from drug possession to murder to basic theft. Others, I'm sure, are innocent, convicted by a court system designed to oppress and silence voices that speak against corruption.

I park outside the large wall encapsulating the panopticon, surrounded by lush green trees. We walk toward a black metal gate where several officers in grey military uniforms and little French red hats ask us for our ID and our purpose for the visit. Rifles hang on their shoulders.

"We're here to see Gamal El-Tayyeb." Yasmine hands one of them our permission slip from the justice ministry. He studies it intently. "Why would two young girls like you be here to meet with him?"

I shudder at his glances.

"It's for work," Yasmine declares with her shoulders squared.

His eyes wander up and down our bodies, and then he throws the permit at Yasmine and waves us through.

"How did you manage to get that permit anyway?" I whisper as the guard leads us toward the structure.

She shrugs. "I told them it was for my research, gave them documentation on my work. Plus," she pauses, "I paid them a little extra." I grin. Yeah, she quickly learned that you could pretty much be anything here.

"Sit here." The guard gestures toward a wooden table in the middle of an open field near the prison yard. "You have fifteen minutes, not a second more."

The prison is panelled by white walls on the outside and angled in different directions, like multiple Vs connected to each other. Clothes and other fabric hang from the metal bars between white walls, opening to what I imagine are cells on the inside.

Gamal enters, escorted by another guard who directs him to sit at our table. He's wearing regular civilian clothes and walks toward us without any cuffs or restraints. My arms tense around my body and I look at Yasmine for comfort. She seems unafraid.

Gamal sits and stares at us. His face is devoid of any expression.

Yasmine clears her throat. "Marhaba Mr. El-Tayyeb. Thank you for agreeing to meet with us."

He smirks. "What else do I have to do here. It's not every day that two beautiful girls come to visit me. What can I do for you?" He clasps his hands together.

My pulse quickens and I eye the guards spread throughout the yard. I have already identified all the ways we could run and escape if needed.

Yasmine hands him an envelope with cash and a bag of bread. "This is just a thank you for talking to us."

He nods and takes the provisions.

"I think maybe you knew my father, Akram Hassan. He was a journalist and he went missing during the war."

"Of course, I remember Akram. We were like brothers."

Yasmine looks at me with wide eyes and turns back toward him. "Um, as you know, he went missing during the war, but I recently found something that makes me wonder if he's alive."

"No," he says.

"No what?" I ask.

"No, he didn't go missing. He ran away. Who told you that?"

Yasmine's breaths quicken. "Do you know something about what happened to him?"

He scratches his chin. "You should ask your Uncle Saleem."

"Mr. El-Tayyeb, I'm sorry. I don't understand. Everyone he knows says he went missing. They searched for him. Who is my Uncle Saleem?"

He laughs and it rattles me. "Of course you don't know who that is. Why would you? Your father hated him and his whole family." He laughs more, then abruptly, he puts his hands on the table. "He wanted people to think that he went missing; it's the only way they were going to get off his back."

"Why would people be on his back?"

"Have you read any of your dad's reporting, dear? If you read closely, he accused some of colluding with the Phalangists, of taking bribes. Powerful people wanted him dead. He had evidence, and it threatened the entire establishment. Your father believed in the Palestinian cause and the pan-Arabist movement. His family didn't like any of it."

"Where did he go? Do you know if he's still alive? When was the last time you heard from him?" She's speaking frantically.

"Haven't heard from that arse in a long time. He's probably living in Syria. That's where he was going to go."

"What did Saleem do? Which of his family members were colluding?"

"I don't know. He never told me. He was very paranoid in the end and kept everything, all his evidence, sealed somewhere. He always thought someone was after him."

"Is there anyone else who might know? Who might help me understand this?"

"Look, it's been a long time. You know, back then, people got into a lot of shit that wasn't worth it if you ask me. Look what I got for it. I struggled for a movement that abandoned me in the end. It was for the cause, they said. Ha! I'm a sheep dog now. There was no cause. It was all a ruse to give more power to the powerful."

"Was Baba involved in what got you here?"

He shakes his head and smiles, displaying a gap surrounded by browned teeth. "No, he wasn't involved in that. Your dad thought that the pen was more powerful than a bullet." He slams his palms on the table and we jump. "Ya bint, it doesn't matter what he was involved in. It's better if you don't know. None of it matters now anyway. The powerful ones, those devil war criminals, they are still in power today and the plebes, the powerless, are even more oppressed now. What do you want with this? Live your life."

"Time's up!" one of the guards announces as he grabs him by the arm.

"Wait, but what was he involved in? Please tell me!" Yasmine pleads for more information, but it's fruitless. He smiles and shakes his head like a mad man as he is led away.

We walk back out through the metal gate.

In the car, Yasmine whispers, "I don't understand." She puts her seat belt on.

"He's obviously not fully there in the head. He's probably hyped up on drugs or something. Didn't you see his eyes?"

"Why would you say that, Reem? He obviously knows something. Maybe Baba told him that he was leaving. Maybe he's right and Baba went to Syria."

"We don't know anything for sure, and I really wouldn't trust this guy. He seemed crazy; he probably had a dream with your dad in it and confused it for reality."

She shakes her head and I begin to drive back toward the road moving uphill, surrounded by arz trees and bushes. "Do you know who 'Ammo Saleem is?"

I stretch my hands out on the steering wheel and clench my teeth. "He was your dad's brother and he's a minister. They live in Beirut, his family."

She stares at me for a moment. "Why are you just telling me this now, Reem? I've been asking you questions about my family and you've just been keeping this from me?"

"Yasmine, I don't want to have anything to do with your dad's family and I don't think you should either. I didn't tell you about Saleem because your mom didn't want you to know them, and what right do I have to undo everything she did to keep you away?"

"It's not up to you!" she shouts.

I realize then how entitled and naïve my cousin is. She's obsessed with forming some idealistic portrait of her family, absent any narrative holes. What she doesn't understand is that this isn't possible. She doesn't get that not knowing the details is a blessing.

"Yasmine, you should listen to people who tell you not to go digging into the past. Just leave it all behind. You're confusing yourself."

"Why should I leave things in the past? That's easy for you to say Reem. You grew up with your family. You had relatives around you. You live in the same place your parents lived."

"So what? You think I would choose that over what you have?"

She looks at me with hurt and betrayal in her eyes.

I lay a hand on my breastbone. "I don't mean it that way. I'm grateful that Mama is still alive. I just … you have a lot, and I don't understand why you can't be content with it. It's kind of selfish for you to be constantly asking people about their past. Some of us just don't want to think about it or talk about it. Just because it doesn't cause you pain doesn't mean you have the right to traipse around asking people to suffer just to fulfill your curiosity."

"You think this is about curiosity?"

"Well, yeah, what else? What good can come of this? What benefit does it bring to you? We don't all just get to leave in a few months and go back to our nice lives in Canada."

"It means everything to me." She rubs the back of her neck. "What if Baba is alive?"

"He's not." My eyes are on the road, but I sense her piercing glares.

"You don't know that. And this isn't just about curiosity. It's about everything."

"Okay, khalas. Whatever you say. Can we just not talk about it anymore?" I don't have the strength to convince her. She crosses her arms. We drive into the Bekaa valley in silence.

As I drive I allow myself to picture what my life would have been like had our places been switched. Would I have been obsessed with learning about the past, wanting to know every detail about my ancestry? The thing that she doesn't understand is that even with the access I have to people and places, there's so much that's been left unsaid. There was a time, when Teta and Jeddo were still around, that I would ask them about their home in Al-Khaliṣa. My grandmother would stroke my hair and speak to me of a time when they flourished, tending to the land. Her father was once the town's leader and she thrived, benefiting from the honours that being his daughter afforded her.

I didn't get anything more than that. They never spoke about how they fled, how their homes were now overtaken by Israeli settlers, or what it meant for them to live in Lebanon, unwanted with nowhere else to go. We heard more jokes about how they played music to muffle the sounds of gunshots during the civil war. They had turned the memories of their lives into comedy to survive, and that's all I got. I didn't get details that were too painful to remember, like my aunt's mysterious brother who she only met once, the third child she lost in childbirth, or the son that was shot in the head in front of her. Those events were locked up. Years had gone by and those stories had become whispers, rumours, floating away into our community's subconscious. We all lived on the edges of the shadows that contained their pain, their children creating new rounds of trauma and heartache.

We drive up and down hills and around valleys, the same mountains and valleys that were once connected to all of the lands of this area. Once upon a time, my great grandparents frolicked across these hills to pick za'atar and maramiyeh from Mount Lebanon. They moved from Damascus to Jerusalem without the need of a paper that told them where they belonged or gave them a right to exist.

A few hours later, we arrive at a hotel in the hills of Baalbek. Yasmine had booked us a room, insisting that we spend the evening and get the most out of our sightseeing. Except now I'm not sure if we should be in the same room for the night. My anger at her entitlement has festered deeper over the course of the drive, and I worry about saying something hurtful.

We drop off our bags and go to dinner at a nearby restaurant. We walk onto a patio shaded by a canopy of brown hemp cloth. White plastic chairs contrast the red tablecloths. We sit at the only table available, avoiding eye contact with each other. A waiter comes over and sets down a bottle of water. I order an argileh.

"By the way, that stuff is worse than smoking a pack a day," she says.

"It helps with my stress. I'll quit when I'm older. If I live that long."

The waiter comes back with a tray of pita and appetizers of za'atar, labneh, and pickled vegetables. A lingering, heavy silence fills the space between us.

I take two puffs of the apple-cinnamon tobacco. I decide to bring it up again. "I don't understand why you're obsessed with this, Yasmine. You have a good life. One that's better than a lot of people's here. Why can't you just be content with it?"

"This has nothing to do with contentment. You also don't understand what it's like to live a life so disconnected from where you came from. I know I have a good life, but it's also been filled with feeling like I never belong anywhere. I just want to know where I'm grounded. I want to know about Baba to understand what I inherited from him. I want to see what Mama saw and know her more intimately." She shakes her head. "And what if he's still alive? I'm just sitting here, wasting time. I need to know where those letters came from and if there's any truth to them."

I fiddle with the fork on the table. "Maybe I don't understand, but you have to stop forcing people to explore painful memories. Some of us are still living through this hardship. We don't want to think about these things. I just want happy things. I don't want to talk about the past."

We don't look at each other for a few moments of silence. Then she says, "I'm sorry. Maybe I shouldn't have forced you to come with me."

"I don't mind coming, Yasmine. I like hanging out with you. You listen to me in a way that other people don't and you believe me when I tell you about my ambitions. You make it seem possible to do things out of the ordinary. I just don't like this. I don't like dwelling over the things we don't have control over. I don't like forcing people who are obviously suffering so much to talk about their suffering."

"I get it. I'm sorry. Maybe I was being a little selfish."

"Yes, you were."

She looks at me, surprised. Someone has to tell her.

"Thanks," she says. I'm not sure if she is being sarcastic.

"You're welcome, and I'm only telling you this because I love you and someone should be setting you straight, especially when you're in a place you are not familiar with."

"Okay, I get it. Thank you." That time sounded genuine.

When the bill arrives at the end of our meal, I grab it. Yasmine had already paid for everything else, but she yanks it from my hand as quickly as I pick it up. "Let me cover it, Yasmine," I demand.

"No, this is my apology to you. Or, think of it as my payment for dragging you here to argue with me."

"You could never afford me, if that's the case. Please Yasmine. Just let me pay."

"*Bas*, forget about it Reem. You can get it next time." The waitress comes and takes her money without paying too much attention to our bickering. Yasmine smiles victoriously.

We spend the rest of the afternoon walking across ancient Roman ruins, structures that have lasted for a period beyond my imagination. Yasmine's excitement is splayed in her features and my heart widens with increased admiration for her. In the past, my outbursts of anger have distanced people from me. I'm often unfiltered in my speech and it has hurt people. But Yasmine doesn't seem to take it personally. Maybe she isn't so selfish after all.

CHAPTER 09

The air in Trablous morphs into a warmer, thicker breeze over the next couple weeks of May. I sleep with the windows open, dozing off to the humming of cars, bird song, and rippling waves. I develop a ritual at night where I pray Isha' and read Baba's letters over and over again, searching for clues, for messages that might speak to me of his ongoing existence on this earth, of where his feet might be trailing over stones or gravel or mud. I have skimmed old news articles only to come up empty. I don't ask Reem for more information about my Uncle Saleem and we have an unspoken agreement not to talk about Baba —or Ahmad, who is still missing.

Instead, I take comfort in meeting with Ziyad downstairs in the courtyard most mornings. At first, our meetings had happened by coincidence. I'd see him there, he'd invite me to sit with him, and we would update each other on our time here. Then, we started waiting for each other, and I now expect to start my days in his company.

This morning, I'm about to head downstairs when my phone rings, a Lebanese number on the screen that I don't recognize.

"Hello?"

"Marhaba. Is this Yasmine Hassan?"

"Yes, who is this?"

"It doesn't matter. I have information about your father."

My pulse quickens. "Who is this?" I demand again.

"I told you, it doesn't matter. Look, I have information about what you're looking for."

"Why should I believe you?"

"That's up to you to determine. If you want to know, bring a thousand dollars and meet me by the blue door of the Suleiman Masjid in two hours."

"I don't have that kind of money."

"Find it."

The phone goes silent. I stare at the screen, flabbergasted by this random person's demands. But I can't ignore it. I have to at least find out what this person is holding. I pull my fanny pack from under the mattress and count my money for the summer. I could spare a thousand, I think, if I don't make any frivolous purchases, eat at home, and walk everywhere instead of taking taxis. I pack the money into my bag and head downstairs.

The hotel is at maximum capacity now as tourists and students flock here for the summer. Ziyad waves at me from one corner. I sit down, clutching the bag against my chest.

"You okay?" he asks.

I run my hands over my hair and remember that I hadn't braided it last night, so my curls feel like they have formed a cloud around my head. I pull out a scrunchy and wrap my hair into a bun.

"Yea, I just woke up a little frazzled. I'm feeling a little…" I waved in the direction of my head.

"Did something happen?"

I scan the room for peculiar faces. How did that person get my number? Where did they get the information? "I just … I got a weird call this morning."

"Anything I can help with?"

I put my elbows on the table and lean forward. I'm glad he's here, but I don't want to involve him. "Yes, you can tell me all about what you were up to yesterday. How was class?"

"Hmm, well, your cousin Reem is an excellent instructor. She's witty and really smart. I learned that laban here apparently means yogourt, but most of the Arabic world uses it to refer to milk. The classes have saved me from accidentally putting yogourt in my coffee."

"What else? Have you gone sightseeing yet?"

"Not really, but there's a soap museum in Saida that I want to go visit. Maybe we can go together."

Intissar sets a cup of coffee in front of him and a plate of mana'ish in the middle. "I see you two are getting comfortable with each other." She winks at me. "I'm going to find him a good wife, inshAllah," she nudges my shoulder with her hip.

Heat creeps into my cheeks as I consider the rumours that might spread through people seeing us together every morning. "We're just friends, Khalto."

"Ah, do you already have someone?"

This was the fourth time I'd been asked about marriage since I got here. Intissar, at least, has the courtesy of waiting to get to know me before prying into my love life. I shake my head. "No, I don't want to get married."

Her eyes widen. "What you mean you don't want to get married?" She smiles quizzically. "You don't want kids? They are the essence of life. A woman has nothing without a husband. Trust me, you'll get lonely. Besides, you're too pretty to be single forever." She lowers her voice and leans into me. "Find a nice Arab man and settle down."

"Maybe, one day." My lips press together, forming a white slash.

Ziyad pulls out a book and pretends to read while intermittently glancing up, shifting in his seat. I wonder how much of our Arabic conversation he's absorbing.

After telling me more of the same for what feels like an hour, Intissar finally walks away. I sit in contained embarrassment and rage.

"She's sweet but can be a bit much sometimes." Ziyad breaks apart a cheese mana'ish and hands me the bigger half. "I heard that you had gotten married from my friend Omar. I think he knew your husband."

"You know Omar? Omar Mahfouz?"

He nods, "Yeah, he's been a good friend. He was there when I converted."

"When did he tell you I got married?"

"Oh, this was a long time ago, like right after I graduated. I heard good things."

My heart races at the mention of Tariq being a "good" guy. That's what he seemed like to most people, and when people said this, it was a constant reminder of his power and influence in our community. It's part of why I lost friends when we separated and why people labelled me as an ungrateful woman. How could a generous sweet talker be anything but good to his wife? How could someone who donated so much of his time and money to the community be anything but a good husband?

In the court of public opinion, I had lost — even now, in front of Ziyad. If I tried to convince him, he'd never understand, and why should I even waste my time? His privilege blinds him to the oppression that a woman might experience. How could he really understand?

But I know the truth: Under that charisma, Tariq flaunted a dark soul. He had no control over himself. All the happiness and power he sucked out of me would eventually fester in his heart and drown him in loveless misery.

Never again will I be in that position. I can trust nobody.

I put my books in my bag. "I'm sorry, I should go."

Ziyad's eyebrows furrow. "Are you sure? I'm sorry. Did I say something?"

"It's nothing. I have to go." I walk so fast getting out of the building that I trip on one of the steps.

My mind returns to the morning's phone call, and I begin to trek along the path going north in the direction of the marina toward the mosque. I rub my forehead and swallow the lump in my throat. Why does it feel like Tariq is everywhere?

About a minute into my walk, Ziyad runs up to me, breathless. "I'm sorry, Yasmine. I didn't mean to — " he stops when he sees my teary eyes. "Oh, shit. Yasmine, I'm so sorry. I didn't mean to upset you." He brushes his hair back. "I heard some other things too. I didn't know if they were true, so I just went with what seemed like a safer statement. I don't even know why I asked about him, honestly. I'm sorry." He pulls out a handkerchief and hands it to me. There's something engraved on it and when I look closer, I recognize his initials.

I hold it up. "The hell is this? Who even are you?!"

"What?" he shrugs. "You mean you don't have personalized napkins?" His features upturn and I wipe my nose with the soft cloth.

That's when I notice someone staring from a few feet behind. He's staring straight at me, as if he wants me to know that he's there. I look directly at him, and we enter a sort of staring contest. I wait for him to come closer and tell me he recognizes me or something. Instead, he gives me a slight smile and turns the other way.

"You okay?" Ziyad asks.

"I'm not sure." I turn and we continue our walk. My shoes click against the sidewalk with every step. "I wasn't crying because of what you said. It's other stuff. Tariq and I got divorced six months ago, and I'm still dealing with some of the legal stuff."

His breath slows. "I'm sorry."

"Don't be. It was for the best. But also, don't believe everything you hear. Just because someone speaks louder doesn't mean what they say is true."

He nods, his hands in his pocket. He looks at me with a curiosity that makes me uncomfortable.

"So, you're sad about the divorce? We can talk about it if you want."

"That's not it. I'm not heartbroken or anything. Between us, he was awful and there are still some complications that I'm trying to sort through. He doesn't seem to want to accept the divorce. There are rumours spreading about me, that I cheated, that I was ungrateful, that I didn't want to give him kids. None of it is true, but I've just been biting my tongue on all of it."

"Yasmine, I'm sorry. I hadn't heard any of that and I believe you."

"Good. I don't want to talk about it anymore."

He nods.

"I'm going to a masjid. I'm supposed to meet someone there.

You're welcome to join."

"Who are you meeting?"

"Someone ... I'm not sure. I also want to talk to the imam. He apparently knew my parents and I have questions."

We take the path by the waterfront passing residential buildings and restaurants. At first, we mostly walk in silence and then it occurs to me to ask him about his name. "I hear Reem calling you Minjoon. Do you go by that now?"

"I go by both. I used Minjoon in my Arabic class because everyone was a foreigner, and it felt appropriate to act like one. Whenever I tell people here my name is Ziyad, they look at me like I'm lying."

"Do you have a preference?"

"You can call me Ziyad."

I fiddle with a strand of my neck hair and look over at him. I notice his watch. It has three dials set on a green background with a dark brown leather wristband. I catch myself staring and look away.

"So, what do you do back home? You still haven't told me about your actual work, which is not your writing hobby."

The question makes him noticeably uncomfortable. "I'm kind of in between work right now. My existential crisis extends to my career."

I slip him a curious look and we remain silent for a few minutes.

"So, want to hear about the time I was chased by a camel?"

I smile. "Sure."

"I was in Dubai for a work-related thing, and they took us out to the desert for an 'Arabian experience' with camel rides and food and entertainment. It was kind of weird and a little orientalist. I had a lot of Arab friends so I knew that the culture couldn't be diminished to camels and belly dancers. The trip was catered to a specific audience, if you know what I mean."

"What do you mean? What kind of audience?"

He shrugs. "You know, like rich influential white people. Others on my trip enjoyed it, so I'm not trying to be judgy; I just think it was kind of weird."

"Okay, go on…when does the camel chase happen?"

"We were meeting the camels and preparing to ride them. One of the tour guides gave us food to feed them. Not gonna lie, I was a little scared. They are huge, way bigger than I imagined, and the thought of putting my hand close to that thing terrified me. But I didn't want to embarrass myself, so I did it. Except then I ran out of food and there wasn't any left and, I don't know, I guess this one particular camel that I was feeding was really hungry because she started nudging me. I actually thought that she might kill me, like trample all over me in her rage for more food. So, I started backing away slowly and she followed me until I started running and then she picked up her pace. At that point, I didn't care about my image anymore or what people were going to say. I just bolted and she continued to chase me until one of the tour guides calmed her down. It was all caught on tape; there's a video of it."

Laughing, I said, "Remind me to take you to visit some donkeys here."

"I think I can manage a few donkeys."

"Suuuuure."

As his story finishes, we reach the masjid. The building sits perched on a hill, on the edge of a busy road. It has an octagon-shaped fountain in the front courtyard where people make their wudu. The adhan blasts through the megaphone announcing the beginning of Dhuhr prayer and people move swiftly toward the front, setting up neat rows. Ziyad rolls up his sleeves, takes off his shoes, and begins his wudu by the outdoor fountain. I wrap my shawl around my head and tell him that I'll find him after prayer. There's still time before my meeting with the mystery caller, so I move toward the women's section of the prayer hall to join the congregation.

The mosque is small but ancient, from the Ottoman era. A large dome adorns the ceiling and circular chandeliers are set throughout. The walls are covered in blue and gold ceramic tiles. Quranic verses are sketched elaborately in gold ink along the top of the walls. It survived the fall of the Ottoman empire, French colonization, a civil war, and invasions from the Syrians and the Israelis, showing no signs of tribulations.

There's no partition between the men's and women's sections and I find a spot in the back with two older women and another who looks to be about my age. We greet each other with a salam and stand in prayer on green carpets laced with thin white lines.

When the prayer ends, I sit cross-legged in the back. People begin to leave and I spot Ziyad in the front right corner, prayer beads in hand. The imam stands below the mihrab, with a line of men waiting to speak to him. I scan my surroundings for suspicious watchers. Was the caller a person of faith? Did they come here to pray? Ten minutes later the room has quieted down, with a few worshippers in a corner reading Quran. That's when I get up and walk toward Imam Amin. His face looks like he has seen a ghost when he sees me.

"Assalamu 'alaykum Imam. My name is Yasmine Hassan."

"Bint Akram and Samira?"

I nod.

He opens his arms as if he is about to give me a hug but then he clasps his hands together instead and speaks to me in Arabic. "MashAllah, you look so much like your father. What are you doing here? How is your brother Yusuf? How is your mother? Is she here?"

I briefly update him on our lives. He seems to fill with pride and joy at first, but this quickly turns to sorrow when I tell him of Mama's death.

"May Allah have mercy on her soul and reunite her with her loved ones." The imam rubs his beard with his right hand and puts his left arm across his belly. I note his long, cream thobe and green kufi. "Your mother was a kind and gentle person. InshAllah, she finds peace in the afterlife."

"Imam, when I was growing up, Mama always told us that Baba disappeared before she left and everyone assumed he was dead. But I just found out that he might still have been alive at that time. Mama didn't tell us much about his family, and we never had any contact with them. I also found out that you shielded her from his family after he died, to protect us."

"Yes, that was a difficult time. We still don't know what happened to him."

"But why did you need to protect us from his family?"

He sighs. "Let's go to my office. I'll make us some tea."

I motion to Ziyad, asking him to wait. He nods without saying anything, prayer beads still in his hand.

The imam's office is in the basement, windowless and bare, with a desk and two chairs. He brings me a cup of hot tea and leaves the door open. His eyes are downturned, and he doesn't speak. We sit in silence for a few minutes and then I ask him about my father.

"He was fierce and hard headed, but he also had a deep sense of justice."

"Fierce in what way?"

"He married your mother against his family's wishes and that was no small feat. They are powerful people with resources and influence. They wanted him to marry a woman of his stature, or maybe someone from abroad, but certainly not a Palestinian from a refugee camp."

"I heard that his family didn't like her, but did they not accept her after the marriage? After we were born?"

He shakes his head. "The civil war broke out in the 1970s and as I'm sure you know, it was all about which sect should have greater power and influence. Many felt that the Palestinians were another thorn, another group demanding representation when the Shias and the Sunnis already wanted more representation in government. The elites don't like the idea of giving the Palestinians more power, but your father grew deeper into the Palestinian resistance. He wrote articles and sent them to newspapers all over the world. He fought his father and his brothers until they stopped speaking to each other. He even started hosting meetings in his home. He believed that Arabs needed to stay united — Palestinians, Lebanese, Syrians ... we should all fight

Western Imperialism. Some didn't trust him easily. They thought he might be a spy. Others took to him quickly, but your mother didn't want any part of it. She was a quiet woman and all she wanted was to find some sort of rest."

Imam Amin paints a picture of Baba that is akin to a revolutionary artist, full of passion for justice and equality formed on the foundation of pan-Arab beliefs. He tells me of how, in turn, his family became even more disgruntled with his leftist views and actions. There was an attempt on Mama's life, and some were convinced that his family was behind it. Because of this, Mama feared for her life and her children, especially after Baba disappeared.

My fists tighten and my knuckles turn white as Imam Amin describes the fear in Mama's face when she came to him after Baba's disappearance. My breathing quickens and the imam stops talking mid-sentence.

"I'm very sorry, but I have not been in contact with his family since the war ended. I am not sure what they are like now or if they know anything." He pulls out a paper and pen and writes down a name and a phone number. "This is the contact information for your uncle's wife, who's also a distant relative of your father. She came to visit me a while ago." He sighs, "Her husband is now a minister in the government."

"Is her husband Saleem?"

"Yes, you know him already?"

"I've heard about him."

A few moments pass in silence, and I swallow hard trying to diminish the lump in my throat. "Thank you, Imam."

He taps his fingers on the edge of his desk as if contemplating saying something else. I wait.

"I received a call about ten years ago." He's speaking like he's doubting his words as they come out. "The person claimed to be your father. He said he was alive but couldn't come home and wanted to check in on Samira and the kids, to check if they needed anything. I think...." I sit up in my seat, and he takes a deep breath. "I think it was him. His voice was familiar, but I can't be too sure."

"Wait, what did you tell him? Did you tell anyone about this call?"

"I told him that I didn't know anything, that Samira took the kids to Canada years ago but I thought they were doing well. I never kept in touch with your mother. It was for the best that way. Your father was a bit of a controversial figure, and I've managed to find sustenance after the war, a life, unlike many others who struggled to rebuild. I couldn't risk any of it."

"Do you still have the number? Why didn't you tell anyone about this? You could have found us!" I speak frantically, my voice rising slightly.

He doesn't answer, looking at me with pity that I don't want. "I regret it now, but I don't think I believed him then. Or maybe I felt like there was nothing I could do and there was no way to know for sure if it was him." His eyes meet mine. "Yasmine, the war was hard. A lot of people went missing. I know this is hard to hear, but your dad is likely among those who have passed. It happened to all of us; every one of us knows someone who disappeared."

I slump back in my chair.

"Call Laila. She might know something." He says with finality. "InshAllah, please, if you need anything while you're here, I'm at your service."

I thank him, then walk back up to the main prayer area and sit in a back corner. My breaths are heavy. I hadn't expected to be presented with a possibility of Baba's survival on this trip and I don't know what to do with the information. My historian brain insists on filling in the gaps of his life and I realize that his family members may be the only ones who know the truth.

I'm living Mama's worst nightmare. She must have known all of this and now her resistance to my coming here, getting to know the family, makes so much more sense. Did she suspect he might have been alive? Did she think he had given in to his family's wishes? Did she love him? Did she die thinking he'd abandoned her?

Ziyad is in the same spot, now with his book in hand. I walk to the front and nudge him. We put our shoes on at the entrance and walk out. I search for the blue door the anonymous caller had told me about. I have missed his deadline but only by twenty minutes. A part of me hopes he'll be there, another part wishes that phone call never came.

"The hotel is the other way," Ziyad says.

"I'm supposed to meet someone to pick up something." There! I spot the door. It doesn't belong to the mosque but to a jewellery store nearby. The door faces an alley. I jog toward it and Ziyad follows. There's no one there that looks like they are waiting.

"Looking to buy some gold?" the shopkeeper says.

I don't answer, scanning the crowds. Inside the jewellery store, the shop owner is on the phone. My feet are cold in these sandals and a droplet of water lands on my hand. The sky has darkened with clouds.

"Are you okay?" Ziyad says.

"Sorry, I was supposed to meet someone here. But I'm late, and I'm worried they're gone now."

"Someone you know?"

"I wish." Another drop of water hits my forehead.

Ziyad pulls out an umbrella and holds it over the two of us.

"I'm sorry. We should probably go."

"You sure? Do you have a number?"

"No. And it's probably better this way. Come on."

We step back onto the main road. I wrap my shawl around my body, and Ziyad and I huddle closer as the rain begins to weigh the umbrella down. Cars honk as they drive past us. I replay the conversation with the imam in my head. Had I missed something? Could he have been hiding something?

"Are you okay?" Ziyad says, interrupting my thoughts.

I don't say anything at first. There's a hollow sensation in the pit of my stomach and a heaviness on my heart. I worry about what will come if I speak, what my tears will give away. "No," I finally say.

"That's honest, at least," he pauses. "Whatever it is, I'm sorry." We finish our walk in silence. Our shoes squish with the rising water and soil and sand, some of it rising up to my ankles. The stone steps of the hotel glow with the sparkle of fresh water. Ziyad opens the main door and asks if I'd like to have a cup of tea. Truth is, I don't want to go back to my room. The day doesn't feel finished.

It's mid-afternoon and the courtyard is relatively empty. We sit at our usual table by the back, near the flowing jasmine bush. Ziyad doesn't speak. It's something I've noticed he does often. I asked him about it once, and he told me he was taking in the surrounding, noticing uncommon or mundane things, writing descriptions, sometimes in his head, sometimes in his notebook.

Intissar walks over to us in an unusual hurriedness. "There's someone here to see you, Yasmine."

I panic at the thought that she might have given away my room number. "Where?"

"He's by the check-in desk. If you want, I can tell him you're not here. I'm not sure if he knows what you look like."

Ziyad looks from me to Intissar and I know he's trying to figure out what we're saying. I stand and look back at the entrance to see who had asked for me. We lock eyes and he walks toward us. It's hard to unsee him. He must be at least 6'5" but weighs less than me. His lankiness extends to his fingers rubbing his chin.

"A word with madame Hassan please," he says in Arabic. I wonder if he's the one who called, if he followed me from the masjid to find out where I'm staying.

I swallow. "How can I help you?"

"I am a friend of your Uncle Saleem. He asked me to come here and check on you."

"I'm sorry, my uncle who? Are you the one who called me to meet by the blue door?"

"Saleem Hassan. I don't know anything about a call. Your uncle is aware that you don't know him well. They know your mother kept you away. He would like to see you. I have a number for you to call and arrange a time." There's something in the tone of his voice, or the way that he barely looks at me, that has a mocking quality to it.

"Why couldn't my uncle come and see me?"

"He's a busy man."

"And how did you know I was here?"

"Do you know who your uncle is?"

"You just told me his name."

He rolls his eyes. "Your uncle is a powerful man and we knew of your arrival as soon as you landed."

My heart begins to race. Had people been following me all along? If they knew I was here, why had they waited this long to contact me? Why didn't 'Ammo Saleem reach out to me directly? Was he trying to establish some sort of hierarchy? Make sure I knew he was in control? I quickly trace all the places I'd been in the last few weeks, all the people I'd met, looking for the culprits, the informants.

I swallow. "Give me his number, and I will think about calling him."

He pulls out a slip of paper from his pocket and hands it to me. "Here. I'll give you a few days, but know that I'll be back if we don't hear from you."

He leaves and Ziyad takes a step closer to me. "Was that the person you were supposed to meet?"

"I'm not sure."

"Are you okay?"

I sigh. "I think some of my relatives want to see me."

"And that's a bad thing?"

"It's complicated."

"Wanna sit and have some tea?"

His face is warm and welcoming, but I need to go back to my

room and sort this whole thing out. I smile. "I think I'm going to head upstairs. Thanks though."

Back in my room. I pick up the letters again, looking for clues about what Imam Amin had said earlier, something that could tell me who 'Ammo Saleem was. I glance through a few of them, trying to see evidence of an assassination attempt or any stories of his family. In the sixth and last letter, I find something.

Samira came home shaking today, her eyes empty. There was a riot in the street as she made her way home from the market. I don't know if we'll ever get to a point when seeing the things that we see — people shot, cars blown up — won't shake us anymore. The fear in her eyes reminded me of the time she got attacked last year. She had gone to the market early in the morning and was followed on her way home. She says it was a kid, but that didn't mean anything. The young and old are both carrying weapons. He asked her if she was Samira and she nodded. She shouldn't have answered the question. She should have lied and said something else. We practised this; I told her to keep her identity secret so many times. Nobody needs to know who she was, what she was. We practised proper Lebanese pronunciation daily: "Bonjour, banadooouurraa, not bandora."

The man attacked her with a knife. Alḥamdulillah, an older man pushing a grocery cart saw him and came to her rescue. I still think about who sent that kid to attack my wife. I think it was S and his aides. Baba tried to talk to him, to stop him, but he's too self-engrossed. All he can think of is himself. I think it was a warning, because it happened right after I threatened to publish my articles. I never got to write about what actually happened anyway. Baba was frail and I worried that my articles about the "Lebanese family" would eventually be tied back to him. That would have sent him over the edge. It wasn't his fault. I don't even know if he knew about his eldest son's betrayal. He's gone now, but I don't have the means to write the way I used to.

His eldest son. Was this "S" my uncle? And why, of all people, was my mother the scapegoat in this drama? Mama had gone through so much to survive and ultimately suffered the consequences of Baba's choices whether it was intended or not. She bore the pain and the heartache so that Yusuf and I didn't have to feel that pain.

That's why she kept it from us. It's not because she just hated this place.

Now that I'm sitting here alone with jumbled thoughts, teary eyes, and a pain in my chest, I wonder if she was right to keep me away. If Reem was right to tell me not to pry into everyone's secrets. I should have respected Mama's undeclared wishes to keep these secrets buried like so much of this country's history.

I look around the apartment in search of someone to talk to, someone to tell me what to do, and I think about knocking on Ziyad's door. Only, I haven't told him any of this yet and I don't know what he'd make of my family's past. And I don't know if I want to open the door to the type of intimacy that would entail if I welcome him into some of my deeper emotions.

I sit on the edge of the bed in the solitude of my room, cold and empty with Uncle Saleem's name eclipsing my thoughts.

CHAPTER 10

It smells like burned olive oil and eggs. Mama is making breakfast in the kitchen and she's entered the second stage of her grief. When Ahmad disappeared again, she'd fallen back into the same pit of sadness she fell into after Baba died. There's an intensity to it at the beginning when she doesn't talk to anyone and spends her days locked up in her room with a dull, distant stare on her face. If I ask her to talk about it, she responds by saying she's fine in an exaggerated cheerful tone. I worry about her most in those early stages, like she's on the cusp of something worse. And then, gradually, something shifts. Her limbs move with intention and she returns to her routine of cooking, cleaning, and visiting neighbours, even while a lingering sadness clouds her movements.

I walk into the kitchen and sit next to Fatme. Mama sets down a plate of scrambled eggs, another of labneh, and a bowl of olives. Fatme tells me about the school project she's working on to build a motor. I tell them about my students and we settle into the safety of small talk, ignoring the giant void, the empty chair.

Later, in the classroom, I listen to my students recite a sentence in Arabic about their time in Lebanon. Minjoon describes his trip to the masjid and Saroise speaks about her visit to Ehden. She's mid-sentence when the force of my tension snaps a pencil in two in my palms. The room goes quiet, and I set the mangled stick down on the desk.

"Sorry, bad habit," I say. The students don't respond. "Okay, well, it's almost two and you are all free to go. Good class, everyone."

The room clears swiftly. I turn the light off, sit in my desk chair, and stare out the window. The wind rustles trees and it looks like another storm is brewing over the sea.

The door abruptly opens, and I jump in my seat. A familiar figure stands in the entryway. He's wearing ripped jeans, with his beard trimmed and his hair freshly groomed, hunched over with his hands in his pockets, looking very much like a sad puppy. I invite him in warily.

"What do you want?" My tone is stern.

"I'm sorry for leaving like that Reem, but I had to that day."

"Why? You couldn't at least call?" I tap my foot impatiently.

He closes the door. "I think there are some people who are after me."

I sigh. I don't want this paranoid version back. I don't need stress and worry beyond what I'm already handling. I have graduate school applications to get through and money to save and I just want my older brother back. Or gone. Our lives had been fine without him breaking the consistency and the routine that I had created. "Why would anyone be after you, Ahmad? You've been gone for so long that nobody cares that you're here."

His brows knit and he moves closer to me. "You don't know anything, Reem. You don't know what I've been through."

I yell, "You know what, I don't, and you don't know what I've been through this whole time! I had to work three jobs just to keep everyone afloat. Do you know that I've been living off a few hours of sleep most nights? Do you know what I've had to endure and sacrifice just to keep Mama from falling into her pits of misery? Do you know what it takes to keep my own dreams alive?"

"I've been trying, Reem." His soft tone contrasts mine and his eyes wander around the room. "It's been complicated."

"Okay, so what do you want now?"

He sighs. "I went to see 'Ammo Saleem. I was hoping he might help, or at least have advice on what I should do."

I can't believe he went to see him. People like Saleem only care about themselves and what they can get out of every interaction. They're chronically chasing power and wealth as if it's unlimited, as if it's their right. People like him are the reason this country can't evolve. "Eh, and what did he say?"

"I wanted to know if there was a possibility of getting a new ID card, with a different name. He knows how some of these things work. He was nice about it. I felt like he understood, that he would help."

I scoff. "Did he help?"

"He couldn't with the ID card, but he gave me something better. He said that there's a way to get Lebanese citizenship and change my name that way."

"I could've told you to just buy a fake passport."

He shakes his head. "Not a fake one." He pulls out a stack of forms from his bag. "There's this lawyer who might be able to take care of it for us. He said that we could claim Lebanese citizenship if we could prove that our grandparents lived here, and were just visiting Al-Khaliṣa in 1948. This lawyer has helped other Palestinians. He forges documents that indicate residency here from the Ottoman era."

I'd heard about this; some of my friends from grade school had gotten their own citizenship and moved out of the camp. I'd always assumed that it was because those people had connections and knew people in high places who could just forge documents for them.

"So you spent four weeks talking to Saleem? Why have you been gone for so long?"

He lowers his head. "I feel bad about what you said that day I came back, about all the responsibility you had to shoulder, so I asked Saleem if he had any work for me. He told me that he was renovating one of his restaurants in Faraya. Construction type work, painting, cleaning, that kind of thing. It didn't pay much, but I saved almost everything to bring back and told him to keep me posted on any other opportunities."

A pang of guilt hits me. "Couldn't you at least have called?"

He rubs his face with the palm of his hand. "Reem, it's complicated. The things I did in Syria, they got me in with the wrong crowd and let's just say that I didn't leave on good terms."

"I can't help you if you won't tell me what happened, why you ran when you saw that guy."

"I don't want you to get involved," his eyes wander around the room, "but if I tell you, you can't tell anyone."

I raise my hands. "Tell me what happened."

"I was the first to get out of jail because I gave the police names and information about the drug dealers that got us into this whole mess. The people who ran the company I worked for, they were smuggling drugs into Jordan and Lebanon. I didn't know it, but they blamed me and a few others when the police raided the factory. I told them I'd tell them everything if they let me go, and I did, even though it took me so long. Now, the haramiyeh are after me, but there's something even worse Reem." He pauses. "They wanted to get back at me and so instead of coming for me, they told the Syrian government that I was involved in extremist activities."

"What do you mean by extremist activities?"

"That I was associated with terrorists, planning a suicide mission, trying to preach those ideals to Syrians, convincing them to turn against the government. They told them that I was a member of Fath Al Islam. You know I would never — do I look like someone who can fight? I just want to be left alone, make money, and live. I don't want to be involved in politics. I don't know how I got into this mess. Ya Allah." His tone is aggravated. "The Syrian mukhabarat are after me now. They want intel on Palestinian resistance in their country as if I know anything."

"And how is citizenship going to help you with that?"

"I need to get a new identity. I called the lawyer that 'Ammo Saleem recommended, and he said he can do it. I explained the situation and it can be done. Then I'm going to use the passport to get out of here. You can do that too."

"But what if I don't want to be Lebanese?" Taking on the citizenship of the same people who have actively excluded me and my family for years feels like a betrayal.

His patience is starting to wear thin, and I see it in the force of his hand running across his face. "Why do you need to resist everything, Reem? Do you have any other options right now? Yes, yes, you want to go abroad, but don't you think that even your chance of that would be greater with this citizenship? You could at least get a proper job, and Fatme could study whatever she wants. We could buy a proper home for Mama and live like full human beings in this godforsaken place."

He's right, but I don't want to give into this plan so quickly. I don't want handouts from the Lebanese people. I want to carve my own way out.

Except, the thought of being able to get paid a higher wage, to get a different job, to buy a house is alluring. And, the truth is, my plan is very long term; it would take me years to get there, whereas Ahmad's plan makes it all seemingly within reach.

"Mama would never agree to this you know. It's like turning her back on what her family's been fighting for and accepting a handout from the very people who hate us."

"They don't hate us, and don't worry about Mama. I'll talk to her." He waves his hands in the air dismissively. "I got a list of the documents we need. It's a pretty simple process, but…." He hesitates for a moment. "It's expensive."

"How much."

"Ten thousand. American."

I laugh so loud that I'm sure the people outside on the street hear me. "And where do you think we can get that? I don't have that kind of money."

"Do you know anyone we could borrow it from?"

"Ahmad, just stop! You disappear on and off; you've been absent from all of our lives and now you come back acting like you're the only one who knows how to plan anything, and you demand all of our money. Forget it. We've been fine without you. We don't need you, and I can figure things out on my own. Do us all a favour and just stay away." I regret the words as they come out of my mouth, but I push him out of the way and walk out.

Once outside, I linger in my car, chewing on my nails. Students sit on the lawn in front of the building, laughing and smiling at each other with their expensive backpacks and cellphones. One of them looks at me with a wide smile and waves. I reluctantly wave back.

My phone rings. It's from the Hallab, my second summer job at the world-famous restaurant that sells knafeh. Sometimes people come to visit from overseas and buy kilos of their sweets to bring back to their loved ones in Canada, Australia, or the Emirates. This year though, the manager calls to tell me he won't need me. They hired a few additional staff members a few months back that are staying on for the summer.

"How about you pay me less than last year?" I plead.

"I'm sorry." I hear the remorse in his voice, but he's unable to give me anything. If I had known earlier, I would have found something else to make up the extra cash. "Good luck Reem. I'll let you know if anything changes." The line goes dead, and I clutch my phone until my knuckles turn white. More students walk out of the entrance. Their smiles haunt me; it's like they all know and pity me. I turn the ignition and drive.

I meet Yasmine at her hotel. She's sitting at a round table near the water fountain in the centre of the courtyard. It must be nice to spend her days here, leisurely enjoying all the free time she can carve out of her life. Her fresh curls fall across her shoulders. She's peeling a pomegranate.

I sit at her table, and she immediately asks me what's wrong. I tell her about what happened with my job and Ahmad. Her hands dig into the flesh of the fruit, carefully taking seeds out of their white shells and placing them gently like pearls in a bowl.

"So, what do you want to do about it?"

"This is not about what I want."

She uses a spoon to scoop seeds from the bowl and passes it to me. "I mean, what are you going to do about what Ahmad suggested?"

I want to tell her that I'd like to ignore him. That I want to finish my applications. That I want to work this summer and accumulate the money to travel. I want to find a way out of this country and to sponsor my family and find the space to spend my days picking pomegranates and reading in a hotel courtyard.

Yasmine pushes the tray aside. "What do you want to do about Ahmad? Do you want to work with him and this lawyer to get your citizenship?" Yasmine's voice is always soft. I try to picture her anger but come up empty and then I wonder if this was what she was like with Tariq, despite everything he'd put her through.

"I can't," I say.

"Why not? Why is it possible for you to get into graduate school abroad but this isn't?"

"Because I don't have the money."

Yasmine lets out a deep breath and hands me another spoonful of pomegranates. "Let's see if we can figure something out."

What? Her response makes me hopeful and confused all at once. Does she think money grows on trees? Is she just trying to comfort me with false pretenses?

"Do you want to come with me to Beirut? I'm going to visit Tante Laila and her husband."

I don't understand why she's asking me this now. It has nothing to do with what I just told her.

"Yasmine, why are you saying you can figure something out?"

"I'll talk to Yusuf and see if we can come up with the money, inshAllah."

"I can't ask you to do that," I say.

"Why not? You can pay me back if you want, but I can and I will."

I'm speechless. And filled with regret for not being more grateful for her presence in my life.

After a few moments, she says, "So will you come with me?"

"Why are you going to see them?"

"Because they're family and I need to know them. I have questions to ask."

"I can't this week. Do they know you're coming? Her husband isn't the friendliest and you shouldn't just show up."

"I did call and they're expecting me."

"They are not your people."

She runs a knife across a fresh pomegranate and taps the edges. Her eyes shift up to me and back down to where her hands crack the fruit open. "Whether you like it or not, they are my blood."

"Government officials here are not like the ones you have back in Canada, accountable to people and stuff. They steal money from the poor and use it to vacation in France. Saleem is the minister of the interior. He's supposed to be managing civil infrastructure and supporting our cities. Instead, he plunges all this country's money into his brother's company in Saudi Arabia, contracting them to build the fancy new towers and shops in the Hamra. They take money from us and spread it back to themselves. Meanwhile, the economy here continues to flounder. They don't funnel any resources back into the healthcare system or education or even entrepreneurship. We could be exporting resources to the entire region, but they're too busy buying themselves Louis Vuitton and hoarding electricity in their neighbourhood."

She scoffs. "Our governments in the West aren't as clean as you think they are either. They've just found better ways to manage their reputations."

"Your dad's family never liked Mama or your mother." I continue hotly. "They're traitors who like to blame Palestinians for this country's problems instead of looking at themselves in the mirror. I don't know the details, but there were some issues that might affect you."

"I know about that. Imam Amin told me some of the story."

I sense she's unwilling to explain further, but I don't blame her. There's no point in fuelling the flames of my hatred for her family. In the end they are hers as much as I am.

"Is there someone else you can ask to go with you?" I ask.

"I might ask Ziyad. He has a car."

"Good. Also, what's the deal with you two?"

"What do you mean?"

"Do you like him? Because I think he likes you."

She purses her lips. "I like his company, but we're just friends." Her feelings aren't as transparent as mine and I suddenly want to dig into this more.

"Sure," I say. "What about Tariq? You never talk about him anymore."

She shrugs. "I prefer not to talk about a man that's been the bane of my existence." Over the years, Yasmine had been vague about what happened between them. She reached out on a few occasions and we spoke about how her relationship was rough, how he was arrogant and neglectful, but she never shared details. I had suspicions about what he'd done to her, though.

"Why did you marry him if he was the bane of your existence?"

She takes a deep breath. "He was nice at first, really nice. I thought I hit the jackpot at a young age. He was a good practising Muslim man with a good job and we generally liked each other."

"Isn't that what all marriages are like though? You love each other at first, only to eventually hate each other a few years down the road? Or in some cases, you never love each other and end up enduring until one dies and the other rejoices in relief."

She laughs. "That's a sad outlook. There are also happy marriages where people love each other."

"Sure," I roll my eyes.

"Anyway, with Tariq, it was worse. He was really mean. He got angry sometimes and took all of his frustration out on me. He called me names. He tore down my self-esteem, and he was controlling."

"Did he ever hit you?"

She turns her face away from me. "There were some instances. I don't like to talk about it. But he was brought up in a space where it was normal. The things he did. He grew up in a home like that, and he was taught that the world owes him something."

I cross my arms. I've seen a lot of women lose too much in their marriages. Situations that were worse than what she is describing. But I understand why many of them stay in those relationships. Family pressures, reliance on a man who could support in material ways. There aren't many options for those who leave. But Yasmine is different; she has access to resources, education, and even a brother who supports her. "Why did you stay with him for five years?"

She shrugs. "I believed that marriage is supposed to be a space where you can find love and mercy and comfort, Reem. With Tariq, it was really good at first, and maybe I wanted to find a way to go back to those times, to find the love and the mercy and the comfort that was lost. I was really young when we got together and I didn't know much about anything. I had no idea what was normal." She shakes her head. "It was Yusuf who actually started to notice things. I became quiet and distant and he picked up on it, and then I started going to therapy and I realized that it wasn't normal to be treated that way." She puts the last of the pomegranate seeds in her mouth. "Anyways, it's all in the past now."

My feelings are mixed as I absorb her words. The men in this country are not all gems, but they've been through a lot and I was not raised in the kind of home Tariq was. "Baba never lifted a finger to anyone. He was so sweet and did everything for Mama. Sometimes, I wonder if I'm just remembering through the eyes of a nine-year-old, if I forgot the bad times. But I have no memories of him raising his voice even."

"Then he was probably really a good man, Reem. They do exist. You remember him the way that he was."

I sigh, thinking of my life right now. "I don't know if I can ever get married. Not until I've unleashed myself from this prison."

Yasmine lays her hand on my arm. "I hope you find someone who brings you warmth and comfort and makes you laugh without any added burden. I want you to find someone who brings you ease, but take your time."

I think of her words as I drive myself back to the camp.

At home, Ahmad is in the living room with Fatme. Mama hums to herself, her face leaning over the steam from the large pot of tomato sauce. She picks up a plate of rice-stuffed zucchini and drops it in the sauce. I take a deep whiff. She wipes her hands on her apron. "Did you see? Your brother is back. I knew he would come back." We both stare at Ahmad seated on the red couch and at Fatme setting up the monopoly board.

Yes, he is. I want to tell her that I'm also here. That I've been here for the entirety of the time that he's been gone.

I move toward the living room and Ahmad looks up. "Wanna play?" he says.

"I will, but I'm the banker this time. None of you can be trusted." I cross my legs and sit at the other end of the couch.

"Food is going to be ready soon, so don't get too sucked into the game!" Mama yells.

Now I want to tell them that it is all going to be okay, because I will find the money, get our citizenship, and get us all out of here. But I can't find the confidence to say such words and the only thing I can picture is us sitting on this floor for the rest of our lives.

CHAPTER 11

I didn't think that my uncle's wife Laila would want to see me. It was as if she hadn't known about the strange call or the man who accosted me at the hotel. When I call, she invites me to dinner, desperately pleading with me to come see her. I have never felt wanted quite like that. She speaks to me with a fervour that makes it seem like I matter to this family. She tells me that they had been looking for me and Yusuf. I don't know what that means and I don't probe further, because I relish the feeling of being desired and potentially loved.

I tell Ziyad about the dinner and he volunteers to come with me. We meet Friday afternoon in the parking lot by his red hatchback. The car smells like the lavender from an air freshener and it meshes with his eucalyptus citrus scent that I'd recently gotten accustomed to being around. We'd become comfortably in sync over the last few days. Ziyad is like an open book when it comes to most things. He talks to me without any filters, and I find a security in that, like I know what I am getting. But I quickly learned that certain topics are off limits: what he does for a living and his father. The dad part I sort of understand. Something happened between them that was too painful or personal to discuss with me. The work thing doesn't make sense, and it bothers me more than it should.

He takes the oceanfront highway to Beirut and, at first, we sit in a comfortable silence. I inhale the ocean breeze and the smell of salted fish through my open window. He plays Korean music and translates some of the lyrics while occasionally singing along. His voice is a pleasant surprise, full and melodious.

"You have a beautiful singing voice."

He flashes a crooked smile and turns the volume down. "Are you nervous about meeting your relatives?"

I shrug. "I'd be lying if I said I wasn't, but I'm more curious than anything." I brush dust off my dress. "Have you contacted any of your family here? Does your dad know you're here?"

"No," he shakes his head. "I'm still not sure if I'm going to bother, honestly."

I decide to go for it. "What's the deal with you and your dad?" I want to hear some of his own family drama, to find something else that tethers us — a common consequence of war and displacement.

He raises an eyebrow and glances at me quickly. "What happened with Imam Amin the last time we were there? Or that blue door situation?"

There's an implication in his question, like he's trying to gauge if we were mutually going there — agreeing to be vulnerable with things we had kept from each other, baring the emotional turbulence that haunts us both.

I tuck a loose streak of curls behind my ear and tell him about my dad, the disappearance, about the letters, and everything I know and don't know. He listens intensely as if consumed by a suspenseful tale, taking in every detail. When I finish, he takes a deep breath; his chest expands in front of the steering wheel.

He doesn't offer advice or tell me what to do. "I'm sorry," he says. "At least I know my dad. I know where both my parents are and what they're like." He grips the steering wheel tighter. "So, I gather tonight is not just about meeting the relatives. You think this uncle has information about what happened to your Baba?"

"Yup."

"Okay," he breathes in again. "I haven't seen my dad in over six years, and I've spoken to him twice in that time. We always had a weird relationship. He had a very specific image of what I needed to do to become successful and it was like I constantly failed him. He told me a few years ago that I didn't turn out the way he wanted, like there was some sort of script I was supposed to follow."

"What did he want you to do?"

"I don't even know — become like him or something? I know

he wanted me to work in his business, but when my parents divorced, we lost touch. He never came to visit us, and we barely spoke on the phone. It was always awkward. And then when it was time for me to go to university, he insisted on paying for it — on the condition that I study in Toronto and major in business or something like that. I thought it was because he wanted to be around me, finally. But then I realized it was because he had this whole vision that I would graduate and begin working under his wing."

Ziyad is talking faster, like he's relieved to be spilling all this out. "Honestly, when he offered to pay and asked me to come to Toronto, I looked forward to doing Sunday brunches and getting to know his wife and playing with my half-brother. None of that happened. He was always busy with work or out of the country most of the time. I think I went over there for three dinners a year. I kind of gave up after that, finished the degree, and went back home. When he found out that I wasn't going to work with him in the company or do anything, really, with my degree, he was so mad and disappointed." He runs a hand through his hair. "He didn't even come to my wife's funeral. How messed up is that?"

"Oh, Ziyad. I'm sorry."

We fall silent for a few minutes.

"Is your family back home supportive?" I ask.

"Yeah, my sister is cool and we're close. My mom has always supported me in everything."

"That's really nice to hear. I'm glad you have someone. Have they supported you with your career choices? What did you end up doing after graduating anyway? I always imagined you becoming a journalist or a famous writer or something."

The mood lightens and a smile dances on his lips "Did you imagine me a lot after we went our separate ways?"

A sudden heat rushes to my face. "Not really. I mean a few times, I did."

"I thought about you a lot," he says.

Our car drives past the Camille Shamoun sports stadium. It's a large oval shaped football stadium that had been rebuilt in the late 1990s. It was now the centre of sports and concerts. A large billboard advertises an Elissa concert.

"Sometimes I wonder if Baba is buried under that stadium."

"What?"

"There's a mass grave under there," I whisper.

Ziyad turns off the radio.

"They buried the dead here, under this stadium, during the civil war. All of those murdered during the Sabra and Shatila massacres. They were brought here and left in unmarked graves."

"Still, to this day?"

I nod. "They rebuilt the stadium after it was destroyed in the 1980s, but the bodies remain."

He opens his palms and recites Fatiḥah. I join him. It is the only thing possible in our powerlessness.

Soon, we're in the streets of Beirut. The car slows amid the sluggish traffic in an underpass. The ocean view is replaced by cement walls and the scent of salted fish is masked by the odour of gasoline until we come out of the snarled traffic. We pass the road that leads to the airport, and the Burj Al Barajni camp, through the Hamra where the narrow streets are lined with cafés and shops. There's a Starbucks with a patio filled with people next to a Body Shop. A few minutes later, we pass a Hermes store near a stone covered walkway, and I ask Ziyad if he's lost. He checks his map and realizes that we missed a turn.

"Oh, I think we're in the Wadi Abu Jamil neighbourhood," I say.

Ziyad laughs. "I have no idea what that is."

"It's the Jewish neighbourhood. I only know because of the synagogue." I point to the building on our left with the coffee-coloured roof tiles. It could be a church but there aren't any crosses or pictures of Mary, nor are there the typical markings of a mosque like a minaret and dome. "The Israelis bombed it during the civil war in 1982. I read somewhere that there are plans to restore it."

"How old is it?"

"This building specifically, I think, has been around since the early 1900s."

"It'd be a shame if they let such a historical structure go to ruin."

"There's a lot of history here. Remind me to take you to some of the old Roman ruins in the Bekaa."

"I'd love that." He loops around and goes back in the direction of the waterfront. Soon, we're in a residential neighbourhood by the corniche with five-star hotels by the water and tall shiny buildings on the other side of the street. He turns into an entrance with a gate and stops the car.

"Is this it?" I ask.

"I think so." The sign reads Le Palais de la Mers. Someone exits a booth by the entrance and walks up to us. We give him our names and he returns to open the gate. We circle a fountain and stop the car near a building entrance. This area of Beirut doesn't have any remnants of the war. Most of the infrastructure was built in the nineties. This part of the city likes to promote an image of progress, tourism, and capitalism and draws the wealthy from the Gulf who spend their summers here. There are no buildings with bullet holes, no beggars or litter in sight. The grass is freshly cut, and palm trees surround the compound like we're in an oasis. The amnesia that erases poverty and oppression is most real here. I turn back to see happy families and lovers strolling along the boardwalk, sipping their coffee, or indulging in ice cream on the warm afternoon.

Ziyad steps out of the car and hands his keys to the valet who's waiting for me to get out. I can't find the strength to get out of the car and wonder if this was all a mistake. My breaths become shallow as I consider the tiny apartment we lived in on College street in Montreal and the second-hand clothes that Mama collected for us. How is it possible that I can be related to people who live like this, with their valet parking and fancy apartment building? How could I have been so disconnected from them? And again, I wonder what else Mama had been hiding from us. I'm about to break all her rules by stepping into this apartment and reconnecting the lines that she had broken.

Ziyad leans in through the window and asks if I'm okay.

"Yeah, sorry. I'm just a little nervous. This ... all feels very different."

He hands the valet money and tells him that we need a few minutes. He comes back and stands next to my door. "Take your time," he says. Then, placing one foot in front of the other, I climb out of the car, the valet takes it away, and we walk up the entryway sandwiched by flower bushes, taking the elevator up to the penthouse.

A Filipina woman answers the door. We take our shoes off and an older woman, seeming to be in her fifties, walks toward me with her arms wide open.

"Welcome, welcome! I'm Tante Laila. Yasmine ... look at you," she exhales and kisses me once on the cheek. "I'm so happy you're here and that we finally get to meet you." Another two kisses. "You are so beautiful." Her eyes glisten.

My body hovers away from her and my hands lightly tap her back. She holds me closer. Laila is wearing six-inch heels, a black dress with shimmering sleeves, and a light gold shawl wrapped loosely around her neck. I suddenly feel underdressed in my dark green maxi dress and black blazer.

She pauses for a moment with her hands on my arms looking at me again from top to bottom. "Thank you for coming."

Ziyad is standing awkwardly by the door.

"This is my friend, Ziyad. His Arabic is not that great."

"Welcome, welcome. Sorry, my English, not very good, but my son, his English is good. Come, come in, please."

She motions us into the living room where we are greeted by 'Ammo Saleem and their two adult children, Samir and Elissa. Windows wrap around the living room with golden silk curtains draped on each side. Above me sits a crystal chandelier that bounces light across the room, forming tiny coins over the walls. Muffled voices and the sound of clanking plates come from the kitchen.

The wealth in the apartment is not meant to be hidden. It screams through the marble coffee table, the solid wood furniture, and the silk couches we sit on. Laila tells me they had them shipped from Italy. There's something unjust about sitting here, knowing full well that there are starving children a few miles down the road. That rug though — the red intricate flowery design edged with diamond shapes looks a lot like the one we had at home. Mama would have loved this décor, this stuff she dreamt of having. I used to think it was tacky and outdated, but now it reminds me of her.

"How's your trip been? You've been here for a few months now, right?" 'Ammo Saleem says. I wonder if he's making it known that he's been watching me.

"Yes, I spent the first few weeks getting settled and now I'm trying to focus on my research."

"History, right?" There's a coldness to him, like he's studying me before he can accept that I'm a part of his wife's family.

"Yes, I'm working on a project that's exploring the civil war era."

He leans back in his chair. "Why?"

It's a strange question that I don't get asked often, so I lean into it. "The Lebanese Civil war isn't studied much, at least not by Arabs. There are a lot of gaps in what we know and we're still so near to it that many of the people who were involved in it are still alive. There's a valuable opportunity to collect information that might not be around for another fifty years."

"Do you have a lot of Arab friends back home?"

His questions are interrogation style, as if he's not interested in the answers as much as he is with the way I'm answering. I decide I'm not interested in playing this game. "I have a diverse group of friends." He asks me a few more questions about the philosophers I like to read and how much I know of his government, and I give him simple, curt, but honest answers, all the while wondering if he's the *S* in Baba's letters.

Finally, Laila chimes in to the conversation. "You know, I think that you will be the first doctor in the family, mashAllah. You're smart, like your father. He was obsessed with books and had a large collection, you know. We kept some of them — at least the more interesting ones — and I would love to share them with you." She gives me a genuine smile.

One of the maids walks out and serves everyone a choice of juice or soda adorning a silver tray. I pick up a cup of orange juice and respond, "I would love that."

"What about you brother Yusuf? Does he also like to read?" Unlike her husband, Laila asks questions with a genuine compassion, like her heart longs for the information.

"We're different in many ways. Yusuf is an accountant. He's always been the more successful one. He just got engaged and bought a house. InshAllah, we can all visit together one day."

"It must have been hard, without your mother all those years." Laila says.

"It was, but Yusuf is amazing. He took care of me like a mother and a brother. We're very close."

"Unlike those two." Saleem points to his children who sit across from him.

Ziyad, quietly ignored, is been left fiddling with a piece of crystal on the armchair next to my cousins.

"Samir, I hear that your English is good. Is that true?" I say to my cousin in English.

"Oh yeah, I went to the Canadian school growing up and then studied at Harvard."

"Ziyad is learning Arabic, but it's not great yet," I add.

"Ziyad? Ziyad?" Saleem repeats his name, finally acknowledging him. "You don't look like a Ziyad." He stares with a predatory curiosity.

My eyes widen expecting to see embarrassment or anger in Ziyad, and I regret having invited him. But he smiles and tells him that he's half Korean and his father is Lebanese.

"Ah, Korea. I would like to visit it someday. I hear the economy is prospering." Saleem sips from his cup. "What's your dad's name?"

"Marwan Haddad. He owns Sabran corporation; they have holdings in Beirut and a branch in Dubai, but they're mostly based out of Toronto."

Saleem nods, "Is his brother George?"

"Yes."

Saleem breaks from his frown and his entire demeanour shifts. "I know your father. We did business together in the 1990s. I brought him clients and we partnered on a few projects in Beirut and Dubai."

Ziyad shifts uncomfortably in his seat.

"Are you in business with your dad? Yasmine, you did good befriending this guy. His dad is pretty big around here."

Ziyad clears his throat. "Not really. I own some shares, but I'm not in the real estate business. I went down a different path."

This is news to me, and I let out a forceful breath just as Laila announces that dinner is ready. On our way to the dining room, one of the maids looks at Ziyad with eyes widened and a bemused look on her face. He gives her a gentle bow and smiles back, saying something to her in a different language.

We sit next to each other at the long wooden table. Saleem is at one end and Laila at the other. Samir and Elissa face us.

I sit next to Ziyad and look at him. I had always known that he came from a wealthier family, but not at this level, not with reach all the way here. He shrugs and says under his breath, "I'll tell you later."

As he smiles and makes small talk with my uncle, I look at him differently. His dimple is in full display as he thanks our hosts for the food. Saleem speaks to him candidly. Suddenly, Ziyad represents so much of what I hate about the world: this unapologetic display of influence and money, the comfort with which people judged who among us is better than the other.

I'm reminded of the first time I saw him outside our usual meeting grounds at the Colombian. I was at a campus restaurant finishing up an assignment one night, and he had been there performing on stage for the restaurant's improv night. I remember watching him, laughing at the performance from my booth at the back. Ziyad lit up the stage with his sarcastic humour and charismatic energy. The performance ended and he joined a group by the bar, surrounded by a crowd of friends that cheered him on. There was this one girl who lingered by his side, drawing closer to him at every opportunity. She laughed at everything he said, excessively touching his arm. He didn't seem to notice. Or maybe he liked it. They spoke loudly over their food and drinks, and I went back to my assignment.

He had spotted me in my booth on their way out and asked to join me. I was about to tell him to sit when the girl who had been drooling over him earlier walked back and tried to grab his hand. He flinched and rubbed his hands together.

"You're not coming with us Ziyad?" She'd said it while looking at me, so I said I needed to finish my assignment anyway. He broke eye contact and briefly covered his face with his hands before returning to the group. I remember thinking that's where someone like him belonged: on stage or with a large group of people, not with me in a corner booth, reading.

Now, I wonder if he belongs with people like this family, talking about real estate and buildings and growing the economy with disregard for how it impacts people like Reem. And it hits me then: I don't really know him.

The maids put out a dinner spread of wara' inab, roasted lamb chops atop fragrant saffron rice, kibbeh, and a few varieties of salad. None of the family members acknowledge them. Everyone is clearly aware of the role they play, except for me.

A few moments pass while everyone scoops food onto their plates. Ziyad excuses himself to go to the bathroom. A part of me wants to talk more about how this household works, but I think of Baba then and how he's the reason I'm here.

"Tante Laila, would you please show me pictures of Baba after dinner?"

"Did your mother never show you pictures of him?" Saleem asks.

"No, she didn't have very many pictures of anyone really. She said she had to leave it all behind when we came to Canada."

Saleem frowns.

"I will go and grab one of the photo albums after dinner." Like a peacekeeper, Laila rests her stiffened arms on the table.

I put my fork down and ask if anyone knows the details of what happened to Baba. It's as if a cloud of fog rushes through the room. Forks drop and mouths stop chewing.

Saleem slams his knife against the table. "We don't need to talk about that right now, but what I will tell you is that your mom was a liar."

"Baba!" Shouts Elissa. This is the first and only thing she says all night.

"Your father was a good man, and your mom took you and your brother away for no good reason. Your father would have never gotten into the trouble he did if it wasn't for that woman. He would have just stuck with the family." Particles of spit fly out of his mouth.

"That can't be true." My voice is dull, flat, hiding the fire and the ache in my chest. "Mama was good to us."

His gaze pierces me and I wonder what I've unleashed. I've been looked at this way before. That look that says, you are dumb. You have failed the only task that proves your merit as a woman in this world. Saleem's eyes move from one side of my face to the other — he's wondering why I can't just listen and take his truth. Just submit.

"If she loved you, she would have left you here with people who could have actually taken care of you the way you deserve. That woman was no good."

"Saleem, that's enough," shouts Laila.

"I think the girl deserves to know what her mother was really like. These kids were deprived of love and family and influence because of her."

But I know that "that woman" was the byproduct of a society that had stripped her of love and compassion and care. And despite the loveless life she had experienced, she had found mercy in herself. She had pulled it out of the throes of her desperation and given it all to me and Yusuf. She had worked tirelessly throughout the years to make sure that we were clothed and fed every single day. She had joined us on field trips where I got to share my mother with friends. Our needs had been met. She showed up. That is more than I can say of my dad and the people who sit at this table with me. I want to shout all of this back at them, but instead I calmly say, "How well did you know my mother? I'm talking about Samira Aswad — that's the same person you seem to be talking about, right?"

"Yes, we knew Samira," says Laila, "but we don't need to talk about this right now."

Saleem's expression hardens. "If you came to talk about this, then you shouldn't have come at all."

A rush of heat floods my body, and I reach for a napkin to absorb the sweat of my palms. As Ziyad returns from the bathroom, I stand.

"Thank you all for the dinner. We should go."

Ziyad looks confused. My plate is still full, and he hasn't even filled his yet. I fight back tears with a strength I didn't know I had. I look at my cousins as a goodbye and make my way to the door. Ziyad follows quickly.

"Just wait," cries Laila as she gets up to follow me. "Let me give you one of the photo albums. You can take it with you and just return it when you come back to Beirut." She grabs my arm in the hallway and lowers her voice. "I just want to ask you one thing, habibti. Did your mom ever give you letters or notes from your dad?"

It's a strange question. "Mama didn't give me anything from

Baba's life." I put my shoes on and Saleem approaches the door.

"Yasmine, let me tell you one thing. Both your parents are now gone, and I don't think there is any good in you trying to find out about their lives. That will bring no good. We can share happy memories of them, but please, don't dig into the difficult histories. You will only find pain and struggle," Saleem says.

"How do you know that Baba is dead?"

"Because we know. Where else would he be?"

"Did you have him killed? Did you make him disappear?"

Saleem takes a few steps forward and jabs a finger inches from my face. "Who you do you think you are, girl? Do you think that just because you were educated in Canada, you know better than everyone else?"

I swallow. Laila put his arm down and whispers, "Bas."

"No, I will not shut up about this. Listen here, if you're going to step foot in my house again, you better learn to respect your elders and the people who lived through more than you can even imagine." He shoves Laila out of the way and walks into a room across the hallway, slamming the door behind him.

Laila says, "Please wait a moment." She hurries toward the living room. Ziyad puts a hand on my shoulder. I don't look at him as Laila returns with two large books. "Thank you, Tante," I whisper as she kisses me once. Then I grab the books, and we walk out of the building.

Outside at the roundabout, I stop in my tracks and breathe deeply. Ziyad waits. After a few minutes, I tell Ziyad to go ahead without me, that I'll find my own way back home. He chuckles. "I'm not going to leave you stranded here. It's late. Where will you go?"

I don't know. We stand in silence in front of the building. I hear the ocean and I want to jump in. Let it take me to the depths that terrified Mama. The car stops in front of us and Ziyad apologizes to the valet asking him to hold the car for a little bit.

"Wanna go for a walk by the water?" Ziyad asks.

I walk ahead of him with a sense of urgency, stomping my feet, moving like I have somewhere to go. He trails behind me quietly. Rage bubbles inside, but I can't figure out where to place it or who to blame.

"What happened back there, Yasmine?" he finally calls from a few feet back.

"Nothing. It's none of your business."

"Okay, but I thought we were friends."

"Didn't that make you uncomfortable? The way they live? Knowing that there are others who struggle to get basic things just down the road?"

His facial expression is a mixture of confusion and sadness. "I don't control that. I'm not sure what you're asking me here, like, generally if I agree with it? No, but I also don't distribute wealth, and I can't tell people what to do with their money." He plants his feet apart. "Is this about their money or is this about something else, Yasmine? You also have a lot of privileges from your life in Canada. Do we want to talk about that?"

I blow out a loud breath. "That's not the point here."

"But it is. If you're mad that they have money, then let's talk about my money or your life in Canada. Your comforts, your healthcare. Let's talk about it." His eyes narrow on my face. I wasn't expecting him to retort this way. "Or is this may be about how you feel not having had access to this family growing up?"

I turn to face him. "Are you saying that I'm jealous?"

He lowers his shoulders and takes a step closer. "Of course not. I'm just trying to understand what happened. Did they say something about your dad? What is this really about?"

I search for the source of my frustration. It's everything. It's the way they speak of my mother. It's the way they presume to be better than everyone; the way they think they have a right over knowledge of my heritage. A right that they can't seem to extend to me. But I don't tell him any of that because the truth is, I am a little jealous. Not about their money, but the access they have to each other. And he's right. I have so many beautiful and easy things in my life. Things that Reem — despite her love of life and the people around her and her struggle in life — doesn't have. I can tell him about that, I suppose.

"Reem's brother, Ahmad … he came back and we found out about what happened to him in Syria." I lower my voice. "It was bad and he's in a terrible situation. I think there are people who might still be after him."

"How bad is it?"

I tell him what I know. The words spill out of my mouth: I'm confused and desperate to help Reem. Reem looks to me for assurance, so I had told her that we'll figure it out a few days ago, and yet, I still haven't found a way to fix it.

"I can come up with a few thousand, and I've asked Yusuf if he can pitch in, but it's not enough. They need ten thousand American dollars sooner rather than later."

He nods his head and is silent for a few minutes. "Give me a few days, I'll get it to them, inshAllah."

I'm shocked at his easy demeanour. "What do you mean, you'll get it?"

"Like, I'll get the money, but don't tell them it's from me. I don't want to make things weird. You can tell them it came from you and your brother or something."

"I can't ask you to do that."

"You didn't ask me, and I can do what I want."

"I don't understand you," I mutter.

"What?"

"I don't know; it's kind of weird, don't you think? Do you just have a bunch of money laying around? You're so weirdly secretive about what you do for a living, and you can somehow easily fit in with my rich uncle, and then you just offer 10K out of nowhere for someone you barely know."

"Why are you claiming that I don't know you?"

"I meant Reem. But the truth is Ziyad, I don't know you. I don't know who that was upstairs. And why do I have to find out that you're part of the Arab bourgeoisie like that? Why couldn't you tell me this stuff?"

"I didn't want to make you uncomfortable. And I don't go around advertising my wealth."

I shake my head. "Don't you think there's something unjust about the ease with which you have this money and the difficulties that others go through to get just a portion of it?" I walk to the edge of the boardwalk where my face finds the mist off the ocean. Grains of sand and pebbles move back and forth in waves ending steps from my feet. I tip my head back and release a deep breath. "I'm sorry Ziyad. I'm just ... I'm having a hard time processing everything."

"I get it. Give me a second." He pats the front of his pants. "Don't go too far; I'll be right back."

I cross my arms and watch him run across the street. I'm grateful for a quiet moment as I continue walking. A young couple walks past me, hands laced together. An older man sits on a bench eating ice cream with two kids and a middle-aged woman. It's dark, but the boardwalk is lit with lampposts and alive with people's laughter. Life goes on. I wonder how many of the people here have obscured family histories? How many have either experienced the horrors of the war or knew someone who did? I picture my parents walking alongside me on the shore. Had they dreamt of a time when we could look out onto the open sea, wondering about the possibilities of life that awaited us beyond the shores of this country?

"I found you." Ziyad nudges my side a few minutes later. He's holding two small paper bowls with a lemon wedge and lupin beans covered in cumin. My features soften and I release the tension in my shoulders. He remembered that I'd been looking for turmus back in Trablous. It was one of Mama's favourite snacks. She used to pick up jars of it from the Arab grocery store, marinate them in cumin and lemon juice and we would eat them while watching one of her favourite Egyptian dramas.

Ziyad and I sit on a bench. I cross my feet under the seat and my eyes glisten with unshed tears. I take a moment to acknowledge what I have. This moment of freedom along a beachfront that I had longed to visit my entire life. A friend who remembers the things that bring comfort. A reminder of the power that comes from ripples of quiet with loved ones. When Mama and I watched those dramas and ate the little beans together, the world and its chaos was quieted by our affinity.

"So, how do you eat these things?" Ziyad asks.

"The skin is thick and you're not supposed to eat that. You just grab it, take a small bite and let the inside slip into your mouth. It's like eating seeds, but you don't need to bite as hard."

He tries with one and lets the whole thing slip out of his mouth and fall to the ground. We both laugh.

"Please tell me you know how to break seed shells with your mouth?"

He shakes his head with an embarrassed grin. "I think we'll need to work on that."

"My dad used to eat them a lot. When we were kids, I always found shells on the ground in the living room. My mom hated it so much. Maybe that's why they got divorced."

I push a bean out of its shell with my fingers and hand it to him.

"Ziyad, why are you so secretive about your work? And why didn't you tell me about your dad? You're open and honest about a lot of other things, but you never really talk about your life back home. It's weird."

"It's not stuff that matters."

"I have a hard time trusting people, and I want to trust you. Yet, there's like this random part of you that you keep behind walls."

"You'll never know everything about everyone. You just have to choose to trust or not based on the information you have. There are things in my life that I don't like to flaunt because it makes people see me in particular ways. Other things, I'm just not ready to talk about. It's not about you. It's just personal."

"So, you're not going to tell me anything more?" I slip another yellow bean into my mouth.

"I want you to trust me, but my life back home is complicated. I...." he pauses, considering his words. "I'm just getting through a very difficult time and there are circumstances that I don't like talking about. Part of why I like being here is that I can just be myself without the assumptions that people may have about me based on arbitrary things. That's why I didn't want to tell you about my dad and his connections. I just am who I am." His eyes crease. "It's what I've always loved about being around you. Ever since we were in undergrad, it's like you see me — all the parts, the real version, not the one people expect me to be. You're one of the few people who see that."

"Your whole history matters, Ziyad. I get that you don't want to talk about it and that's okay, but I also just want you to know that everything that's happened in your life until today has shaped you to be the way that you are. All of it matters."

He looks away, and maybe he's contemplating what I have said.

I pick up my phone to check the time and I'm surprised that there are more than ten missed calls from Reem. It's unlike her to waste her minutes with a phone call.

"We should go back," I say.

CHAPTER 12

I don't recognize the man who shows up at my door. He's not from the camp and he speaks with a Syrian accent.

"I'm looking for Ahmad Khoudr." He talks to me like I owe him something.

"Who should I tell him is looking for him?"

"An old friend."

I tell him to wait and try to close the door, but his foot blocks the entryway. He throws a cigarette to the ground and stomps it with his thick black boot. I pretend to be unbothered by the open door and walk upstairs to get my brother.

Ahmad is still sleeping. He looks peaceful, his back moving up and down evenly with his breaths.

But abruptly, he turns to face me. "Are you going to keep watching me sleep or are you going to go make me breakfast?"

"There's a man at the door asking for you."

He pulls the blanket off and sits up on the bed in a white t-shirt and blue shorts. "What man? Who?"

"Some Syrian guy ... said he's an old friend."

His face turns ashen. He pulls his pants on quickly. "He didn't give you a name?"

I shrug. "No, he didn't. Should I tell him you're not here?"

He looks out the window and wipes his face with his hand. "Where's Mama? Is Fatme in school? Tell him I'm not here, Reem."

His reaction tells me all I need to know. Ever since he'd told me about Syria, I believe the fear he lives is real.

"Ahmad, who is this guy? What is going on?" I demand.

"They found me, Reem. I told you, the mukhabarat and the drug dealers are after me. I don't know who is downstairs, but it doesn't matter. One is worse than the other. Please go downstairs and tell them that I'm not here. I'll try to hide or something."

"Stay here. Don't move," I order him. I go back downstairs. The stranger is in the same position, so I tell him that Ahmad is not available.

"It's kind of urgent." A fresh cigarette hangs by the corner of his mouth. "When is he going to be back? I can wait here all day."

And then I hear a loud thud on the roof. We both look up to see Ahmad jumping from our roof to another. He's making a run for it.

"Ahmad, ya ibn il kalb!" The man curses, veins protruding in his neck. "You're surrounded. There's no way out!" He runs in Ahmad's direction, and I glimpse a pistol by his waist.

My heart quickens. I don't understand what's happening; nothing makes sense, but I know he's made things worse by exposing himself like this. We don't even know what this guy wants and my brother has jumped to conclusions. I go back inside the house to find my phone and dial his number. No answer. I dial Yasmine for help. No answer. I pace around the house and go back to his room. I look out the window and see a shadowy figure far ahead. He runs until he disappears from my view.

"Ahmad!" I shout. 'Ammo Ashraf lives a few houses down, so I yell out to him. Someone has to hear me. Someone has to find a solution. Someone has to at least stop the person who's after him.

And then, I hear it. A loud bang that startles birds into the sky.
Bang. Again.
My heart races and my muscles tense.

Someone screams. A woman. I tell myself it has nothing to do with Ahmad; it's only a coincidence.

I know what I must do. I pull a black abaya around me and run in the direction of the noise. My feet slam on the gravel harder the faster I go. Small rocks penetrate my flimsy flip flops, their rigid edges piercing my soles. At the scene, the heat from my body erupts in a deafening scream: Ahmad is on the floor in a pool of his own blood. My shrieks echo through the camp.

Three men stand around his body but they scurry away when I approach. An old woman at her door is in shock. "He shot himself," she announces, "he shot himself!"

"No!" My vision blurs in a sea of blood and sweat. Death can't be knocking on my door again.

I kneel to the ground and my brother holds my hand. His head is in my lap. My hands and clothes quickly soak with his blood and I want to take it all and put it back through the hole in his chest.

"Ahmad! Where did you get that gun? Please talk to me." I sway back and forth, my head close to his. My tears mix with his blood.

"Someone help!" I shout.

Ahmad's eyes open momentarily and he whispers into my ear. "I'm so sorry Reem. It was the only way. I couldn't go back. I couldn't go back. Please forgive me." He raises his index finger and I hear him mutter the beginnings of the shahada. Then, he falls silent. His arms go limp as he bears witness to the oneness of Allah.

I look around, trying to find someone who can help, even as I know it's too late. I try to contain the wound, press down on his chest, search for a cloth. The earth is muddled with sand and gravel. "Ahmad, please." I don't have any more space for pain. My body can no longer endure this hardship. There are too many scars, no more light to pave my way forward.

My eyes turn to the gun on the ground and I pick it up. I hold it in the palm of my hand. The metal is still warm from his grip. I wrap my fingers around the handle and pull it close.

"Reem!" Mama runs over, followed by a crowd of people. When she sees all the blood, she collapses on the floor. A flock of neighbours come to her aid. Someone pries the gun out of my hands.

I watch all of this happen as if from another dimension. My body, my eyes are disconnected from my mind. It's the only way I know to exist in this moment. This can't be how Ahmad's life ends. There's so much more to be done. We just need time. We just need time.

The following day, Yasmine shows up to take me to the funeral prayer. She stops in the entryway and her eyes fall to the broken glass in the kitchen. When I got home last night, I was getting a glass of water for Mama when a vase fell off the counter and broke, inches from my foot. I stood there for several moments wondering if I should clean it up, or step on it. Instead, I dropped the glass of water in my hands and watched it shatter. That sound created an opening, a relief, and I couldn't stop. I took a plate from the cabinet and smashed it on the floor.

Then Mama walked in, picked up a silver tray and flung it across the room. We continued the ritual, breaking every one of our cups and glasses. If I could, I would have torn down the walls. When we finished, we each went to our respective rooms alone, pretending like the pain in our bodies had been left behind in the kitchen with the broken glass.

Now, Yasmine puts her purse down, walks into the kitchen with a broom and dustpan, and sweeps. She tells me that she saw Fatme at the neighbours, and I tell her that she's not coming.

On the car ride, Yasmine holds me in her arms, and I loosen some of the rigidity in my body. She strokes my head and rubs my back. I initially want to push back, but I'm overwhelmed by her comfort, so I let myself go with the stroke of her fingers against my back and her beating heart.

At the masjid, Ziyad asks Yasmine in hushed tones about what to do during the funeral prayer. She doesn't know, so I assure them that the imam will give the instructions before the prayer. I'd been to far too many in my lifetime.

It's a short prayer. There are three declarations of Allah's greatness, followed by a du'a for the deceased, all of those who have passed before him, and all of humanity.

I pray, following the familiar instructions, open arms to the sky, asking Allah for forgiveness, for healing. We have prayed day after day for ourselves and for the dead and the pain, and yet the tribulations continue. I remind myself that this prayer isn't designed to rid me of pain, it's meant to help me live through it.

Ahmad's body is carried out to be taken to our local cemetery, where Baba lies. Yasmine and I stand behind the men. I hold Mama's arm as the imam announces that the women should stay behind, lest they be tempted to hysteria. I look at Imam Amin with rage.

"I'm going to the burial," I say.

He doesn't say anything.

"Sheikh, if you don't like it, you can bury me there with him and then I won't be your problem anymore."

Yasmine whispers something to him and he nods, giving us permission to join the fleet of men carrying my brother's body. Mama is taken home with the help of her friends.

At the cemetery, Imam Amin reminds everyone of the gravity of suicide, that it's a major sin and that we should all strive to stay away from it. As if we have control over it. Does he think Ahmad did this on purpose? Does he think that we all choose this life? My body tenses and I want to show them the hysteria I'm capable of. I want to stand and shout at everyone in the space, ask them what they had done to help us, to help him. This world has been complicit in maintaining Palestinian oppression. We have been living here our entire lives, without the dignity afforded to most humans: a house, running water, regular electricity, the ability to travel. And what about my parents who witnessed their friends' massacres and rapes for years in this country and in their own homeland? What about my grandparents witnessing the theft of their homes at the hands of settlers they had welcomed in their generosity? The world watched and did nothing.

Yasmine tightens her arm around my body, and it gives me the stability I need. When the imam is done, he prays for forgiveness, for my brothers' grave to be filled with light.

The casket is lowered into the ground and it's hard to believe that Ahmad smiled at me just yesterday morning. My life is devoid of meaning, just as Ahmad's was. What is the point of living if the only thing we can do is survive? Soon we'll all be there, under the same dirt, facing our lord, and a part of me looks forward to it. But I don't know if I will have anything to show for my life.

CHAPTER 13

Mama once told me a story of a girl who befriended a bird. She was a prisoner in her home and the bird would fly to her window and sing songs that told stories from her village and places afar — of the old lady who fed stray dogs in the middle of the night and the child who stole bread from the dumpster behind the restaurant. Sometimes, it brought her tales from the island across the sea, of the people who walked on one foot but learned to run at the speed of light. In time, and as she grew older, the girl began to rely on this bird's visits because they assured her of a world outside her room, and in that knowledge she dreamt of possibilities beyond the grasp of her imagination. Then, the bird stopped coming. The girl waited, day after night, but it never came. She cried for many sleepless nights, hoping, wishing, praying the bird would find its way back to her. She would have accepted it in any form. A squirrel, an ox, a donkey — anything just to have the stories back. But what she didn't realize in her mourning was that she had stopped growing. Two years passed and the girl remained the same height and weight; even her hair refused to get longer. When she gained the courage to climb down her window and run to the sea in search of her friend, her body began to regain its strength.

 I'm sitting in the courtyard of the Athar, wondering if Ziyad has become my bird. It's been a week since I last saw him. After the funeral, we all went our separate ways. The next morning, I waited for him in the courtyard for our usual breakfast, but he didn't show. I sent him text messages that he left unanswered. I'd been waiting a bit longer every morning, only to leave with an extra coffee in my system. Today, Friday, I don't order his cup or an additional cheese pie. Instead, I take a taxi to the camp. It drops me off on the outskirts and I'm left to navigate it on my own this time. Reem had been meeting me at the entrance, but today, I've told her I'll find my path. I walk along the sidewalk that edges the wall circling the enclosure, looking for the entryway into a narrow path. I know it by the writing on the right — "Palestine will be free" — and I follow the letters, the soles of my sandals muddy. After spending several minutes wandering alleys, I stop by a house with an older woman sitting on the steps in front of a brown metal door.

"Assalamu alaykum," I crouch down.

She leans forward and folds the edge of her white scarf behind her ear.

"I'm looking for the Khoudr family's house. Can you direct me?"

"Ah, you're here for the 'azā?"

I nod.

She stands. "Come, I'll take you there. I need to visit them anyway. It's awful what happened to that boy." She shakes her head and grabs my arm. She leads us past the large centre, the shops and parking lot now familiar, and into an adjacent path that eventually brings us to Reem's home. The painting of the white bird is finished; it's flying above the open sea with an olive branch in its mouth.

The sounds of Quran recitation echo from inside the home. The hallway is crowded with shoes and the main floor hosts chairs filled with men. Khalto Fawzia is nowhere in sight, but I spot Reem making coffee in the kitchen.

I walk into the kitchen. I'm not sure what to say to Reem, how to console her grief. Her eyes are puffy and wet, and she no longer maintains the façade of happiness and carelessness. I want to hold her grief and tell her to lean into all of that anger. The weight she carries is too heavy and I can't erase it, but I can help her unleash it.

"How are you?" I ask simply.

She's moving in robotic motion. Stir the coffee, pour it into the pot, set it on a tray. Her legs shift and I follow her up the steps to where the women congregate. She sets down the tray and leaves. I lift the copper pot and pour coffee into each of the white ceramic cups, decorated with green petals and red flowers. I distribute the drinks to those who accept. When I'm done, I find Reem in her room.

Reem is sitting on the floor. She's looking out the window at the satellite on the adjacent roof. I rub her shoulder and she puts her hand on my arm.

"You can cry if you want."

She leans into my chest. Her scarf falls to her shoulder, and I bring her closer to me, absorbing her pain. Her hands tremble and I hold her closer.

"You know, after Mama died, I didn't know how to survive. I didn't know what to do with all the love and the pain she had left behind. Where to put it. I mean I was just a kid, but I still bottled up all that grief, all that love that had nowhere to go." I rub her curls with the tip of my fingers. "Just let it all out, habibti. It's hard, but in time, we'll learn how to navigate the world with that weight."

"I'm so tired."

"I know." I feather her back with the tip of my fingers and we stay that way until someone asks us to replenish the coffee. She wipes her face with a tissue, pulls her scarf back onto her head and we return to the kitchen, make another pot, and serve it to the guests. I watch her move about the house, serving guests with her shoulders hunched and her hair knotted under the loosely wrapped hijab.

Once everyone has been served again, I pick up one of the Qurans on the table and recite quietly from Surah Yasin. I draw tranquility from the familiar words that Mama read to us whenever we fell ill. Those same words brought my heart to stillness in the moments of agitation after I left Tariq.

The next few days move in that same monotony: a repetition of prayers, condolences, and hugs.

The ‘azā and visitations for the dead end days later and Reem asks me to give her space to grieve alone. She stops answering my calls, but I continue to drop off food at their house. No one answers the door, so

I leave the food with the neighbour.

Ziyad also doesn't answer my calls. At least with Reem, I know she is at home. But my mind wanders — what might have happened to him? I shift from anger to worry.

My days fall into a routine — lonely trips to the internet café and back to the hotel. On days when the power is out for longer than usual, I don't bother lighting any candles. I sit in the armchair starring out the window, moonlight casting its glow. Boats float in and out of the marina, birds fly over and nestle on rocks.

On one of those mornings, I make a trip back to the mosque. I wonder if maybe the blue door man is waiting there for me. I have been waiting for another call to come from the same person, but it never comes. Imam Amin is dusting the old shelves when I arrive. He greets me and invites me to have tea in his office.

He asks about Reem's family, telling me he knows that they must be haunted by the death in the same way that many in the community are.

"They are not well, Imam, and…" I pause, hesitating in my speech. "I think they were upset about what you said about suicide being a sin."

He sits silently for a moment as I wonder if I've overstepped my boundaries, but I'm tired of these rules. I just want to say what needs to be said.

He takes off his glasses and sets them on his desk. "You know, even truths have a time and a place and sometimes as Imams, we try to play the game of figuring out when it's appropriate to tell someone a truth and when to be silent and compassionate." A tear lands on his beard. "I was worried that people in the community might have misunderstood my compassion for them as approval of what happened, because I don't approve. I wish that Ahmad came to one of us." He waves his hand in the air. "There are politics involved that you may not understand, but I think, perhaps in this case, I should have erred on the side of compassion and not worried about what people might think. Allah knows our intentions. Maybe I need to be reminded of that." He clasps his hands over the desk. "I'm very sorry about everything. Please tell them that I am here for them, and I will visit when I can inshAllah."

He looks down at his desk, making small imaginary circles with the tip of his index finger. "What else can I help you with?"

I lean forward in the chair. "Actually, there is something else I wanted to ask you on a related topic. What would you say to someone who was struggling to understand why bad things happen to them? Like good people, who do good things, but the world keeps pushing them down and their circumstances just get worse?" My voice trembles at the last part because I'm afraid of the answer.

He rubs his beard reflectively. "Sometimes, we know that we might suffer in this world as a way of cleansing our hearts, but it is not always directly tied to good or bad actions we take. We really don't know the cause or Allah's intention and anyone who claims they know is arrogant. The Prophet, peace be upon him, suffered much through his life and he had no sins; he lost his beloved wife, his protective uncle, and most of his children, even his homeland. Sometimes, these tribulations and these trials are designed to bring us closer to Him; they allow us to know the different parts of Him and ourselves. Sometimes, the only way someone can experience mercy is through relief of tribulation. One comes with the other." He sighs. "But ultimately, I don't have a clear answer for why this specific tragedy has happened. I don't know, Yasmine."

He pauses for a moment, and I say nothing.

"Know that Allah is compassionate and merciful. We are all here temporarily. All experience life in different ways. InshAllah Ahmad finds peace in the Ākhira."

There's an ambiguity in what he is saying and I'm not sure I understand how to process it.

"It's a lifelong process, to know yourself. To be good to people. It will take a lifetime, but that's part of the struggle of life."

"Thank you. I won't keep you any longer," I say.

"Please, any time. I promised your father that I would protect you."

I stand.

"Did you meet with your aunt?" he says quickly, before I turn to leave.

"I did, but I'm afraid they weren't as excited to see me."

"Saleem?" He whispers prayers or condemnations under his breath.

"It's okay. There's a lot I don't know. Maybe I need to accept that and move on."

"They never got along, those two, but I thought with time they'd have gotten over their quarrels."

He's speaking about my father as if he still has the opportunity to forgive, but that is only afforded to the living. "What did they disagree about?"

"Your father had been investigating Saleem's acquaintances. But it doesn't matter anymore. None of those crimes can be tried now, anyway. It shouldn't matter."

"What was he investigating?"

"He never told me. People liked to spread rumours, but I'd never seen the evidence and he kept it all to himself."

"Okay. Thank you, ya Imam."

I turn to walk away but pause in the entryway. I take a breath and face him again. "Imam, remember my friend Ziyad? He came with me on that first night and I think he'd been coming since to the tajweed classes. Have you seen him the last few days?"

"He came four nights ago and excused himself from class for the next four weeks. It's too bad. I enjoyed his questions, mashAllah."

Relief washes over me. At least this disappearance act was intentional. I try not to get angry that he didn't give me the same courtesy warning.

On my way home, I take the long path and stop by the marina.

Traffic has increased over the last week with an increasing number of boats and street vendors. There's even a stall selling turmus now, and another with Lebanese ice cream — the kind that's made with gum so it stretches. I step closer to the railing and notice a familiar figure sitting on a nearby bench.

"Hey stranger," I call.

He startles out of his thoughts. "Hey! Salams!" He wipes his face. "Sorry, the mist from the water sometimes gets in my eyes. Come sit." He scoots over and gives me a forced smile.

My heart sinks at the sight of his grief. I have never seen him like this — a miniature of himself.

"Are you okay? I messaged and called you a few times." I pass him a tissue from my purse. "Sorry, I don't have your fancy handkerchief."

"Sorry, I didn't mean to just go MIA. I wasn't feeling well." He avoids my gaze. "I hope you've enjoyed the time to yourself though, without my incessant questions." The corner of his mouth lifts.

"I was actually really worried. It was weird not having you around." I surprise myself by admitting this out loud. "You should have answered my texts or at least told me you were going to disappear, especially after … everything."

His head tilts toward the mid-afternoon sky, filled with clouds. "Sorry, sometimes I just get overwhelmed, and I need to spend time alone. I've kept my phone off."

"Did something happen?"

"The stuff with Ahmad," he pauses, "it was a little triggering."

I wait in silence for more. Triggering of what? I don't ask. But as I wait, my hurt builds. I needed him after Ahmad's death. I want to yell at him for abandoning me in my time of grief. Does he not understand what his presence means to me?

I suppose I don't, either.

We sit quietly and listen to the bird songs, and I try to ignore the pull between us.

CHAPTER 14

Weeks have passed since the funeral like a dark cloud moving through a storm, ushering in a warmer breeze. I'm sitting in a restaurant at the palm beach resort, waiting for my cousin Elissa to show up for our scheduled meeting. She had called me a few days ago to share condolences for what happened to Ahmad and asked to meet with me. I agreed out of a desperation to hang out with someone while Reem mourns and Ziyad spends more time alone.

Sitting outside, I stretch my legs under the table and take my shoes off to feel the soft ridges of the wooden floorboard. The restaurant sits on the edge of the resort; below us, water crashes. A pair of silver, bedazzled heels stop a few feet away.

"How are you, Yasmine?" Elissa sets her black Louis Vuitton bag on the table. She's in a bright pink blazer worn over skinny jeans. Her long blonde hair is parted to the left and I wonder if it's naturally straight or if she spent an hour on it this morning. She's not the type of person I normally hang out with — cutely packaged entitlement.

"I'm good, alḥamdulillah."

She puts her hand on top of mine on the table. I wonder how much of her demeanour is fabricated to get something out of me. Over the last few months, I've learned that people here rarely mean what they say. Their words are filled with embellishment.

"Thanks for meeting with me. I know this is kind of weird, but ever since that dinner, I've been meaning to call you."

Her admission surprises me and I find myself wondering if she's being honest. "Your dad knows how to reach me."

She looks down. "I've known about you for some time now, and when I heard you were in town, I was excited to see you, to meet this cousin of mine who lives in Canada. I want to know everything about you and your brother and your life back home."

"What do you want to know?"

"I don't know. Anything. Do you have any hobbies? What are your studies like? I'm thinking of going to graduate school in Canada, but I'm exploring some options. Would you recommend it?"

"It depends. What do you want to study?"

"I did a double major in science and politics, and I was thinking of pursuing a medical degree, then coming back to work here. We need good doctors."

I raise an eyebrow. "There's a lot of good schools there, and if you decide to go down that route, I'd be happy to help you."

"That's very kind of you." She pulls out an envelope from her purse as a waiter arrives and takes our order: American Nescafé coffees for the both of us. The waiter leaves and she leans in closer, pushing the envelope toward me. "So, there's another reason I actually wanted to come and see you — beyond just getting to know you, of course."

I eye the envelope on the table. "Okay?"

"Mama wanted you to have these. There are pictures and other things that she held onto or that were left behind in your parents' old house."

"Why now? Why didn't she give me these earlier?"

She scrunches her mouth. "Baba doesn't know."

"And she's worried he'll be upset if he finds out?"

She nods. "My family is complicated. I know things about Baba. I've been trying to collect evidence of a money laundering practice among the ministers. It's something I got obsessed with a few years ago, but haven't done anything with it. It's more of a curiosity than anything else and I don't know if I'll do anything. I'm not sure if Baba is involved yet, but you said something the other night when you came over, and I'm wondering if you know something I don't."

"I don't understand."

"I have a friend who I met when I was studying. She works for Amnesty International now, and we've been working together. You're a historian working on this country. And also, this thing with your dad — I might have found something."

"What kind of money laundering, and what does my dad have to do with it?"

"Look, I know I don't seem like it, but I'm part of an activist coalition. Many of the Lebanese younger generation are trying to pave the way out of corruption to create a more sustainable future. I tried to talk to Baba about this, but he won't tell me anything. He does not necessarily believe that a better Lebanon is possible. So, I've taken it upon myself to find a way and see if I can convince him to be a part of that change."

I scoff. "I doubt your dad would want to help build a better future."

She sighs, like she was expecting me to say this. "I know about your dad's conflict with him. He's not as bad as he seems. He just has a lot of defences up all the time. He didn't dislike your dad by the way, just the way he wanted to expose some of his family members."

A part of me doesn't want to hear this explanation. I'm not ready to show mercy to her father, so I change the subject. "Can I open the package?" I ask.

She pushes it across the table. "Open it."

Inside, there are pictures of my dad with his family and others of her father at meetings with important-looking people, documents from a bank in Saudi Arabia that show transaction histories between the minister of interior affairs and a company called Qibr Construction. "What is this?"

"Evidence."

"Of what?"

She tells me that Qibr Construction is a company based in Saudi Arabia that had received ninety percent of new building contracts from the Lebanese government. The company is owned by Wael Jambal's nephew, the former leader of the fascist party of Lebanon who had orchestrated numerous massacres of Palestinians, benefiting from and aligning themselves with the Israelis.

"Why are you giving me this?"

"You're a historian. I thought you might have use for it. Maybe you can piece it together with other events."

"Does this company have anything to do with your dad?"

"Not that I'm aware of."

I read through the document in greater detail and as my eyes wander from one line to another, from one name to another, I recognize familiar ones: Hassan Khalil, Hussein Ahmad, Ramy Salamat. They're all in my father's notes. They had gone missing along with others in his list. He had been looking for them, or looking to find out what had happened to them.

Finally, I ask, "Who are these men?"

She shrugs. "I don't know. There are accounts in their names. I don't know who they are. Do you?"

"What do you know about my dad?" I ask instead.

She pulls out another picture. "I found this a few months ago. I'm not sure what it is, and I am not sure if I should give it to you."

It's a man in blue bell bottoms, an afro, and a black button-up shirt. He's standing in front of a shop. "Al zamman" is written in Arabic script above his head.

"Who is this?"

"Look at the back," she says.

"Akram Hassan, Damascus, 1992." I read aloud. My heart drops. He was alive in 1992? "Where did you get this?"

"In Baba's office. I went there one night, looking for certain things, and I found it among a pile of documents shoved in a back drawer."

"Aren't you afraid of going against your dad? Your family? Everything you have?" I point at her purse.

She sighs. "I'm not the only one. There are a lot of people in this country who want to see a democratic Lebanon, freed from its corruption. We've been working on this for a while. Between my dad's connections and all our mutual friends, I found ways." She clears her throat. "Yasmine, I know other things about your family."

"What kinds of things?" I speak in a whisper, looking around the restaurant. "Can you find out more information about this picture? Why was he in Syria? Please, can you find out from your dad?"

She scrunches her face. "I'm not sure, I can try. Sometimes, Mama also has a way and it's easier to get stuff out of her than him. It's where I heard about all the other stuff, but I can't tell if it's true or not. A lot of them blame your mom for radicalizing him. I hear this often. They blame her for pushing him into investigating these family ties, into threatening to expose them. They believed it was all her influence."

We pause while the waiter puts another cup of coffee down.

Elissa looks at me. "But the truth is, his family didn't like how open he was about everything. They didn't like how he kept revealing the decisions that people made, how he would write about it, collect information, create an outcry. Anyway, I've also heard that Saad — this is my dad's eldest brother — was a spy for the Mossad and colluded with the Lebanese Front." She clears her throat. "Their family was very well-off during the war, and when some of the massacres were happening, they were taken to Israel, and they stayed there for a bit and then returned. How else would that have happened if they didn't have connections?"

"But I don't understand why everyone thinks my mom corrupted him."

"They didn't like that he was marrying her. They didn't like that she was Palestinian living in the camp. They made assumptions about how she was using him for his wealth and influence and then I think they couldn't understand why he was such an activist and so I think they blamed it on her." She takes a sip of her coffee. "I don't know, they probably wanted him to marry some other girl and got mad that he defied them. From what I hear, your dad was a little hardheaded; he did whatever he wanted."

"How do you know this? And what about your uncle Saad? Is it true?"

"I heard Teta talking about it every now and then with my mom. As for the other stuff, I have no evidence, but your dad maybe was wanted because he was going to expose Saad or something else. I don't know."

"I need to go to Syria," I say abruptly.

"And do what? This picture is from 1992, in Damascus. Do you know how big that place is?"

"Do you know if we have relatives there? Maybe someone knows. I can start there."

"I don't think we have any family there, but you might on your mom's side. I'd start there."

She's right, but this is information I need from Reem, who I haven't spoken to in weeks. I need to do something now with the information that Elissa is giving me.

"Are they still alive? Teta and Jeddo?"

"From Mama's side you mean?"

I nod.

Elissa sighs. "No, Allah yirḥamon. Teta passed away a few years ago. She had Alzheimer's and was bedridden for a year before she died. Jeddo died in a car accident almost five years ago." She shakes her head. "He shouldn't have been driving."

A whole generation of people in this family are gone. I need to collect what's left of the stories; it's the only way to find Baba.

"Listen," Elissa sits up straight. "I want us to be friends. We can work together. Share information."

There's a sincerity in her voice and I want to believe her. "Thank you so much for bringing this to me and for telling me about the rumours. I have so many questions about Baba … I don't even know where to start. Can you see if you can find information about where this picture was taken?"

"I'll see what I can do, but I don't think I'm going to find anything. You should ask your cousin Reem and start with family in Syria."

I remember Reem's words about stirring up memories people would rather forget. I'll just need to find a way through their grief, in time.

"Listen, don't dwell on this too much. Our families don't define us. I know maybe you think it defines you, and you are your own person. For a while, I got really angry at Baba because of his role in this government. It's filled with bad people who aren't interested in anything beyond stealing money. I used to have a lot of anger about being associated with him, about being his daughter. It took me a long time to get over that, and now I've just converted my anger into action. I want to fix things. But it's a slow process. It takes a long time."

"So, you got over it?" I ask with slight sarcasm. "I can't get over not knowing where my dad is."

Elissa's lips curl into a smile. "Not totally, but I learned that I can be my own person and that I can use my privilege to do good things. He's obviously not going to change no matter how angry I get, but I can do good things with what I got from him. I'm still trying to figure out what that looks like. People aren't black and white."

"Have you heard rumours that Baba might still be alive?"

"I think that might be a little far-fetched. Maybe he was in 1992, but I'm not sure now. I feel like we would have heard, no?"

I tap my finger on my bottom lip. "Yeah, maybe. Thank you for this. You know, you're not what I expected you to be."

She giggles. "I know, I know. It's because of the blonde. I wonder if it gives people a certain impression of me. I've been thinking of going back to my natural colour. Maybe I should; maybe then I might attract the right kind of guy."

"What kind of guy are you trying to attract?"

"A nice one; one that's smart and not looking to get into my pants. Someone who respects me."

We both laugh.

"What about your friend Ziyad? He's cute. He looks like a Korean actor from a show I watched."

"He's an old friend, but yeah, he's one of the nice ones. How do you know about Korean shows? Do you speak Korean?"

"No, no, I'm not that smart. I have a friend who got me to watch it with her, with subtitles obviously. She's cool; she taught English in Korea for a while. You might like to meet her. She's originally from Chicago but came back to live in Lebanon last year."

We talk about our lives for another hour. I find that I'm no longer annoyed by her purse or her shoes, and I regret my earlier assumptions.

It's past Maghreb when I return to my apartment and there's a paper bag hanging by my door. It's a welcome sight that I've missed. Inside it I find a bag of nuts, fresh figs, and bars of homemade soap from Saida. I walk inside and set my belongings on the dining table.

I pull out the pictures from the envelope from Elissa and look at them again. One draws my attention more than all the others. It's of Mama and Baba sitting on a beach somewhere. He's wearing jean cut-offs and Mama is in a long, flowery dress. They're leaning on each other, immersed in their love and happiness. I wonder if they knew then what their life would become. Would it have changed the decisions they made? Had Mama loved Baba's stubbornness, and did she eventually regret her love?

I want to believe that there was something deep that connected them, despite the choices they made.

Here, in this tiny apartment, with the birds chirping from a distance, and cars honking incessantly, I'm reminded of all that I have. A lead on Baba. A cousin whose investigative skills are beyond mine. Reem, who holds the key to the trail into Syria. I pull out my phone and call her, but as usual she doesn't answer. I send her a note telling her that I miss her, that I want to see her.

I remind myself that my priority is to be there for her, and that I will not pry into the family history unless it's safe to do so.

CHAPTER 15

I see Reem on an unusually rainy day in early June, after those first weeks of silence. A windstorm had rolled in at an unusual rate, leaving the streets and alleys of Trablous drenched in water. I convince her to go out with me for lunch.

At the table, I hand her the money for the citizenship process — the money that Ziyad had given me. She takes the bag from me gingerly, her eyes downcast. She doesn't eat anything, and we sit in silence for the remainder of our date, her eyes swollen from the ache of her brother's loss and the burdens she carries. I search for the courage to ask her about family ties to Syria. I had planned to show her the picture of Baba from the nineties. In my fantasy, she would drop everything, call some aunt, and come down to the border with me in search of my missing father. Instead, the space between us weighs that desire down and I find that I can't ask her for any favours.

At the end of our lunch, she asks me not to invite her to any more of these outings and I agree to respect her wishes. She has clearly given up on her future, on her grad school application. She is living her life in stillness. She tells me that she goes to work and returns home immediately after. Her social life has died along with her dreams. She is stuck in the moment of Ahmad's death.

For me, time has moved forward in Ziyad's company. I spend much of my free time with him, mostly over breakfast and dinner and the occasional trips to the souq or a bakery or a bookstore. I know that I have begun to develop a mild reliance on him, and it doesn't matter. Our time has given me space to think about my future and has prevented me from spiralling into scenarios that take me to Syria without any lead, without any information, thrown into a pit of the unknown — one that inevitably ends in heartbreak.

Outside of my time with Ziyad, I work my way up to a better relationship with Tante Laila and her family, thanks to Elissa who insisted that I come and sleep over at their home on a few occasions. I hesitated the first time she invited me, but she assured me that her father would be away, travelling for work. We have been scheduling and coordinating my visits with the times he's away and I use these as opportunities to find out more from Laila, but I keep my secrets to myself.

Whenever it is just Elissa and I, we compare notes. I collect information on the list of names from the documents she had handed me at our first meeting. Thanks to Baba's letters, I am able to tie the names to specific people and events. To my relief, I confirm that the "S" in Baba's letters isn't Saleem, but a man named Saeed who appears in many of the pictures with the family. I suspect that he might have been some sort of double agent, feeding information to the Phalange militias in return for money and protection. At the same time, he seems to have given Baba some of the militia plans, which were foiled according to the archives I consult. I do some additional digging but can't locate him anywhere in Lebanon. There are rumours in Saleem's circle that he moved to France. I am still not sure what he had been doing with the information or why it might have gotten him killed, but I now have a more complete picture of Baba. He didn't just abandon his family. He was passionate, he loved Mama, and he believed in Palestinian liberation. He was also a beautiful writer. I find myself dissecting his words, unearthing his love for the language through his coded use of dialectics and metaphors.

It's now early July, and I am in my hotel room. It is early morning, and I'm holding my phone in trembling hands, staring at Reem's number on the screen, my thumb hovering on "send." I woke up today drenched in sweat not from the heat, but something inside me. The walls around me spin and when I get up, I throw up all over the floor. I stumble when I try to clean it, so I return to my bed instead. The sweltering heat of the summer bores into my bones, but my body continues to shake.

Reem answers my call at the third ring, and I tell her I need help. Thirty minutes later, she's standing at my door.

"Oh my god, you look awful. Why didn't you call me earlier?" She pinches her lips, her hands on her hips, and sets a bag down on the kitchen floor. She puts her hand on my forehead. "You don't have a fever. That's good." Her eyes wander around my apartment. "But this place. Ya Allah. Just go lay down."

I can barely stand and return to the bed. "Just hang out here with me for a bit." My voice is raspy. "You don't need to do anything; just don't leave."

"Of course, of course." She tucks me into bed with my blanket on top of me. "I can stay here tonight. I won't leave you." I watch her mop the floor, clean the dishes, and put away the laundry sprawled across the living space. She then steps out and returns with bottles of water, clean towels, and bags of food to stock up my fridge.

I'm in and out of sleep for most of the morning. It must have been well past noon when I hear a knock. It's Intissar. "I brought you some soup and tea." She marches in.

A tingling warmth spreads throughout my limbs.

"Habibti, does anything hurt? I can call the doctor."

"No, my stomach doesn't hurt anymore. I think it was maybe something I ate or drank."

"Alḥamdulillah. Drink this soup then try to eat something."

"Did Reem tell you I was sick?"

"No, Ziyad told me. Oh." She raises her finger like she just remembered something. "He told me to give you this."

She hands me a book, with a sticky note on top:

One of my favourites, hope it keeps you company while you recover.
Feel better.

I turn my head to find Reem, who is sitting on the couch, my eyebrows raised.

She nods. "I saw him in the lobby before I came up and told him." She shrugs. "He said he texted you this morning and you didn't answer."

"Tayyeb. Get some rest girls. I put some extra bedding on the couch for Reem. You know where to find me. I'll check in on you tomorrow inshAllah."

I put the book on the edge of the bed and pull the tray with soup and crackers toward me. The warm sage tea goes down my throat smoothly, coating my empty stomach with a hot layer of relief. I lean back against the pillows and watch Reem pull out a mattress on the floor. The air conditioner hums above her.

"I didn't think you would come," I say.

"Of course I would come if you needed me."

"I know, but you've been distant lately. I'm not mad; I was just worried."

"It's been hard and I just wanted to be alone for a while. I don't want to have fun or do anything leisurely, but I will always be there for you. I'll never forget everything you've done for us."

I extend a hand toward her, and she holds it tight. "Good. I'm glad. But I'm here if you need to talk about it some more."

She leans over and lays a gentle kiss on my forehead. "Thanks. I think I'm finally in the stage of accepting it." She walks away to change in the bathroom.

I push the tray of food onto the floor. A few sips are all that my stomach can withstand, and I lean back against the bedrail with Ziyad's book on my legs. For the rest of the day and into the night, Reem sits on the mattress watching a Syrian drama and I read through the *Samurai's Garden*.

I text Ziyad before falling asleep.

> Thanks for the book, and also the introduction to Japanese/Chinese politics. The story is beautiful and cozy, exactly what I needed.

He responds almost immediately.

> Which part are you at?
>
> I'm at the section where Stephen visits the leprosy village. Loving the nature themes. Thank you for lending it to me.
>
> How are you feeling?
>
> I'm ok. Able to eat and drink now.
>
> Good, your seat is always saved downstairs. I'm getting tired of having one-sided conversations with myself. Intissar tells me that I need a wife and that my books don't count as companions. I think she may think I'm going crazy.

I stifle a laugh.

> Well, it depends on the book, I guess.
>
> Nah, I'd have to agree with her on that.
>
> Oh yeah?
>
> Not necessarily the needing a wife part, at least not right now, but that the books won't make up for the loneliness of singledom forever.
>
> I don't know, I still have to disagree.
>
> Well, today has been proof for me. None of these books or the conversations with random strangers has made up for the void created by your absence.

My cheeks grow warm. The last time I felt like this, I ended up heartbroken in a marriage that sucked the life out of me.

> Goodnight, Ziyad.

I turn my phone off.

The next day, Reem spends the morning teaching and then returns to my place after class. She's returning to life and speaks to me about what happened over the last few months, without mentioning Ahmad. She tells me about her students and the upcoming weddings of friends and family, never missing the opportunity to remind me that she's not interested in being set up with anyone.

I call Elissa to come for a sleepover. Reem is staying over too, and I hope to broach the topic of Syria. We're all in our pyjamas under blankets, but Elissa is looking at her laptop. The television plays a Syrian show and there's a bowl of chips in the centre. Reem gets up to use the bathroom.

Elissa turns her computer to me. "This is the Korean actor I was telling you about a while ago. Remember? Doesn't he look so much like your friend?"

My eyes focus on the picture. The guy is wearing a suit, his hair is styled back, and he is smiling at the camera, his half dimple on full display. Save for the light brown hair, the person in the picture looks exactly like Ziyad. "What's this guy's name?" I ask.

She turns the computer back to her and reads the text under the picture. "Minjoon Haddad." Her eyebrows crease. "Weird. He's got a Lebanese family name." Then she quickly turns back to me, mouth agape. "Wait. No way. Is this your friend, Yasmine?"

"You got me," I lift my hands in surrender, pretending like I knew all along despite the anger starting to course through me. "But don't tell anyone and don't mention it. He doesn't want people knowing." I'm not trying to protect him. I'm trying to save myself from embarrassment.

"Are you guys still just friends?" Elissa asks, adding a wink.

"Yup," I say vehemently.

Elissa laughs as she closes her laptop and stands up. "My mom likes to say that marriage is all luck. You don't know what you're going to get until it's too late. Some people have it good, and some people don't." She shrugs her shoulders. "But Ziyad looks promising, if you ask me."

"I don't know. It's not for me right now. Too much trauma from the last one, if you know what I mean."

"Whatever. You can say what you want, but the heart wants what it wants." She walks over to the other side of the room and sets the blankets on the mattress next to my bed. "Hey, why don't you come next week and bring Reem with you? We'll go to the women's beach. It might be good for her, from what I hear."

My lips dance from one side to the other. "I think that would be a good idea, but I don't think she'll be okay staying at your place. It's complicated, with your uncle and all."

Reem walks out of the bathroom. "What are you two talking about?"

"Want to go to Beirut next weekend?"

She shrugs. "I'll check with Mama."

"You should stay at a hotel; it might be even nicer for you Reem. Oh, like the Movenpick. My friends and I go for dinner there sometimes. I can come and pick you up if you don't want to drive."

"Yeah, you'll need to, because my car broke down a few weeks ago." Reem switches off the light, a subtle hint for us to stop talking. She returns to her spot on the couch and turns over to sleep. Elissa complies and lies down on the mattress.

I don't fall asleep. The image of Ziyad on Elissa's computer is cemented in my mind. Last week, we went to the local souq in downtown Trablous and found a little bookstore hidden among a series of shoe shops. The store was windowless with just a few rows of books, all in Arabic, and we spent several hours there. We read the book titles row by row, and I translated them all for him.

He ended up buying a little children's book with a story of a pig who pretends to be a cat, making his way through different families until he finds a Muslim household and is able to be honest about who he really is, freed by the knowledge that they wouldn't eat him. It was a sweet story of belonging and identity. Now, I think about his choice. He promised that he'd be able to read and translate the entire story for me by next summer, and with that promise had come the realization that we had made plans for the future, beyond our departure from this country. That night, I had let my mind drift to a time when maybe I might let myself be loved. My heart had expanded at the possibility of holding a relationship with someone who cherished all of me, of living in velvety comfort with someone who provided physical, spiritual, and emotional sustenance.

But now, that picture — his secrets. He'd left me out. I could not be a part of his life. This meeting in the obscure future couldn't be anything more than a reunion of friends with very different lives.

I chastise myself for having those fantasies and eventually fall asleep.

I avoid him for the next several days. We go a week without talking or seeing each other and the one time I answer his call, he tells me that he's leaving for Beirut for a six-week intensive Arabic program at the American University of Beirut.

"Hey, everything okay?" he asks.

There's a pang in my stomach as I scramble to think of how to fill the six-week void, and then I remember that it's better this way.

"Yeah, you know, just trying to sort things out, spend time with Reem, be there for her."

"Okay." He sounds disappointed and we listen to each other's breaths for a few seconds. "I'll see you later I guess."

"I guess. Safe trip."

CHAPTER 16

The day after the sleepover, Yasmine is better, so after restocking her fridge, I decide to go home. In sort of a twisted way, I'm glad she got sick. It forced me out of this darkness that I'd been steeping in and it gave me the courage to look at things in a different light. Mama and I hadn't talked much about how Ahmad's death impacted us. We rarely spoke to each other about the things we found difficult, but I don't want to keep doing that. Today, when I get home, I find Mama kneeling on the floor in prayer and I sit down next to her, waiting for her to finish. She sends greetings to the angels on her shoulders and I rest my head on them.

"Mama, are you still sad about Ahmad?"

She recites her dhikr, counting with a string of beads, her rocking soothing and familiar. We stay like this for a few moments. "There's nothing we can do Reem. It's Allah's will. He's gone now."

"Yes, but you weren't like this when he disappeared, and you weren't like this when Baba died."

She sets her beads down, turns to face me, and cups my cheeks, wiping away a tear with her thumb. "I realized something when Ahmad died — the way he died, how angry it made me. Ahmad was never angry, not in that way. He took what happened to him and made something with it, just always trying to fix things. He never dwelled on his hardships, and he never complained; even as a young child, he was always so easygoing. Now, I wish he complained more." She looks down at her prayer beads. "I don't know where he got that gun, and I wish I knew. I wish I had taken it away. I wish he told us what was happening. The anger hasn't gotten me anything, ya Reem. Our life is what it is, and we just need to accept it. I want to learn that from him. I don't want to dwell on the anger because, I think, maybe my anger got him killed, maybe he saw how desperate and sad

I was — I don't know." She rubs her thighs and begins to cry. "I think maybe he gave up when he saw that I had given up, consumed by my anger and regret."

I hug her from the side. "Oh Mama, it's okay. It was not your fault." I hold onto her and caress her hair. We rock back and forth in each other's arms.

Mama and so many around me survived the civil war, living victoriously in spite of the devils that rule this world. It's in my blood to resist and I will continue to do so, grabbing opportunities wherever I can find them. My students are all examples of this. They are self-interested, pursuing things that serve them and their futures. Why should I be any different? Why should the burden of our suffering prevent me from seeking freedom and opportunities?

I vow to not let Ahmad's death be in vain.

I will persist.

Later that day, I call the lawyer and pay him the fee that Yasmine gave me and begin the process for getting citizenship. It had been just sitting in a bag at the bottom of my closet and I decide it's time to put it to use.

Elissa shows up at my front door shortly after noon on a Tuesday. I say my goodbyes to Mama and join her and Yasmine in the back of the car. I can't exactly describe what it is that made me agree to this trip. Perhaps it's the allure of pretending I'm a tourist and escaping my life for a few days. Or maybe it's just so I can be close to Yasmine, in the sanctuary of her comfort. Her words, her gentle touch, and her presence form a nice buffer to my anger and grief.

On the car ride, Elissa recounts horror stories from her dating adventures.

"Gosh, it was awful. No, it was gross; he was barely shaven, his hair was a mess, and he showed up in sweats. And he kept picking his teeth with the tip of his argileh, and then he had the audacity to offer me a puff." She shivers. "He called the next day to ask if I was still interested. I was like, what?! How are you that delusional?" She looks at me through the rearview mirror. "Reem, what about you? Anyone in the prospects?"

I return a curt smile. "No. There was a guy I've known for a while, but after everything that happened with Ahmad, his family didn't want the thing to move forward so we cancelled everything. Honestly, it's probably better this way." I rest my chin in the palm of my hand, staring out the window. Hamza. I had reached out to him after Ahmad died, even though he wanted to stay here and I didn't. I guess I had lost hope of ever leaving this country then. We were good together, and we could have been again. But when his parents found out about what happened, about the suicide, his family didn't want to have anything to do with us, so we stopped talking.

Elissa drops us off at the hotel about an hour later, and we agree to meet at the women's beach the next day.

We're staying at Le Commodore, a luxury hotel in the centre of the Hamra district. It was Yasmine's idea and her face fills with glee when we walk in. The lobby is adorned by brown walls and underwhelming couches and chairs.

"Do you know how much history lies within these walls?" she asks.

I've heard stories about this place and its role during the civil war. It had once been a journalistic hub. Some of the greatest journalists of the 1980s and 1990s stayed here while they reported the violence that plagued this city. The building is tucked between taller ones, and it provides the right kind of camouflage to go untouched by the destruction that inundated the streets.

"Think of all the conversations that took place here. Think of all the things those people witnessed. It's marvellous, isn't it?" She smiles wide and looks at me like she expects me to be just as impressed.

I shrug, but she doesn't notice. To me, it's like any other bougie structure. Many of the buildings around us still have bullet holes embedded in their walls. I mean, I live with people who witnessed the war, so I don't need a building to tell me about it.

"This place was considered to be the safest place in Beirut for a long time. When people came to book a room, they were asked if they wanted a room on the car bomb side or the artillery side," Yasmine continues as we walk to the reception.

West Beirut had seen a lot of violence. I guess to some extent, it was surprising —miraculous even — that this place is still here.

We check in and wander around. There's a private pool with reclining chairs and luscious plants climbing the surrounding terrace walls. Yasmine takes a deep breath looking out on to the pool, and I think we both realize that we needed the time away.

I poke Yasmine when I see him sitting nearby. "Hey, Ziyad is here. Did you tell him we were coming?" He's sitting in an armchair with a high back, reading a book.

She turns around quickly and squints her eyes. "No, I had no idea. But he's doing the special program at AUB. Maybe this is where he's staying." She doesn't walk toward him or indicate interest in speaking to him.

He lifts his head and our eyes meet. He raises his hand in the air and mouths "What are you doing here?"

We walk over and tell him about our visit. Yasmine is oddly distant, and he seems just as surprised as I am by her attitude.

"Heard you're at the AUB. That's where I studied, you know," I say.

"It's a beautiful campus. I love feeling like I'm back at school, but none of the teachers are as good as you, Reem."

I try to hide my pride. "Thanks."

"Will you join me?" He asks enthusiastically, pointing to the chairs nearby.

Yasmine's lips curve into a smile but her tone is curt. "We would love to, but we should probably just get settled in. I'll see you around though?"

CHAPTER 17

Beirut is a small city in comparison with what I would normally consider a metropolis. But it has the life of one with its dense and diverse population. Filled with shopping districts and historical sites, it's a beach town with endless restaurants and cafés lining the waterfront. There are churches and mosques of different denominations. I love witnessing the enduring history of this country in the varying architecture and I think of the lives of those who have filled its buildings.

On the evening of our arrival, I tell Reem that I'm going to the AUB library for some archival research. The narrow streets are busy with crowds of young and old folks enjoying the cooler sunset, sipping tea and eating shawarmas on patios. The AUB campus harmoniously brings together my two main loves: nature and books. It reminds me of home, the intellectual drive that consumes people here. It's a bit of a dream for me to be here.

Despite the busy crowds filling the restaurants and shops nearby, the campus is quiet and absent of students who typically fill these halls. I make my way directly to the library and pass aisles of metal shelves. My feet skim over the carpeted floors. Wooden cubicles line every free space. I pick up microfilms that contain archived newspapers from Syria from 1989 to 1992 and go to the computers to peruse the contents.

While I scroll, I exhale deeply. I'm at peace here. There's comfort in the solitude, in being surrounded by books that speak of world experiences. I wrap my shawl around me and lean into the screen.

It's here that I see it, in the archives of the *Damascus Times*: an article about corruption among the Lebanese politicians, how their narcissistic drive for status and money was going to drive Lebanon into the ground even though the war was ending. The author's name is oddly familiar: Akram Aswad. That was Mama's last name and Baba's first. The article was published in 1990. After we left for Canada. I squint to get a closer look, to make sure I read it right. Could it be?

I search for other articles by the same author. There's a total of twenty, all written between 1989 and 1992. All related, one way or another, to how Lebanon could rebuild, how it should leverage support from the Palestinian community by giving them recognition. How Arabs needed to reunite to build strength to resist imperial powers. There's nothing about his brother and the corruption that rang through his family, my family. There's nothing directly in the articles tying the author to Baba or his family, but something about it … something about the subjects, the writing, feels similar to what's in his notebook — familiar.

I believe it in my gut. This is Baba, writing from Syria.

I go back to the microfilms and find news archives up till 1995, but there's nothing on Akram Aswad after October of 1992. I rub my chin, silently listing possibilities of what might have happened. Did he come back to Lebanon? Did he begin to use a different name? What if he was still writing? I search for pictures of Akram Aswad but come up empty. I search for a contact at the *Damascus Times* and send an email to their general informational inbox telling them that I'm an academic looking to get in touch with one of their journalists. I click send and sit back in my seat, hoping, waiting for a response.

Someone taps me on the shoulder, and I see a young guy accompanied by a tall brunette. "Yasmine, right?" he says.

It takes me a minute to place him and then I realize it's Tariq's cousin, Faisal. The one from Qalimat. I had met him during the earlier days of my trip at the school's get together.

"Oh, hey!"

"Just doing some work?"

"Yeah, research. There's more content here, so I've been making a few trips to Beirut."

"Too bad you were not here earlier. I could have introduced you to my historian friend that teaches here. But he usually leaves campus early in the summer. How long are you in town?"

"Just for a few days, but I try to come often." I want to connect to this historian; maybe he can help me identify the source of these articles. "What's your number? I can text you the next time I'm around."

"Yeah, for sure. I'm spending the rest of my summer here — well until August at least."

"Great, I'll let you know when I have some time. Maybe next weekend?"

He's about to walk away when I ask something that's been lurking in the back of my mind, threatening to disrupt my peace in Lebanon. "Hey, is Tariq here? You mentioned he was coming into town."

He looks confused by my question, or maybe he's surprised by my interest. "Yeah, he just arrived a few days ago. I'm going to meet him this weekend."

Lebanon is crowded, but it's also a small country and everyone knows everyone. I don't want to think about the odds of crossing paths with him. I rub my arm, feeling a shiver cross my body and trepidation in my chest. "Oh okay. Thanks for letting me know."

Faisal leaves with his friend, and I return to my computer screen, trying not to think about the possibility of running into my ex-husband, of seeing him with his family here, of the judging glares they were sure to give me, of the rumours they might spread. I let myself get consumed by my work and a stack of books. I spend the rest of the evening searching for more clues about where Baba could be, for more articles, for anything.

Hours go by with me in front of the screen with nothing to show for it and slowly my flame of hope is extinguished again.

I return to the hotel empty handed.

CHAPTER 18

The next morning, Yasmine and I both sleep in and order room service for breakfast before making our way to the private women's beach. These resorts are probably one of the best things this country has to offer. I enjoy the salted smell of the sea, dipping my feet in the sand. Uncovered, but safe from the intrusive glares of strange men.

Yasmine pays the admission fee and the woman behind the counter makes it a point to tell us that we can't get a refund if a war breaks out.

"What war? Why?" I hunch over from behind Yasmine.

"There was something in the news this morning about HizbAllah kidnapping some Israeli soldiers and some fighting at the border in the south," she says.

"Ah, the usual." I move back. We've gotten used to random acts of Israeli aggression ever since their occupation of the south ended. They happen annually and if we stopped our lives every time they threaten to annihilate the people of this country, we'd be living idly. Bridges are bombed, cars explode, and politicians are assassinated — regular occurrences that one must plow through.

We walk into the resort, walled off on both sides by large concrete walls. A large pool dominates the centre of the space near a café. Reclining beach chairs are strategically placed everywhere else. White sea birds line rocks ahead and chirp above us.

I take off my hijab and wrap it around my neck. My toes sink beneath the atoms of sand and pebbles. Yasmine reclines in a chair to my right. "This is nice. Thanks for bringing me here." The sun's warm rays settle into my skin.

She rubs sunscreen over her legs and I turn to look at her with suspicion.

"What?" she says.

"Where were you last night?"

"I was at the library at the AUB, doing some research. Like I told you."

I cross my arms. "Did something happen between you and Ziyad?"

She raises an eyebrow. "What do you mean?"

"I mean, are you two still just friends?"

She closes the cap of the sunscreen and hands it to me. "I wasn't with Ziyad yesterday. I was at the library, like the true nerd that I am." She smiles with warmth in her eyes. "And yes, we're just friends. He's…" she pauses for a moment. "I don't know, he's nice and all, but he's a bit complicated."

"What do you mean, complicated?"

"I don't know, I think he's figuring himself out and we live in different countries and I'm pretty sure he's not interested in anything serious." She lays back in the chair and puts her hat over the top of her face. "Which is probably a good thing. He just converted and he's a widower, and he should eventually find someone who fits his lifestyle. I'm not it."

"But do you like him?"

"I don't know, maybe a little, but I don't want to." She bites her lower lip, which I can see below the hat that covers her eyes. "You know, Reem, I'm still trying to get over Tariq. I need to be alone for a while. Ziyad and I are really good friends, and we've benefited from each other's company, but I think that's where it ends for us."

I give her a once over and wait for her to continue.

"Also, Tariq is in town and that's been on my mind lately."

I sit up. "What do you mean? In town where?"

"I met his cousin at that student party you invited me to, and last night I bumped into him at the library. He told me that Tariq is visiting."

"Does he know you're here?"

"I have no idea."

"Tayyeb, don't let it bother you too much. It's a big country. It's probably just a coincidence."

"I wish it was that simple, Ramroum."

"I hate this so much for you, like — how far is he going to follow you?"

Elissa calls out from behind us, and we turn to look. She's glamorous in a sheer dress over a pink bikini, oversized sunglasses, and a straw hat.

"Ladies, how's the hotel?" She sits in the chair across from me and opens a bottle of oil to rub on her body.

"It's good. We bumped into Ziyad there," I say slyly.

"Oh, walla! And?" Elissa says.

Yasmine sighs. "I don't know how many times I need to tell you that we're just friends."

"It's not possible to be that good of friends with a guy, you know that, right?" Elissa lowers her glasses to look at her. "It's weird. Is he not interested in you?"

Yasmine leans back in her chair and puts the hat over her eyes again. "Well, what can I tell you. That's what we are."

"I'm pretty sure he wants to be more than friends," I say.

"Why do you say that?" Yasmine asks.

"Because he always asks me about you, and his face just lights up every time he sees you, including yesterday. It's so obvious. He asked me once if you'd ever consider marrying a non-Arab, and I'm pretty sure he was asking about himself."

"I don't think I could marry him or anyone. Not right now."

Elissa rolls her eyes. "Yasmine, it's not easy to find a nice guy these days, let alone one who's also good looking, especially when you're a divorced woman. He's basically the whole package. If you're not going to pursue this, then I have about five girls lined up that would say yes in a second." We all giggle. "Did you not hear about the argileh teeth-picking guy yesterday? Believe me, I have more where that came from."

We stay at the beach until sunset, snacking on chips and watermelon and sunflower seeds. Elissa tells us more stories from her dating adventures. I talk about my dreams of leaving for the first time since Ahmad died. And it all feels mundane, normal, to be with them. A string of hope forms in their company.

Elissa leaves us at the hotel entrance. When we enter, the newscaster on the television shouts into the lobby. The tension at the southern border has escalated and the Israeli government refuses to give in to HizbAllah's demands of releasing its political prisoners. A bunch of soldiers have died, and Israel has launched a raid at the border.

Yasmine's brows crease as her eyes fix on the screen. She doesn't say anything, but I picture all the questions and possibilities running through her mind.

"I think if they bomb the electric companies, then you should probably book a flight and go back home. That's usually a sign that things will escalate. But honestly, I think you're fine. It will all be resolved soon. It's all talk," I say.

She nods and we go upstairs to our room.

CHAPTER 19

It's our second night in this city and I can't sleep. I'm not sure if it's because of this violence on the news, or if it's because I finally confided in my cousins about Ziyad. The truth is that I'd been having a hard time not thinking about him.

I pray Fajr and give in to my restlessness by going downstairs for an early breakfast. Except, the kitchen is still closed and the only thing I can get is tea. I sit in a large red cushioned armchair facing the pool and open my computer. I type Minjoon Haddad into the search engine.

Pictures of him pop up almost immediately, along with a few pages of articles, half of which I can't read. A recent one announces his "break from the media" after a death in the family. Older ones featuring a younger version of him showcase awards he's received. A few articles describe his secret marriage — a scandal, fans upset that they hadn't learned about it until her death. He doesn't just keep secrets from me, it seems. Strange, how one's personal life choices could generate this level of disdain among complete strangers.

One thing is clear though: Ziyad and I come from different worlds. I want a quiet life; I thought that he had wanted that too. But from these articles, I confirm my suspicions: this is a temporary stay for him, and I am a temporary comfort.

The light from the sunrise drifts across the Beirut sky. I'm the only guest in the lobby. Utensils clank against plates as the hotel staff prepares for the breakfast rush.

That's when I hear a shrieking thud. The ground quivers beneath me. I look up to the sky and the sun shines bright over the pool, bouncing off windows. There's not a cloud in sight.

Smoke.

There's smoke and it's coming from the land. Suddenly, airplanes hover over us. I lean closer to the window and wrap my trembling hands around my body. More smoke. Sirens muffle the silence of fear; the sound of breakfast being prepared stops. I turn my gaze toward the empty lobby. A single hotel worker scurries away. Whispers come from behind the reception desk.

    Another loud thud shakes the ground and my heart races. I close my laptop and tuck it under my armpit. Someone turns on one of the televisions. The frantic voices of reporters announce that Israeli war planes have destroyed a bridge in Beirut. Reports of attacks on the airport are being verified. Then, a clip of an Israeli official announces that if their soldiers aren't returned immediately, they will turn Lebanon's clock back twenty years.

    I stare in disbelief. It can't be. This can't be. Nobody is that evil. Surely, they won't destroy an entire country for a few kidnapped soldiers. They want to negotiate, initiate a trade to get them back. That's what HizbAllah wants too. They'll fight at the border and then it'll all be over.

    Another boom. A pop. Something shatters. My knees buckle and I sit down, pinching myself.

    "They are trying to get the airport," someone says. "It will be fine. They will bomb it a bit and then go away."

    Sirens ring through downtown and then gunshots pop things into the open sky. I stand up and look for others. It's just me and hotel staff in this lobby and we all congregate behind the concierge desk.

    "This is not normal. This doesn't happen. This is bad," one of them says frantically.

    Another boom. I wrap my fingers around a chair, my nails digging into the fabric. I am now at the mercy of violent beings that do not care about the living bodies occupying Beirut, this city of love, laughter, intellectual fodder.

    "Some of the roads have been bombed," another staff member whispers, voice filled with dread.

    We were just at the beach the night before. Everything was normal; there was no indication that things could progress so drastically and so quickly. My mother sacrificed too much to give us a good future and a life absent of the wars that she had endured. I picture a hypothetical headline: "Canadian woman goes on a vacation of horrors."

A loud boom sounds in my vicinity and I see more clouds of smoke through the window in front of the concierge desk.

I, out of all people, a historian who studies war, should have known this could happen. It happens here more often than it does in the movies. It happens to people like Reem all the time; it happened to my parents. There's no guarantee of a happy ending, no guarantee of survival.

My arms tighten their grip around my limbs, and my mind spins, exploring possible outcomes when the reality of the situation finally hits me and I begin to think of all the things I should do.

My breath quickens, but I don't try to calm myself this time. I can hear Mama.

Mama was perpetually preparing for doom. She prepared us for this by leaving a door open to chaos, uncertainty, and tribulation. We were always preparing, waiting for something to happen. She'd stock up on unnecessary things, extra pots we didn't need, canned food, bags. All sorts of things were piled in the closet. "For packing things" she'd say. "Just in case."

I didn't need the things she hoarded. In this moment, when my world is actually falling apart, I want her knowledge, her wisdom, and her touch. I let her voice shout at me, telling me to run, to plan, to figure out an escape. I let all the voices that scream so intently in my ears spur me into action. It's all I have.

CHAPTER 20

My heart sinks into my stomach when I hear the second explosion. I know that noise, I know how close it is. I rinse the soap off my body, shaking under the hot stream of water. I don't want to be caught naked and exposed. This happened to one of Mama's neighbours when they were younger. She was in the shower when tanks entered the neighbourhood and gunshots rang through. She ran out of the bathroom and out of her home, so confused by the need to survive that she didn't notice she was naked until someone wrapped a sheet around her. I won't become the source of stories told for generations to come.

Another boom, this one closer as it shakes the ground. I pull on my pants and look out the window. I don't see anything other than the row of buildings. I can smell smoke, though. The sun shines casting its glow in between structures.

Yasmine is still not here. That girl just keeps wandering around without telling anyone where she is going. I turn on the television and newscasters confirm what I think is happening. The Israeli government is retaliating for the soldiers kidnapped near the border, and we are at war, they say. I wonder what that means, for we've been "at war" with Israel for as long as I can remember. They have plans to take a chunk of this country, absorb the land of mountains and fertile soil down in the south, and HizbAllah won't let them. Then, the reporter says the airport has been bombed, and I understand the gravity of this war they have declared. A shiver runs down my spine.

We're stuck in Beirut until this ends. Yasmine is stuck in this country for the foreseeable future.

Knock, knock.

I jump off the bed, wrap my hijab over my wet hair and look through the peephole. It's Ziyad. I open the door slightly. His hands rub against each other. His hair is dishevelled, as if he rolled out of bed and ran down here.

"I think they are bombing the city."

"Yeah, no kidding genius." He looks worried, terrified, and confused as he enters the room "Sorry, obviously we're both scared," I say.

He spins around the room. "Where's Yasmine?"

"She was gone when I woke up."

"Where could she have gone?" His breaths are quick.

Boom! Another explosion. Automatic gunshots. We scream and lunge toward the floor. A whistling. Screams from afar. The cracking of rubble. We turn to face each other.

"It's far," I say.

I've learned over the years to predict the proximity of a bomb. A boom, even one that shakes the ground, is not close enough to harm. I fear the ones that tell you they are coming. The white noise of an engine in the sky, a whistling sound that increases in volume causing your muscles to contract, gunshots from an anti-rocket machine shooting into the sky. And then there's the force of something powerful meeting the earth and obliterating all that it touches.

I don't tell Ziyad that right now. We get up.

"Those gunshots must have been the anti-missile guns going off automatically. They are set throughout the city," I try to reassure him.

"We have to find Yasmine." He runs his hand through his hair and turns around. "I'll go check the lobby. Maybe the hotel people know what's going on."

I grab my things, throw them in a bag and catch up with Ziyad in the hallway. "Wait. You should go gather all your things. Carry valuables, especially your passport, at all times."

"How bad do you think this is?"

"I honestly don't know, Ziyad. Bombing the airport is unusual, but time will tell."

"I don't understand. Why? What happened? How does war just start out of nowhere?"

"It is not out of nowhere. Israel is unpredictable. You know they bomb things every now and then whenever they have a confrontation with Hezbollah or for some other made-up reason. Their goal has always been to cripple our society. Did you know that there's a community down in the south that funded and put together solar panels to generate their own power to have sustainable access to energy for their farm lands? And then you know what Israel did? Bombed it. They have nothing to do with HizbAllah, but Israel claims the terrorists are building solar panels. We've been living the horrors of their domination and expansion for fifty-eight years. Believe them when they say they are going to destroy the country."

He was quiet for a moment. "So, what now? If the airport is destroyed, what do we do?"

"I don't know. InshAllah they'll fix it, and it'll start running again, but for now, let's hunker down and meet downstairs. Get your stuff and I'll find Yasmine."

In the lobby, crowds of people congregate in front of the reception desk and others face television screens. I spot Yasmine behind the desk talking to someone. The air is filled with tension and anxiety; people are shouting, some are crying, holding each other. There's panic now. And yet, Yasmine seems composed, maybe the only stable thing in this space.

Our eyes lock and she runs to me. "They bombed the airport — well, the runways. They've been at it all morning." She looks around. "Have you seen Ziyad?"

"He's fine. He's looking for you somewhere in the crowd."

He comes out of the elevators a few minutes later carrying a packed bag and rushes to us. "Are you okay, Yasmine?" He looks at her like a person who just found out their dead lover had come back to life.

She swallows. "Yes, yes, let's go upstairs and figure out what we're going to do. It's too crowded here. I'm getting claustrophobic."

We walk past the jumble of bodies quivering in fear. Ziyad's hand hovers behind Yasmine, like he's restraining himself from touching her and absorbing the comfort of her back against his palm. I realize then the profoundness of his love for her. This isn't a crush, or some sort of infatuation.

When we're back in our room, I tell them we should go back to the north, where it's safer and I'm closer to Mama.

"Not yet," Yasmine says. "It's not safe. They are targeting moving vehicles on the roads, claiming that HizbAllah is using the roads to move supplies." She takes a deep breath. "Also, we don't have a car. I doubt Elissa is going to drive us back in this state."

"I have a car," Ziyad says.

"So what? We just wait then?" They don't understand that there are things that need to be done. We can't stay here. It's only going to get worse. "It's not safe here; there are targets in Beirut. HizbAllah has an entire base a few miles from here and the Israelis are going to target that entire neighbourhood. We're not safe here. Plus…" I pause and a flash of guilt crosses me. "I need to get back to Mama."

I should have never left her. I should have known better than to accept Yasmine's offer. People like me don't vacation. I'm angry at myself, angry at her for convincing me to come here when I could have been back where I belong, taking care of my family.

Yasmine reaches for my arm tenderly, her fingers feather across my shoulders. "Ramroum, don't worry. We'll go back. We just have to figure out the best route and strategy. Who knows, this might not last and we might be able to go back soon. The hotel is letting people stay here indefinitely."

I lean into her, my eyes filling with tears. "I need to go back to Mama. She's probably going mad with worry right now."

She holds me and my tears soak her shirt. The sound of an aircraft whizzes past and I sense her shoulders stiffening. She pulls me closer, until there's no space between us save for the air we are breathing. We close our eyes.

Another boom!

Paintings on the wall tremble. Ziyad pushes us into the tiny space between the door and the bathroom, away from windows. His arms hover over us. We stay quiet until the sounds of the anti-missile guns stop.

Yasmine asks Ziyad if he has a Canadian passport.

"No, not on me. Not a valid one anyway. Why?"

"I got in touch with the consulate services this morning. I gave them your info. Do you have anything that identifies you as Canadian? Drivers licence? SIN card? Anything?" She pauses. "Did you register with the Korean embassy when you came?"

"People know I'm here." He rubs the back of his neck.

"Of course they do," Yasmine says. Another boom shakes the building. "How close can those be?" Yasmine looks out the window. Ziyad grabs her by the arm and moves her away.

The buildings in our vicinity are still standing, but now there's visible fire and more smoke in the sky. I tell myself that this hotel is in a tourist area; there are embassies nearby. They wouldn't bomb a hotel filled with tourists. That would just be bad for their image. They wouldn't do anything that would garner international outcry. They've always treaded a thin line: create destruction but just enough that they can justify their "self defence" stance. Bombing civilians in a tourist neighbourhood? Surely, they wouldn't.

CHAPTER 21

Ziyad's hand lingers on my arm, keeping me away from the windows. I smell his sweet eucalyptus citrus fragrance and try to ease the tightness in my body. We'll get out of here, I assure myself. We have to. I need to get Reem back to Trablous and I can't die here. I can't leave my brother an orphan without siblings.

"Let's go back downstairs," I say. There's something about being on the sixth floor that makes me uneasy with airplanes flying around carrying all that artillery. Reem tells us to avoid the elevators even though they are running because "you never know." She walks next to me, her legs shaking with each step, with each staircase. Mine are stiff.

In the lobby, we sit in silence surrounded by forks clinking, voices murmuring to others, others shouting. Some stand by the entrance with luggage by their sides, waiting for an opportunity to flee. Minutes turn into hours and my mind moves at a creeping pace. We spend the rest of the day organizing. Reem tries to contact her mother, but the lines are all down. I try to get hold of Yusuf to let him know that we're alive, but those attempts are also fruitless. We all send messages to our loved ones hoping that someone will eventually get them. The power goes in and out. When it's on, we charge our devices and try to send out more messages. My heart beats hurriedly in contrast to the slow-moving time. With each passing second, death becomes less distant. The world, our world, is on fire.

Twenty.

There have been twenty hits so far, close enough to annihilate us. Half of those are close enough for us to hear the balls of fire erupting in a nearby building. I think about who's lying under the rubble. I picture their last moments spent in fear. I pray that Allah grants them the status of a shahid.

That word. I hate that it gets translated into "martyr," but there are no words in the English language to describe a person's dying act being the witnessing of injustice. This witnessing becoming their ephemeral end. That is why they get privileged status in the afterlife: they bear witness to oppression. May we all witness and hold the truth until our dying breath.

The sounds taper out that afternoon. They are further and I feel a glimmer of hope. I step outside for some fresh air. It's quiet on the pool deck and the still air absorbs my thoughts, calms my beating heart and cools down the heated blood running through my veins. A few people stand on the other side of the pool, smoking. Despite the air of doom that settles around us — it smells like burning rubber and gas — the sky is free of clouds and I lean back in a chair, embracing the warmth of the sun.

Only, my leg won't stop shaking. There's coursing energy looking to get out. Deep breaths: in for five seconds through the nose, out through the mouth for seven. It's not enough, though, so I get up to do jump squats because that tension has to go somewhere.

Ziyad appears next to me and starts doing the squats too.

"I guess it's a good idea to start working on those leg muscles. I suspect there might be some running in our immediate future." He chuckles, but I can't laugh. "Sorry, you know I make awkward jokes when I'm nervous."

We keep moving — up, down. My breaths turn into panting. I reach twenty and stop. Sweat beads across my forehead. "Exercise helps with my anxiety."

He stops when I do, and we sit in the reclining chairs facing the pool. "You seem quite controlled actually, so it must be helping."

I'm both glad for and exasperated by his words. There's nothing calm about this. About me. I only *appear* this way. That's what I'm going for, but it's exhausting and lonely.

I exhale a long breath. "I'm just trying to be sensible for Reem, to figure out a way to get us back." My tone is sharp, so I try to soften it. "What's your plan? I mean, to get out of here. Did you contact the Korean embassy?"

"I tried but can't get through. I don't think there are too many Koreans here. I'm not sure what to do. What about you? Do you want to wait to see what the Canadian government says?"

I fold my arms. "I don't know." I regret the sharpness of my words, but I can't find the filters. And my rage at his secrets has returned. "We should go our separate ways when we make it back to Trablous."

His body stiffens. "Yasmine, are you mad at me about something?"

"Do you know something I should be mad at you for?"

He raises an eyebrow and gives me a side glance. "You've been avoiding me. You haven't returned my texts. I've been wondering if it's just me, if I'm being needy, but now I know it's not all just in my head."

"What texts? I didn't get any texts."

He pulls out his phone and shows me. There are messages almost daily. "Good mornings" and "how are yous." One of them says "I miss you." I didn't get these messages. I take my phone out and show him. We're both baffled by the emptiness on our screens.

"I'm sorry. I don't know why I'm being like this. Everything has been weird," he says.

"I don't think this situation is the only thing that's weird."

Ziyad looks confused.

"You've been lying to me," I say.

He doesn't say anything for another few moments and we watch new smoke pass through the sky overhead. Normally, I give a lot of thought to the words that come out of my mouth. I think about my sentences and construct them in a way that conveys exactly what I think without hurting anyone. But it seems like in this country, they just spill out. "You lied to me about what you did for a living. You've lied to me about who you are."

A flash of contempt or anger crosses his face. "I didn't lie to you Yasmine." His voice is low, but deep. His jaw clenches. "I just left certain parts out. Is that what all of this is about? You could have just asked."

"I did ask. I asked you when we were in Beirut and you lied by omission."

He stands and faces me, his entire body turned toward me. "You don't have any right to all the details in my life." His hands land on his waist. "And if you're mad because you think, somehow, I've deceived you about who I really am, then I'm even more glad I kept it from you."

"What's that supposed to mean?"

"It means that you are making a whole bunch of assumptions about who I am now, and somehow everything I have been for the past few months was not real. Why do you think I'm here, in Lebanon? Because it was a safe place to study Arabic, to live a quiet life where nobody would notice me on the street. I just want to exist, and now that you've seen a picture of me online or read an article or something, I'm suddenly a liar who's been deceiving you. Forgive me if I wanted to keep our relationship authentic." He sighs and lowers his voice. "This is what you've always done. You did it in undergrad when you made assumptions and cut me off, and now you're doing it again."

I swallow a lump in my throat. "That's not why I am upset, Ziyad. I mean yes, it's a little weird to find out that way, but I'm not making judgements or assuming that you're someone else." I take in a long breath. "You can be both, you know? One doesn't negate the other. I don't understand why you feel like you need to pretend you are someone else. You're you and you're also some big shot rich guy."

He runs his hand through his hair. "So what are you mad about then?"

"I thought we were friends. I trusted you with some very personal details about my struggles and feelings around my family and finding my dad. But you couldn't trust me." I look down, and I have no rage left. "I don't know, maybe that's a me problem. Maybe I felt like I did have a right to some parts of your life, but I get it. It's none of my business. Whatever."

His stern expression loses some of its severity and he returns to the chair.

"Yasmine." A pause. "I'm afraid of what would happen if I opened up to you more than I already have."

I'm more scared now than I was this morning and the tightening in my chest returns, but there are no explosions.

He sighs. "I'm in love with you. I came to Beirut to create some distance between us. Because…because you've made yourself clear." He shakes his head. "This wasn't supposed to happen. It doesn't make any sense. I thought I had gotten over you after so many years but it's like when I'm with you, I make sense. I've never been around someone who…" his voice cracks, "who makes all the mundane things in life seem so beautiful."

"Ziyad…" I try to choose my words carefully now. "I had to cut you off years ago because my heart was leaning toward you. I loved our time together, I loved the way you made me feel. I love how free I am around you. But we were young and Tariq was in my life and he seemed like the much more responsible choice. And now." I sigh. "Now, my heart has been doing the same thing, but I don't know how to make it work when memories of my ex chase me. I've never lived on my own. I went from being under Yusuf's care, straight into the arms of Tariq and then finding out this about you. There's so much of your life that I don't know. Our circumstances don't make sense. I don't know how to make this work." I had admittedly thought about it many times. I had run through multiple scenarios and none of them seemed feasible for either of us. "Ziyad, you're going through a significant life change. You've only been Muslim for what? Eight months? You're figuring out who you are, who you want to be. Who knows, in a year you might find me repulsive."

He scoffs and I see the beginnings of a smile. "That's impossible."

"We don't even live in the same country, and we are both stuck in the middle of a war zone." I don't tell him that I'm still in the middle of my messy divorce or how hard it was to leave Tariq even though it was the best thing, too.

A quiet fills the space again. A man wearing a sombrero walks out with a cigarette in one hand.

"Aside from timing though, like if we weren't in this situation and this was a different time, would you have a different answer?" His brown eyes fill with an intensity that makes my heart quiver, and I have to look away. I wish he didn't ask me that question. I don't want him to ask me anything else. I just need to get out of here. I need to find a way out of my divorce with Tariq. I need to find a place to live. I need to find my freedom, and it doesn't include him. At least, not now.

"We should go back inside."

He doesn't break eye contact. "Yasmine." His voice is deep and shaky. "Can you please just tell me if you feel the same way. That it's not that you just love our friendship?"

"Ziyad, what's the point of asking something like that at a time like this?"

"Because I'm looking for something to hold on to, some hope of better things, in better times."

I stand. "Right now, we need to figure out a way to get out of here. Come, let's go back inside. We can talk about this another time."

A moment that feels like hours passes in silence and he remains in the chair, biting his lip. I walk away and it takes every last bit of my strength to go against my desire to tell him that I wish we weren't in this situation, that I'm not broken and traumatized, that I can be a good partner to him, that I want to wake up to him every day, that I want him to hold me, make me feel safe, and tell me everything is going to be okay.

Instead, I take those voices and bury them in the hollow pit of my stomach.

CHAPTER 22

Reem and I spend our first night huddled together under the same blankets. We wear our shoes, our bags hanging off our shoulders and our arms wrapped around each other. Bombings increase at night. Our bodies become rigid and our sleep disjointed.

At some point in the night, someone knocks on the door. Ziyad is in the hallway with one hand in his pocket and another wrapped around the strap on his bag.

"Hey, I just wanted to check in on you."

"We're okay. It's hard to sleep through it all, you know?"

He nods.

"You okay?"

His hands tremble. "No, not really."

I cross my arms and look back at Reem sleeping with her hijab tight around her head. "Do you want to stay here? There's an extra bed." I create an opening by shifting my body to the side.

He bites his bottom lip. "Only if you think it's okay."

"Honestly, it's probably best that we all stick together." I nod my head toward the empty bed and invite him in, shutting the door. "We're sleeping with our shoes on in case we need to run."

He swallows and lays down on the bed, staring at the ceiling. The air conditioner muffles some of the noise, but our bodies flinch at every bang and at every whistle.

"The far ones sound like fireworks," he whispers.

I turn my head slightly toward my side. "We'll make it out, inshAllah."

I see the rise and fall of his Adam's apple. "I'm going to miss you, you know. I've missed you for seven years. I'm not sorry about that, but I am sorry about putting you in that awkward situation downstairs."

"I'm sorry too, Ziyad."

"I know." He closes his eyes, and I struggle to catch my breath.

The next day ushers in renewed hope and turmoil. By now the phones work intermittently. I'm sitting alone in the lobby area in an armchair with my laptop in front of me. Reem has gone upstairs to make phone calls and Ziyad has decided to change out of his clothes. I brainstorm ideas to get us out of here.

Unexpectedly, my phone rings. An unknown number. I wonder if it's the blue door man, if he's calling to tell me that my uncle has provided us with a safe way out. And then I remember how the Israeli military calls people from an unknown number, to have their location marked as a target. This makes me want to fling my phone into the wall. I don't know what to do and my hands tremble. Why would they want to attack me? Maybe they have the wrong number? I don't answer it.

Then a text message bings.

> Yasmine, it's Tariq, I'm in Trablous. I know you're also here. I've got a taxi taking us to Syria in a few days. Come with me.

My hands get clammy and cold, and I almost drop the phone. I look around to see if anyone has noticed, but it's like I'm living in a time loop. The couple at the table next to me don't seem to notice me. I take a deep breath and read the message again. I don't respond. He sends a few more messages expressing worry. Then he asks if I need anything. And then he starts begging me to return his messages and calls.

Reem comes back downstairs.

"How's your mom?" I ask.

"She's okay, but she's getting hysterical. Her blood pressure is rising. I feel bad for Fatme. I need to get back. I can't just leave them."

She leans forward in the chair. "Listen, you and Ziyad, you can get out with your passports. There are rumours that embassies are going to be evacuating people. I need to get back, so how about we just split? I'll find a way to return and you stay here."

I shake my head. "No way Reem. I won't leave you."

That's when I realize that the only viable option I have is Tariq. He figured out a way to get us out of the country so maybe he can figure out a way to get us out of this city. I promise Reem that I'll get her back to her family and we talk for a while until she goes back upstairs.

When I'm finally alone again, I respond to Tariq. I tell him that I'm in Beirut and don't know if I'll make it out in time. My phone buzzes almost immediately.

Where in Beirut? I'll get you out of there.

Can't, roads are being bombed it's not safe.

There are special routes. My cousin just arrived this morning. Tell me where you are, I'll send a car.

I send him the hotel address and tell him that I'm with my cousin and a friend, that we all have to leave together.

I'll find something and get back to you.

Tariq has always been reliable, I'll give him that. I consider what accepting his offer of help will mean to him. He'll use it to try and get me back. I picture him assuring me that he'll take care of me, and he knows that's what I'm looking for. Time will pass, and he'll tighten his grasp on my life. He'll lash out at me for cooking the wrong thing, for not being home waiting for him at the end of the day. He'll ridicule me in front of his friends for spending hours with a book.

It'll all be worth it to get us back to Trablous.

The third day is much the same, explosions violating our sense of ease. I spend my time in the lobby, chatting with anyone I can find. I want to know how others are getting out, how they're planning to leave. Some are arranging for taxi rides outside of the city into nearby villages. Some are finding passage to the Syrian border. The main highway, the fastest way along the coast, has become a death zone. The Israeli government bombed several bridges and overpasses and it's too exposed. Anything moving is a target.

Ziyad and I avoid talking to each other. We sit and address our conversation to Reem, who acts as a buffer. We make a pact to only leave the hotel once it's safe for all of us, and then go our separate ways from Trablous.

On the news, announcements are called for planned evacuations for Australians, Irish, Italians, and other Europeans. No promises from Canada, aside from a request that citizens register with the embassy.

"It's because they realized your true roots: you're an Arab and you'll always be an Arab," Reem says in response to my frustration about updates from the Canadian government. I know it's not true. That's not how our government works, that's not how our democracy works. But something about her statement fills me with hopelessness.

One afternoon, I get a call from Elissa. "Are you okay?"

I don't know how to answer. What does it mean to be okay in light of the current circumstances? To be alive? To have breaths with which to witness the carnage?

I don't answer and she tells me that they've gotten safe passage through the UAE embassy. "Yasmine. I convinced my dad to get you onto the list of evacuees. I tried to get Reem on the list, but Baba didn't think it was possible." There's pity or remorse in her tone.

"Don't worry about it. We'll figure something out. I can't leave Reem here. Someone I know is trying to get us out to Syria."

We promise to see each other again in the future, I wish her luck, and we end our call.

I remember once reading about something called survivor's remorse. A psychological state that comes from living through traumatic events — guilt for making it — like you didn't deserve to live when everyone else was perishing. I wonder if Elissa is feeling it and how much she truly cares about us. How is it so easy for them to just pick up and leave the country when we were just trying to figure out how to leave the city?

On the fourth morning, I go back down to the lobby with my laptop and sit in my usual spot. There's an older man sitting at a table next to mine. It's the first time I've seen him. After a few days, we've all gotten to know the hotel staff and most of the guests. We've all been sharing stories and tips about where to get food and how to book a car to get us out of the city. Half the guests have already left. A few others remain, foreign nationals or people who live in the south and have no interest in going back.

"Marhaba," I say.

He smiles. "Ahlan."

"I haven't seen you around here."

"I'm a driver, I'm taking a family out to Trablous."

"Oh, subḥanAllah, we've been trying to find a way to get there."

"I can take you if you want, after this trip."

I tell him that we have a car, that we're just looking for the safest route. He says there's a network of drivers who have been keeping each other informed on which roads are still safe. Then, he pulls out a map and begins to draw a route leading eastward and into the mountains. Then he draws across another path in a different colour in case the first one is no longer viable. He finishes drawing up the route, writes down his number and gives me additional tips. "Early morning is the best time, unless you're comfortable driving in the dark without headlights on, but I don't recommend it. You'll need to drive very fast. There's no time to stop, at least not at first, but eventually when you get up to the villages it's safer and you can take breaks."

I thank him and he refuses the money I offer for his intel. I make duʿa for him instead. And just like that, we finally have a plan. I send Tariq a message and let him know that we've secured passage back to the north.

I gather my things and go to our room upstairs, making a stop at Ziyad's room to tell him to join us. Reem is sitting on the bed watching television when we get there.

"I found our way out," I say. They turn their heads, waiting for more. I unfold the map on the desk. "There are two routes we can take. Reem, I'm hoping you can drive because you probably know these roads better than either of us. We can leave tomorrow morning, early, right after Fajr. Right now, these roads are safe, but they won't be for long."

I don't get the excitement that I'm expecting. Instead, they seem hesitant. "There was a family that was just killed on one of the roads near Saida. Their van was a target. Moving cars are not safe. You sure you don't want to wait for the Canadian embassy?" Reem says.

"It is not that safe to stay here either. People are leaving. We'll soon be stranded in a ghost hotel with everything exploding around us." Of course, I know the roads are not safe, I know that moving vehicles are being targeted, but what choice do we have?

"Reem, this is our best shot. I won't leave you. I will go back with you to Trablous and we can figure things out from there. The longer we wait, the worse the roads will get." I turn to Ziyad. "Ziyad, if waiting is what you want to do, Reem and I can find a ride out of here. You don't have to come with us. The taxi driver already offered to take us if we can pay the $4K fee. I still have money from my research grant that I can use."

He looks up at me with certainty, and my heart does something in that moment.

"I won't leave you," he says.

I return to Reem. "So? It's better we do this now, before more of the roads become inaccessible."

"If we stay, we risk dying here. If we go, we risk having our car blown up. Are you asking me if I prefer to die here in this hotel or on the road?"

Yes, that is exactly what I'm asking. I nod and swallow hard, trying to keep my momentum and the energy that continues to flow through me despite having gotten very little sleep the past few nights. "Once we are back in Trablous, I have a car arranged to take Ziyad and I to the Syrian border." I don't tell them that this car is the one offered by my ex-husband.

Reem rubs her thighs. "Okay, but can we please pick up my cousin and her baby daughter first? They live in the Burj Al Barajni camp and the bombings in that area are very bad. I talked to Mama this morning and she told me they were trying to find a way to come to us in Trablous."

"That would add to our trip, Reem. You know it's more dangerous in that area. I don't know. We'd be risking it," I say.

Reem crosses her arms in front of her chest. "I can't leave without her. They are really having a hard time. If you guys want to go, fine, but I can't go without her. I won't leave them. She has a baby." She speaks fast with distress in her voice. I look at Ziyad for the final vote. He's hunched over with both fists in front of his face. He nods in agreement.

"Okay, we leave at sunrise. Reem, tell your cousin we are coming."

"InshAllah," Reem says.

"InshAllah."

CHAPTER 23

My cousin Mariam doesn't answer her phone and won't return my text. Despite this, we still make plans to get her. She knows we're here and I won't leave without her.

I call Mama and tell her of our plan.

"May Allah be pleased with you." She says and I take it as a sign of her approval.

We get up at the crack of dawn and pack our things into the trunk of Ziyad's red Yaris. I throw in bottles of water from the hotel.

Before stepping into the car, I warn them all that the Burj Al Barajni camp is the largest in the country. It's in the Daḥieh neighbourhood and is being heavily bombed. We'll take the main road to cross the city because it's the only one I'm familiar with and it's the fastest way to get there.

I put my hand on the car and sigh. "Are you sure you are willing to risk your lives?"

They both nod but tentatively. Then Ziyad sits in the back seat, and I take the wheel with Yasmine by my side. Yasmine holds my hand.

"InshAllah, we'll be okay." Her voice is soft and soothing.

I don't know where she's come up with that confidence. If you asked me how she might react in a situation like this a few months ago I would have laughed, fully expecting her to have crumbled in an instant, but I was wrong.

"Bismillah," I say as I turn on the ignition. I turn left at the main road, praying that Allah is with us, protecting us in his infinite mercy. Yasmine recites Āyat al-Kursi and the other prayers for protection she has memorized. The sounds of bombs grow louder the further inland we travel. I press my foot on the gas pedal and watch the speedometer creep up to 180.

The Bay Rock Café whizzes past me and I know this area, yet it's unfamiliar. This city that had once been a beacon of life and light is gone. There are only remnants of life, indications that people were once here. Litter on sidewalks, an empty ice cream stand and broken streetlights. The silence of fear. There's an eerie quietness that's pierced only with the occasional sound of war crafts and the barrage of bombs. We're riding in the only car on the road. We are the only people. An open target. I lift my index finger and make my shahada. The bombs grow louder. The steering wheel vibrates in my palm. I wonder if we should have stayed in the safety of the hotel.

I look at Yasmine, who looks deep in thought, and I don't say anything. Instead, I push my foot further down on the gas pedal, barreling forward at 200 km an hour. I find new strength in my limbs, a rush flooding my veins. No one speaks for the rest of the 15-minute car ride until we make it into the camp. It feels like a miracle.

When we get out of the car, the air smells like burned rotting wood and metal. Smoke fills the air. We agree to stay together. Ziyad and Yasmine follow me as I swiftly navigate the alleys of this camp. It's quiet. No children in the fields or between homes. Shops are closed, windows are boarded. I knock on Mariam's door forcefully three times. What will I do if they don't answer? How will I explain risking our lives for a cousin who didn't even know we were coming? My palms are sweaty, and I'm cornered. When no one answers, I shout out her name.

Seconds later, she appears at the door, carrying a baby, surprised to see us.

"We're going to Trablous, do you want to come?" I ask. There's no time for chatter. My legs move back and forth. Echoes of bombs are constant, and I feel a need to hide, run, just get out of here.

"Umm, okay," Mariam frowns. "Let me just check with Omar and pack a few things. Please come inside."

We walk in and wait in the entryway. Mariam's husband offers us something to drink and I can't answer. Yasmine smiles at him and graciously declines. I'm still searching to understand where she's finding this calm.

Mariam comes down shortly after with a bag and her daughter Yara wrapped in her arm. She glances at her husband with tears in her eyes. "Please be safe." He kisses her on the forehead and then their daughter. They say their goodbyes.

"I'll find a way to join you with Mama," he says.

We make our way back to the car, speedwalking through the narrow alleys the same way we came. Yara looks at me from across her mother's shoulder and smiles that sweet baby smile, oblivious of her surroundings in her mother's arms.

I see the car. But the noise, the whistling — it's too close. It's so loud, it penetrates my ear and sinks into my brain. The earth shakes and then anti-missiles shoot into the sky. We crouch down to the ground instinctively.

And then, I'm flying, floating by the force of a hot wind, and my body slams against the floor. This is it. This is the end and I'm relieved that it's come swiftly.

I'm flooded with fear when I realize I'm still alive.

There's a ringing in my ears and my skin burns with flaming rage. Pain shifts from one side of my body to another. I lie on the ground, nothing but a grey cloud of smoke in my vision. Another boom blows near me again and, this time, I don't move.

I hear the faint sounds of a child's cries. Yara. Someone needs to get Yara.

Smoke spreads further, creating a clearer path in front of me, but I can't stand. My legs are like noodles in water. Someone grabs my arm and lifts me up, placing a cloth over my mouth. It's Ziyad, carrying me into the car. His black hair is a dusted grey. "Yara!" I yell out, but he doesn't hear me.

He puts me in the passenger seat in front of Mariam and I see the sweet baby face, wet with tears. Mariam caresses her and sings lullabies.

"Yasmine," I shout, coughing. "Where is Yasmine?" I open the door to go look for her and someone from the outside closes it again. I see Ziyad carrying Yasmine's limp body. Her eyes are shut. There's blood everywhere. I scream, hoping that my shriek might wake her or bring her back to life "Yasmine!" I can't lose her too. Not like this. I should have died … ya Allah, take me instead.

Ziyad puts her in the back and takes the driver's seat. "I'll drive," he says. "Reem, just tell me where to go." His eyes are sharp and focused. Blood streaks from his eyebrow.

I lean back to see if Yasmine is breathing. "Is that her blood?"

Ziyad looks like he's about to crumble. "I don't know. Oh god, I don't know." His voice is shaky.

Mariam puts Yara on her lap and checks if Yasmine has a pulse, then tries to find the source of the blood. "It's her arm, she has a bunch of scratches and blood is coming from her arm." She removes a tiny blanket from her bag and wraps it around the wound. Then she searches the rest of Yasmine's body, looking for other injuries. "I think it's just her arm, and she's breathing. I think she'll be okay, inshAllah."

Ziyad hands her a bottle of water and tells her to try to clean the wound.

"Maybe she's just in shock. She hasn't been eating. InshAllah, she'll be fine," I say. I don't convince myself; for all I know, she could be taking her last breaths. "We need to move. We need to get out of here."

In front of us, smoke streams out the top of a building a few houses from Mariam's house. The ceiling is gone and the cement is blackened. A woman walks out of the front. Her face is red with blood, her arms in the air. She's shouting something incoherent. Ziyad looks at me. "We should help her. What if there's someone else inside?"

"No, we can't do anything for them. What are you going to do, kill yourself to get back inside? We need help. Yasmine needs help."

"Let's just see if she needs anything," whispers Mariam. "That's Khalto Samar, I know her."

My face turns pink with rage and I curl my fists. Obviously, they need help. We all need help, but we can't do anything. The longer we linger here, the more we're at risk of also dying. We need to move, fast. "There's no time to help." Ziyad and Mariam don't seem convinced. The car is not moving. I raise my tone. "Her house was just bombed. Her face is bloodied and who knows how many people she's lost. All these people need something. Look around! There's nothing you can do about it. Nothing. We're all living in this misery, and we'll continue to live in misery forever because nobody cares. Don't you know that our lives are worthless? This military that just dropped those gifts on us are backed by some of the most powerful people in the world. The best thing that can happen to us is death right now." I'm sobbing now.

They say nothing. I take a deep breath and speak in a razor-sharp tone, making sure that no one mistakes my intention. "Ziyad, if you get out of this car, I'm leaving you behind here and driving without you. Choose: stay here or go now."

He acknowledges me with a slight nod, turns on the ignition, and we drive off.

CHAPTER 24

I wake up in a moving car, my head pounding. My clothes are wet and moist against my skin. My back rests against the door and my feet are propped up. For a moment, I wonder if it has all been a dream. Am I in Toronto? Passed out in someone's backseat? Then I realize my right arm burns like its wrapped in hot steel.

I can't see very well. Everything is blurry but I make out the shape of a woman and a baby on her lap in front of me. Ziyad calls out my name. I can't turn my head and I'm afraid to move. I blink a few times and see his face in the rearview mirror. His eyes are red-rimmed and there's a streak of blood on his forehead. I want to wipe it away. Hearing my name slip through his tongue — the way my mother intended it, pronouncing the S softly like the flower — in that deep voice, makes me want to keep my eyes open.

"Let's stop here for a bit, Ziyad. We need to get a bit of rest. I think we are entering Ehden," Reem says.

The car comes to a halt and the door behind me opens. Reem protects me from falling with her hand. I find the strength to stay propped up and am relieved by my spine's ability to move.

"Here." She hands me a bottle of water and I take a sluggish sip.

My vision clears. We're in some sort of a village. There are houses backing up onto a valley. Birds sing. A red squirrel runs across the field behind Reem. The house next to us has a giant metal gate protecting a field of grass in the front lawn. It's made of white bricks with orange roof tiles and a garden around it with blossoming trees.

On the other side of the road is a dukani that sits in a forest of pine and arz trees. Beach towels hang on a clothing line out front, and all of its windows are covered with ads for Coke, Pepsi, Unica, and other Gandour treats.

"Where are we? How long have we been driving?" I say.

"We've been driving for about four hours," Ziyad says. "It's safe to stop here for a bit. Let's get you cleaned up." He moves Reem aside and kneels in front of the car at eye level with me. "Yasmine, how are you feeling? You have a bad cut on your arm. Does anything else hurt or feel weird?" Despite the blood on his own face, his eyes are warm.

"We should clean up your wound. I have a first aid kit in my bag." He opens the trunk and pulls out a bag, finds the kit and passes it to Reem. "I'm going to go to that store to see if I can pick up a few things."

"How far away are we, Reem?"

"Maybe another hour, habibti." She pauses to look around. "You need to eat and drink. I think that's why you fainted; you haven't been eating or sleeping much."

Ziyad comes back a few minutes later with a bag of snacks and drinks and a large beach towel with Mini Mouse's face on it. He rips the towel into several smaller pieces and hands a few of them to Reem along with a bottle filled with a white foggy liquid, probably arak.

I pat my body trying to get a sense of how stable it is. Aside from an ache that permeates my entire arm, I tell myself I'm okay. My clothes are wet from the blood that has soaked through it and I wonder if all of this is my blood.

Reem unwraps the cloth around my arm with the tip of her fingers and I gag at the sight of the cut. She pours the white liquid on top of it, and I scream in pain.

"It's okay, it's okay. This will help get it all cleaned up," she murmurs. I'm hardly comforted by her shaking hands. She cleans my arm with strips from the towel and then wraps it with a clean bandage from the first aid kit.

"There's a bathroom next to the store. It's old-school Arab style with a hole in the ground, but you can use it to change if you want to get out of those clothes."

Reem and I both grab a change of clothes from our bags and head in to the bathroom to get out of the rags we are wearing. Mariam nurses her baby in the backseat. We both walk cautiously, holding on to each other. The fresh air fills my lungs, giving my body permission to momentarily ease the tension that grips my limbs.

I put on a pair of loose linen pants and a black t-shirt. We walk back, our arms tangled with each other. Our heels drag against the gravel beneath our feet. My white sneakers are bloodied beyond recognition. I stand in front of the car, my back resting against the passenger door.

A group of men dressed in zaffeh outfits with wide pants and turbans walk out of the house in front of us. One of them carries a large drum, shouting congratulatory chants. Lebanese pop music plays loudly from speakers as the group puts on a performance welcoming a bride and groom who walk out behind them. The couple is followed by a group of people in dresses and suits. The bride wears a large princess dress, with a bouquet of red roses in her hand. Her hair is pulled up into a bun of giant curls. Her husband is in a tuxedo, and they are surrounded by people who share in their newfound joy, throwing flower petals over them.

"This is so weird," I mutter to Reem.

She side-eyes me. "We're far from the action here. People's lives go on. If you're not watching the news, you wouldn't even know that we are at war."

"Are you sure Reem? Like how, why?"

She takes a deep breath. "There is nothing of interest to the Israelis here, at least not for now. This is a Christian dominated village and there's very little HizbAllah activity in Trablous. InshAllah, we're safe for now and we'll be safe when we get home." She looks in to the car, checking in on Mariam and her baby. "Plus, to my knowledge, the Israeli army hasn't physically invaded yet. They are just attacking from the air and sea. If they actually invade, I'd be worried then." She hands me a granola bar and tells me to eat it. "I'm going to go check on Mariam. Stay here and get some fresh air."

I tilt my head up to the sky. Outside, it is hot and humid, but the air is fresh. I listen to the laughter from the wedding crowd and picture the couple's glee in this union. What would their coming days look like? Would they get to go on a honeymoon and find love amid this chaos, or would they be filled with grief from the losses to come? Would it have been worth it then, to have spent a day celebrating a love that might not last?

Ziyad leans against the car next to me. "It's strange, right, that even in times of war, people find ways to move on, to continue to love each other."

I sense the sharp edges of his words. I swallow a lump in my throat. "I'm sorry, Ziyad."

"What for?"

"I don't know." My voice is shaky and coarse. "Everything, I wish—"

"It's okay," he responds before I can finish.

"No, it's not okay. Maybe if this was a different time, then my answer would have been different."

"I know," he looks so sad. We were supposed to have a few more months of touring the country. We were supposed to visit an ancient museum in Baalbek. We have many more breakfast dates planned. I was going to introduce him to Lebanese ice cream, the stretchy pistachio kind.

He pulls out something from behind him. A wild orchid flower, light pink and fragile. "I spotted a few plants back there. I figured we could all use a bit of colour to lighten the mood." He smiles. "Do you like orchids?"

I nod but I'm dazed, my eyes wandering the celebration in front of me. "Did you know that orchids are one of the oldest flowering plants? They've been around for a long time. For all we know, this flower comes from a plant that has been here for hundreds of years."

"They're my mom's favourite. She has a huge garden back home. I've tried convincing her to move to the city a few times to be closer to me, but she refuses to leave her green space and her precious garden.

Even if it means she's lonely."

I'm not sure why he's sharing this information, but it's endearing, and I find myself wanting more. "Do you have a garden back home?"

He shakes his head. "No, I live in a penthouse. There's a balcony, but I'm never there long enough to really care for any plant. I'm afraid they'll all just die on me and then the guilt of killing them will drag me for days."

"So all of your travels, the ones you've talked about, were they all related to your work, or do you just like getting around?"

He takes a deep breath. "Mostly yeah." He folds his arms in front of him. "But I'm tired of it, to tell you the truth. I rarely have time to sit and think and take in everything, enjoy things or care for plants. This, here, this time here in Lebanon is really, really nice. Sucks that it's ending sooner than I planned. All of it."

I nod and smell the flower. It doesn't have a scent, but I sense something akin to a light mildew. The smell of beginnings.

"Becoming Muslim has given me something concrete to focus on that's stabilizing, but I miss writing. I miss the feeling of getting lost in the pages of my words."

"Didn't you say you still do some writing?"

"I've written some poetry that was published, but I don't know. I can't get into it more than that." He turns his head to look at me, but my eyes are on the wedding party. "Being here has made me realize how burnt out I've been, how I never took time to grieve. I've started reading and writing again. Even working on something new."

"Is that what you want to do?"

"I have no idea what I want. But for now, it doesn't really matter. I'm grateful that I can take time to figure it out. I don't think I want to go back to Toronto and work for my dad."

I twirl the flower in my hand. It's a reminder that despite the chaos, the killing, the fear, and everything else that's going on a few hours east of here, life is meant to be pursued slowly. That things will grow in their time.

"Your feelings are not one-sided." I say, finally. "I just can't do anything about it right now, and it's probably best that we go our separate ways after all of this."

I see the rise and fall of his Adam's apple, and he tightens his hold on the water bottle. "Let's just get through this for now."

We stand in silence for a minute. Reem steps out from behind the car and tells us that it's time to hit the road again. Yara nestles in her mother's arms.

CHAPTER 25

Making the trip from Beirut to Trablous typically takes about forty-five minutes if we take the main oceanfront highway. But that road has been bombed in multiple places and cars are too exposed to war ships and warplanes. This trip takes us six hours. We drive inland through the mountains and valleys where our car is camouflaged among the Druze and Christian villages before going north and west again. The end comes as a relief. I'm in disbelief that we made it. We no longer need to sleep with the sound of bombs crippling our surroundings, forcing us to grip our seats, ready for death. It's a vile kind of psychological warfare, one that had me hoping for death because the anxiety, the stress, the fear of what might come next is greater than my fear of death. Allah is merciful and those who drop those bombs are living devils. I'm nauseous and dizzy. My body is not designed to endure this level of fear and anguish. Every explosion, every thud has scrabbled at my limbs, lacerating my physical and mental strength.

At home, I think about asking Ziyad if he wants to stay with us, but then I think about having to explain him to Mama. So, I tell him that I'm grateful for his help, for leading when I couldn't.

I help Mariam and Yara out of the car while Yasmine and Ziyad grab our bags, and I see the way that they are looking at each other. It makes me long for love, to be looked at that way. She says something to him and walks toward me. We start making our way through the alley back to my home. Ziyad calls out to me. I return while Yasmine waits for me, and he hands me a thick yellow envelope.

"What is this?"

"I'm probably leaving tomorrow, so I'm not sure if I'll be able to see you before I go. I had some extra cash for my trip and I won't have any use for it anymore once I'm gone. Please just use it however is best."

I look inside. There's a stack of bills. Normally my pride would have gotten in the way of taking it, but these are dire times, and the banks have shut down. "Thank you." I put the envelope in my bag.

He nods and lingers in front of the car.

I wait.

"Reem, I'm really sorry about your brother. What happened was awful."

He pauses as yet another tear falls down my cheek.

"I've been there, and I know what that feels like. The level of desperation and hopelessness. When you're in that reality, the darkness just takes hold of you and you can't control it."

"Thanks?" I eye him curiously, unsure if he's trying to comfort me, because it feels like the opposite. He doesn't know what I feel. He's alive, so whatever desperation that he went through, he also had the support to get through it. Ahmad didn't have that privilege and he is gone now. I can't run into the safety of another country. I don't have three passports.

"What I'm trying to say is, sometimes it feels really rough and dark like we're in a cave, but in reality, it's a tunnel and there's light at the end, and you'll get there inshAllah. Please keep moving forward and working toward your dreams. And if you need anything — I mean it, anything — please reach out. I'll even pay for your education if you get into a program overseas."

My eyes widen. I wonder if his confidence in me is misplaced.

"Thanks," I say. It hits me then: Ziyad is that dream student I'd been waiting for, the one who would provide me with some sort of pathway. I'm speechless and I don't know if I should believe his promise.

But what's unfolded over the last few months has been a reminder that this is where I belong. With my family, supporting my loved ones. Who am I to think that I can get out and pursue these dreams when everyone else has only uncertainty?

"Just because you've lived through so much doesn't mean the rest of your life is going to remain difficult. Your struggles, your experiences, your resiliency, Reem, they will push you through the rest of it. You've accumulated the strength to change so much."

An awkward silence settles between us. "Anyways. I left my number and email address in that envelope. Just keep me posted."

He gets into the car and drives away. My dream student, leaving behind a tiny spark of hope in my heart.

Mama is still in one piece, physically and metaphorically. She feeds and coddles us until we can't move. She treats me the way she received Ahmad when he reappeared, like a king. I can't help but feel like I'm replacing him. His permanent absence is an eternal guilt in my heart. I miss him, and I don't understand how it's possible for grief to get worse over time.

Mariam and Yara sleep with Mama in her room and Yasmine sleeps with me and Fatme. I can't even close my eyes for most of the night. I watch Yasmine like a hawk, making sure she stays alive. I worry that she has one of those head injuries that take people in their sleep.

Morning arrives — I must have fallen asleep. She's sitting cross-legged on the floor with a pen and her notebook. Relief washes over me at the sight of her alive and well. I turn to face her, but she doesn't notice, immersed in her notebook. "Are you writing a love letter to Ziyad?" I ask.

She throws a pillow at me. "No, I'm taking notes. Someone is going to have to tell these stories, the things that we've witnessed, these feelings. I want to catch it all before it's forgotten. No one will tell our stories the way we tell them."

I smile. This feels normal. "Are you leaving today?" I try to hide the pain at the thought of her leaving.

She puts her pen down and her chest rises in a deep breath. "I'm not sure."

"What do you mean? Did the car guy cancel?"

She shakes her head. "I don't think I want to leave, Reem."

What am I supposed to say to that? Don't go? Please stay here with me in the world of unpredictable futures and no prospects? I hate that the world has made it easy for her to go and impossible for me to leave. So I just ask, "Why not?"

"I don't know, things are okay here, right? Maybe the war will end soon and I'll be able to collect more data. Here in Trablous, I'll be safe." She looks down. "I think."

"But what if the war doesn't end, and it gets worse and the Israeli government invades and they do the horrible things we've heard of them doing and the Lebanese military gets involved and then, probably, it will be even more difficult to get out because the Syrian government will close the border." I sit on my bed. "And then you might have to swim through the Mediterranean to Cyprus. Do you want to go swimming with sharks and Allah knows whatever else lives in that ocean?"

Her mouth curves into a smile. "Yeah, that's what Yusuf said. Well not the bit about having to swim to escape, but that I should take this opportunity to get to safety."

"When did you talk to Yusuf?"

"He called this morning." She rubs her injured arm.

"What's the issue then?" I see her thoughts spinning in her head. She overthinks things. "You'll need to get that arm checked. You probably need stitches and it might be easier to see a doctor once you get to Syria."

"Tariq is the one arranging the car. He called me when we were in Beirut. He's been waiting for me to get back so that we can leave together."

My eyes widen. "Oh."

"I didn't tell Ziyad. I'm hoping he won't notice. I was just planning on telling him that it was a family friend."

"Yasmine, the way I see it, this may be the ultimate way to get revenge."

"I'm not interested in getting revenge. I'm scared of being around him for so many reasons."

I sit down next to her on the floor. "Listen, he's offering to get you out. He probably paid for the taxi and everything. Just use him and then dump him as soon as you get to Syria. Mama contacted our aunt and she said that you can stay with her. She'll even pick you up at the border so you already have a place to stay." I grab her hand. "And then, you go and marry Ziyad and make sure, Tariq, your khara ex-husband, knows about it."

She shakes her head. "I'm not marrying Ziyad and I'm not just going to abandon Tariq. I don't hate him and I don't want revenge." She wipes a tear from her eye.

"Then what?"

"I don't know how to explain it. Ziyad told me he loved me in Beirut and I didn't respond. I just told him that it wasn't the right time. I need to get over one person before jumping into another entanglement. I can't ask him to wait for me to get over whatever it is that I'm getting over, right?"

"You're thinking like a rational person and I'm proud of you for that. I've made jokes about you two, but I get it, wallah I get it. And if you ask him to wait, he might."

"I won't do that. And there's something else, too. I've been wanting to ask you about Syria and this aunt. I found out that Baba had probably been in Damascus in the 1990s and I was making plans to go before this war broke out, but I needed a lead. And now I have it."

I sigh. "Then you have to go."

We both nod and sit in silence. "But, please Yasmine, find a way out and finalize your divorce from Tariq. I hate him and I've never even met him. I want you to hate him too."

"I don't want that. I know the things he did were unforgivable, and it took me a long time to realize that. But those are his demons and he'll have to deal with them for the rest of his life. I kind of feel bad for him sometimes." She looks away. "That's also part of why I'm afraid of being around him. I'm afraid of how he makes me feel. I know it sounds absurd and it's hard to explain for someone who hasn't been in my position. It's complicated, but a part of me wants him to find some sort of redemption. I hope he doesn't die with a darkened heart."

"So then just make sure you're never alone with him. He's not your responsibility Yasmine."

She shrugs. "I know."

"You'll be fine. It's just a car ride. Take a knife with you. If he makes a move, stab him in the eye."

Yasmine laughs and I don't know how to convince her that I'm not joking. Her face shifts and is overcome with sadness now, tugging at my heart. "I'm going to miss you so much, ramroum." She invites me into a hug with open arms. I lean in and never want to let go.

We eat breakfast with Mama, Fatme, and Mariam, who spends half her time staring at her phone.

The destruction in Beirut has only gotten worse since we left. More civilians have died in Lebanon, and I have doubts about the Israeli military's commitment to only target "HezbAllah." But to them, we're all terrorists so they can kill as many of us as possible. When I say this out loud, Mama reminds me that these are the same people who invaded the country more than thirty years ago to slaughter more Palestinians that had fled their grasp years prior. They can't be content with Palestinians living, even in refugee camps countries away. They will only accept us if we jump on their bandwagon and spread their lies and give them permission to colonize our lands.

The war has barely been going on for a week and two hundred innocent lives have left the world as witnesses to grave oppression. How many will be enough, I wonder. How many until the so called free world —that funds and support them — realizes that enough is enough. How many Palestinian lives are equal to theirs?

There are rumours that the Israeli military has entered parts of the south, paving the way for history to repeat itself. Home invasions, kidnappings, hospitals destroyed, slaughter. Oh, the slaughter. We know the stories of mass executions. We know the stories of children who watched their fathers' bodies fall limp on to the ground of the refugee camp. Bloody bodies like discarded cattle. We know all too well how they kidnapped our fathers and brothers, torturing one while the other listened to generated "confessions" of their allegiances to the PLO, or to "Hezbollah," or to Fateh. It's always someone else who's a terrorist. Soon, there won't be anywhere to hide and we'll all be deemed terrorists, our lives worthless to those on the outside who believe the lies fed to them.

And then, before I know it, Yasmine is standing at the door waiting to say goodbye.

CHAPTER 26

I nurse a surge of regret for not spending more time with Reem and her family and guilt for my inability to do anything about their situation. I give them the rest of my cash, tell them I will send more, that I will pray for them. I wish I had more time. Khalto Fawzia hoards stories of Mama and their childhood, stories that I haven't been able to gather. She holds them in the vault of her mind along with all the pain she's experienced in her life. That's another thing I'm leaving behind.

I hesitate for a moment at the door and Khalto Fawzi leans in to give me the first hug I have ever received from her. I don't want to let go.

She pulls away. "Do you know why your mother named you Yasmine?" she asks.

"No, do you?" My heart leaps at the prospect of accessing this intimate tidbit about myself.

She nods. "Most people love the jasmine because of the scent of its blooms. A tiny flower can fill a room with its intoxicating aroma, but that's not why Samira loved it. She was amazed with the way the flowers only bloom for a few days before they change colours and fall off. The next day, new flowers emerge with fresh scents. She loved how it was constantly blooming, never seeming to get tired, save for some parts of the year. The flowers are so powerful, but their lives are short. The plant is so resilient, it has no problem producing new ones after the others die. We're kind of like that, the Palestinians. We've suffered so much loss, but we've always rebuilt and we always will. Your mother wanted you to be like the Yasmine that is constantly falling but always blooming."

I lean in for another hug and hold tight, inhaling another whiff of her now familiar scent — a mixture of olive oil and citrus. I let myself pretend like it's Mama giving me the strength to continue, reminders that she loved me. "I'm so sorry," I whisper in her ear.

"There's nothing to be sorry about. Get home safely and help Reem get into a program."

"InshAllah." I hold her tighter and my tears flow.

Reem walks with me to the taxi waiting out front. "Remember, don't let that ass touch you."

"Okay." We are both crying now. "Please don't give up Reem. I'll be waiting for you."

She gives me a reassuring smile. "I won't, I promise. Even if it's only so that I can see you again."

"And if you need anything, anything. Please..."

She nods. "Yallah, go. The driver is getting annoyed with you. Be careful and text me when you arrive."

I release my hold on her, grab my bag and get into the car.

Tariq waits for me in the courtyard of my hotel. He isn't supposed to be there for another few hours. I need time to pack my things, get ready, and emotionally prepare myself to face him. I hesitate at the door for a moment and think about going back to Reem, avoiding him altogether. And then I remember Yusuf pleading with me to come home in a shaky voice.

I walk toward Tariq sitting at my favourite table by the jasmine bush.

"Salams," my voice is low. "You're here early."

He looks up at me and smiles, his beard freshly groomed. I am surprised to realize I still think he looks handsome. An unintentional flutter ripples across my chest. He is the tall, dark, and handsome type with almond-shaped eyes that capture people's attention. You would never be able to really tell, just by looking at him, that he has a violent streak. I take deep breaths.

"I had time, and I wanted to see if you needed anything." His eyes dart to my bandaged arm. "What happened?"

I shrug. "We had an accident on the way over. I think it's fine. The bleeding stopped."

His fingers graze my arm and I take a step back. "We'll get it checked as soon as we get to Syria. You might need some antibiotics; I wouldn't want it to get infected."

I fake a smile with my lips closed. "Sure, but I need to pack my things upstairs. Are you okay to wait here?"

"Does it hurt? I can come up and help you."

"No, thanks." It still takes strength to say no to him, to not fall into the habit of trying to please him. My hands tremble and he reaches out to hold one. I flinch. He puts his head down in disappointment, or anger, or sadness — I don't know, but I brace myself for what I know is coming next. He scratches his beard and lets out a long breath.

"Yasmine, I waited two days. My family left and I waited for you so we can get out together. I risked my life for you."

"I didn't ask you to do that."

He sighs, takes a deep breath. "Sousou," he calls me endearingly. "I'm sorry."

Those words are familiar. He uses them a lot, but they've often held very little meaning. Change comes for a day, sometimes two, sometimes three, but inevitably the status quo returns because of the hierarchy in our relationship.

"Can you sit down for a minute?" he says.

I can't find the courage to say no again, so I sit, watching the clock.

"I've been going to therapy, working on myself, trying to fix things. I'm just saying this, Yasmine, because I know that it must feel kind of awkward to be here with me and to have accepted my help. I'm really glad that you said yes to my offer, but I also want you to know that I'm different. I'm more in control, and I've been working on it. I've missed you."

He looks broken and hurt, like he's shed some of that arrogance he so proudly carried in the past. I'm not sure what to make of it. I remember Reem's voice, telling me not to let him touch me.

I get up. "Tariq, I really have to go pack everything. Can we talk about this stuff another time, please?"

He gestures with his hand. "Of course. I'll wait here."

I walk up the stairs and wonder what to make of this new version of him. His mother's voice returns to me, telling me that marriage is a sacred union. But I'm so tired. I don't want to give him any more chances. I tried for years to make it work, and I now despise him. Why should I need another excuse to leave the relationship when he's given me plenty? Even Yusuf would never approve of me returning. He gets it, and that's all the support I need.

In my room, I start packing my things. There's a lot to fit into my suitcase. I roll and stuff my clothes. I stack the Turkish teacup set, wrapped with socks, and on top of it I place the wooden jewellery box with Palestinian embroidery. I layer my books and put Baba's letters neatly on top of everything. I try to move quickly, but my body aches. What I really want to do is curl up into a fetal position in the corner of the room and cry forever.

I take in one last view of the open water from my window. Rocks by the shore have grown a layer of green algae. It's too quiet outside, nothing moves except the splashing water. I'm going to miss this place. I pray I'm able to come back soon, to a country free from raining bombs and corruption.

There's a knock at the door and I sigh, annoyed that Tariq is encroaching on my remaining twenty minutes. That frustration turns to a sort of glee when I see Ziyad standing at my door.

"You didn't tell me that your family friend was your ex-husband." He doesn't even say hello.

My heart races. I didn't think he'd recognize him. It's been so long. He's barely ever seen him.

"I…" I swallow. "He reached out to me when we were in Beirut. He arranged everything. I didn't think you needed to know the details."

His eyes narrow.

"Ziyad, just take the ride, please."

He scoffs. "As if you've given me a choice. What other option do I have now? I can't believe you didn't tell me. I can't believe you're taking his help. I could've helped, Yasmine. We could have figured something else out."

"I'm sorry, Ziyad. It was just an easy way out. I didn't think you'd notice. This doesn't mean anything." I let out a deep breath. "Look, the drive is not long. It's about an hour. We get to the border and figure things out from there."

"Doesn't mean anything? How does this not mean anything, after everything?"

"After what?"

He has no words. I know what he's referring to. He knows I know, too, but neither of us will say it out loud.

"Do you already have a flight booked to Toronto?"

"No." I hadn't thought that far ahead, but Tariq might have. "You?"

"Of course. You're just waiting on him."

"What's that supposed to mean?"

"I have a flight booked to leave in five days. It's the earliest ticket I could find and now I wish I had found something sooner."

"You can stay with my aunt. We're all going to hunker down there until we can get a flight out. I don't know what the hotel situation is, but she's got a big apartment and it's just her and her two kids. She said she'd love to host us."

"You and Tariq?"

I avert my gaze. "Yes, probably."

"Yasmine." His voice is low and exasperated. "Are you divorced, like officially, like three times? Or are you still kind of married?"

I don't want to answer his question. Tariq and I aren't even legally divorced yet. We've only been separated for eight months. I had planned to file the paperwork when I returned to Canada.

Something fuels Ziyad's glare. His hands curl into fists and for a brief moment, I'm scared of him. "Just once," I say. "We have things we need to figure out."

"Is this why … you've been leading me on, all the while?"

"No. I told you we've divorced. I have my own place and everything, he's just refusing to sign the legal papers. And I never promised you anything Ziyad. I didn't lead you on, so don't accuse me of something that didn't happen."

His fists turn into open palms and he wipes his face with his hands. "Okay. I'll see you downstairs."

Ziyad and I meet Tariq in the lobby about thirty minutes later. And though Ziyad recognized my ex, Tariq has no recollection of him and I introduce him as the friend we're bringing along.

Tariq eyes him from top to bottom. "How did you two meet?" he says.

"We've been friends since undergrad," Ziyad responds before I can say anything.

Tariq takes a step back and looks at me suspiciously. "Did you two plan this trip together?" He seems repulsed.

This time, I speak before anyone else has the chance to say anything. "No, it was a coincidence. Ziyad and I haven't spoken in years."

Relief overtakes Tariq's face and I breathe a sigh. If he'd picked up on anything, Tariq might have used this to tighten his grip on me. Before I left, I felt like I'd made some headway with him on the divorce. He seemed to accept it and I was hopeful that by the time I got back, we could file mutually and wouldn't need to get lawyers involved. But if he finds out that there's a potential for anyone else in my life, he will never let me go.

"So I've got Yasmine's trip covered, but it's costing us $500 per person." Tariq says.

Ziyad smirks. "Don't worry about it, I'll cover my ride. I can also pay for yours and Yasmine's if that might help, as a thanks for arranging it."

"I got it." Tariq is curt and he takes my bag before leading the way out the door. Ziyad makes no eye contact with me and I'm okay with it.

I look around to see if Intissar is nearby to say goodbye but there's no one else here, so I settle for leaving her a note by the front desk.

The car drops us off at the Syrian border. There's a pileup of people, vehicles, and buses idling in a vast open space covered with sand, weeds, and dust. We step out of the taxi and Ziyad and Tariq both walk quickly around to the trunk for our bags. Ziyad grabs my bag first, then Tariq puts his hand on the side handle and they both somehow manage to lift it out at the same time, but they are pulling it in opposite directions.

I step in between them. "I got it, thanks."

"Habibti, let me get it." Tariq says and I cringe at being called "my love."

"Everyone carries their own luggage," I respond.

We step into a queue, hauling our luggage behind us. It's another hot summer day and my clothes stick to my skin. Relief from the oppressive humidity approaches with the setting sun, but swaths of mosquitoes come to feast. I put on a light cardigan. Ziyad sprays bug repellent all over himself and then passes it to me.

I wait for the sense of relief that's supposed to come. Reem's family said that I would now have stories to tell my friends back in Toronto. To live the experience and learn from it, as if these traumas can be reduced to entertaining narratives for those looking to feel something, some excitement that's absent in their lives. But the relief doesn't come and I don't want to formulate stories or narratives.

The chaotic line moves an inch every few minutes. In front of us is a mother with two children that look to be in their early teens, each carrying a backpack and no luggage. Other kids cling to their parents or cry with exhaustion.

A woman in a flashy yellow vest walks around passing water bottles to people, reminding me that a small bit of love might still be found amid this desolation.

"I wonder if there's an express line for Western citizens. Do you think anyone might notice if I wave around my passport?" Tariq asks.

"Tariq. Please."

He shrugs. "What? I'm serious, we can probably speed up this process."

"Please be quiet," I snap. "We're all going through the same thing. You're not an exception here. Nobody knows who you are, and nobody cares."

He stares back in awe, and pride bubbles in me for putting him in his place. Ziyad is behind me and I notice the slightest crease of a half dimple. We stand in silence for the remainder of the queue.

An hour later, we are at the front of the line. The border crossing is a far cry from what I am used to, no cameras recording me from every angle, no police officers and fancy metal detectors positioned everywhere. There is none of that here. Military officials are stationed with large AK-47s by their sides. A lonesome Syrian flag waves through the air atop a small building made of brick walls, where border officers presumably stay cool away from the sun's oppressive rays of heat.

What a joke. Just by crossing this line, this border that was likely drawn up by some kid in the Syrian army or some old white man, we will be safe? That line is real, but it is also arbitrary, and the rules that dictate who can cross it are unjust. Less than a hundred years ago someone decided this land should be separate countries — the Lebanese belong here and the Syrians belong over there and the Palestinians, who have since lost their country, will live in obscurity among these Arabs, at their mercy.

We hand the officer our passports through the window separating us from the man behind the wall. Tariq pays the visa fees. We're waived through almost immediately, no questions asked. We come from the lands of the free and civilized democracies.

"Are you coming with us to her aunt's place?" Tariq asks Ziyad gruffly.

Ziyad looks at the stream of cars flooding the streets ahead of us. "Yeah, if that's okay for now. I'm going to try and see if I can make alternative arrangements. I just need internet access."

Tariq gives me a strange look and I try not to return to old habits of constantly trying to make sense of his stares just so I don't trigger anything. "What's your aunt's address again?" Tariq says.

I hand him the piece of paper and he then shoves it right back into my hand. "This is in Arabic. You know I can't read it. Why would you pass this to me?" Tariq says.

"Sorry. I'll give the taxi the address," I say, but not too quickly.

I don't know why I gave him the note. Of course I know he can't read or write Arabic and is only fluent in speaking. Maybe a part of me wants to humiliate him. Or, maybe I'm trying to reassure Ziyad in some weird way. And then I wonder if I'm more comfortable poking Tariq when Ziyad is around. I've forgotten what it was like to be around Tariq, always walking on eggshells.

And I don't plan on going back.

We're across the border and still, relief doesn't come. Instead, I wait for the sound of bombs falling from the sky; I look behind me as if someone is chasing us. I overheard people in the line talking about how the Israelis want to come for Syria next, that it's all part of their plan. I know these are only rumours, but my body can't shake the feeling of needing to escape.

Tariq approaches a parked car available for hire. Ziyad is kneeling on the floor with his forehead to the ground, prostrating in gratitude.

I'm flooded with a sense of inadequacy and ungratefulness. At least we had made it out.

"You're not still scared?" I say when he is finished.

He dusts sand off his pants. "Of course, I'm still scared. But I can also be grateful for making it out here. For getting here. For our relative safety."

"Aren't you mad about having to leave people behind?"

His eyes crease reflectively. "Yasmine, I know it was hard to leave Reem. But we can't control what we can't control. You can't give her your passport; I can't make this war stop. All I know is that I'm grateful for being here and I will continue to be grateful for everything I have because that's the only way to guarantee better things to come, for all of us." He pauses and swallows hard. "I'm sorry I yelled at you back at the Athar. It's not my business, and I've been projecting. I shouldn't have put that on you."

My irritation eases a little. "Thanks for saying that."

"Yallah," Tariq shouts.

We load our luggage and get into the car. I give the driver directions in a Lebanese accent. Ziyad, Tariq, and I avoid talking to each other in English, lest we be targeted. The streets of Homs look similar to the ones in Lebanon, only there is no view of the open sea poking through the gaps between buildings.

By the time we arrive, the full moon lights the entryway into Khalto Nawal's building. This is the woman who I think might be the link to Baba. I march into the structure with Ziyad, and Tariq trails behind me. Despite my ex-husband's many connections, he doesn't have anyone in Syria. This is my connection. So here we are, all three of us sheltering in the home of displaced Palestinians after fleeing yet another war.

Two calico cats sit by the entrance drinking water from a plastic bowl. They quickly scurry away when my suitcase wheels over the stone floor. There is no power, so we are all forced to take the stairs. Tariq grabs my bag again and this time, I don't argue about carrying it up the stairs. When he reaches the third floor, he goes back down to grab his own, and Ziyad and I wait for him. By the time we have all our belongings, we're all dripping with sweat. There's only one apartment on the floor. I tap the door with my knuckles.

A petite woman in her fifties with a white shawl wrapped around her head opens the door. "Yasmine?"

"Na'am," I nod, then point to the men behind me. "This is Tariq and this is Ziyad."

She smiles wide and ushers us in. "Of course, come in, come in." The entryway is a square with a body-sized mirror on one side and a closet on the other. It smells like sautéing beef with cumin and saffron. We walk into the living room where the warm air ruffles through the white curtains.

"We've been waiting for you. I hope you're hungry," She points to the large dining table next to the living area. It's covered with platters of rice, hummus, some sort of lamb or beef dish, samosas, and a variety of pickled side dishes. My eyes and mouth water. A surge of gratitude swells in my chest. "Oh Khalto, you shouldn't have."

She appears to be genuinely happy to feed and host us. "Wallaw, you must be starving. Fawzia told me that you were in Beirut, and the drive..." She whistles. "It must have been awful. Please sit."

We do, and we fill our plates. My aunt calls her son Hassan to put my bags in one room and Ziyad and Tariq's things in another.

"I can sleep in the living room, or anywhere," Ziyad says when he realizes what's happening. "There's really no need to inconvenience anyone."

"Nonsense, you'll sleep on a comfortable bed."

I eye him and mouth a sorry when Tariq isn't looking.

"Yasmine, it's really nice to meet you," Hassan says. There is something about his look and the way he says my name, like we're supposed to share a secret. I'm tired of people knowing about me, and not really *of* me. I decide to just ask.

"How much do you know about me?"

He looks at his mother and she shakes her head, warning him not to speak further. There is a secret they hold, and I must know it now.

Then a door slams and Ziyad and I jump in our seats. We eye each other with compassion.

"Relax, there are no bombs here," Tariq says in a mocking tone as he enters the room. I want to throw a cup in his face.

Khalto Nawal gives me a sympathetic look. "It takes a while to get over that. My nephew was caught in the war too, and he came to stay with us for a few days. He just left, but he also jumped every time a door slammed. We'll try to be mindful here." She passes me a plate of stuffed grape leaves . "You can stay with Farrah tonight and Ziyad and Tariq will stay with Hassan."

Tariq thanks her. "I'm sure we'll be fine, inshAllah. You're very kind to let us stay here."

"Are you all just friends?" asks Khalto. "How do you all know each other?"

I nervously chew a stuffed grape leaf, letting the spices and the mushy rice melt in my mouth. No one answers, so I start. "Ziyad is a friend. He was studying Arabic in Lebanon." I swallow. "Tariq is… he's…we used to be married."

"Still kind of are." Tariq murmurs. "You know how it is Khalto, sometimes couples go through rough patches. Make du'a for us."

"Eh, may Allah put love and mercy back into your relationship," she says.

And there it is. That's the cost of accepting Tariq's help for getting us out of the country. How could I have been so naïve? Tariq had never been supportive of the divorce. He had reluctantly agreed to it after I moved out to stay with Yusuf. I had stopped responding to his calls and emails and ignored him until he gave in. I felt like I'd won.

But here we are again, back where I started. He thinks there is still hope for us.

I don't look at Ziyad, afraid of what his face might reveal.

Both of Nawal's children join us for a late dinner — Hassan and Yusra, both engineers. She tells us that her husband travels for work and won't be back for another week. Khalto Nawal describes the city and the things we could do and the places to visit. "The mountains are beautiful during this time of the year," she says.

"I don't know if anyone has an appetite for anything fun Khalto."

"I'm sure we could do something fun," Tariq says. "It might be good for your mood, for all of our moods."

CHAPTER 27

That night, I'm unable to sleep and when dawn breaks, I go into the kitchen, make tea, and take it out to drink on the balcony. No matter what time of day it is, cars seem to be driving, honking, people yelling at each other, and I'm happy with the noise of people who are free to argue in public. The sliding door opens, and Tariq walks out. He sits across from me.

"We should go get that checked." He points to my arm.

"It's fine. I can take care of it when I get home."

"It might get infected. We should go today."

I rub my arm on it, and it does feel worse than it did a few days ago. I also worry that it's infected and haven't bothered to look at the wound since Reem wrapped it before I left.

"Your aunt told me about a good clinic nearby. They are open now. We should go."

"Now?"

He stands up. "Yes, better to deal with it sooner."

"What about Ziyad?"

Tariq sighs. "What about him? He's still sleeping."

"Should we ask him if he wants to come? He was also in that accident, maybe he should get checked too."

Tariq scrunches his eyebrows. "He's a grown man. I'm sure he can take care of himself. Don't concern yourself with other people's business, yeah?"

He sits close to me in the car like he's trying to make a statement. "I was up late last night talking to Hassan. He's interesting." His hand rests on the space between us, half an inch away from my thigh.

"Interesting how?"

"He was close with your dad apparently."

My eyes widen. "What are you talking about? You know that

Baba disappeared a long time ago."

He shrugs. "Honestly, Yasmine, I don't know. But apparently, your dad came here when he left Lebanon. Hassan said he lived in hiding for a really long time and your aunt's family was pretty close to him, providing a bit of a refuge for your dad. They didn't tell anyone where he was, and he stayed under the radar. I think he still felt like people were after him. I didn't fully understand why though."

"What are you talking about Tariq? My dad is dead."

"You know what Yasmine, when Hassan first told me, I thought that you had lied to me about your family. I don't know why, maybe to get my sympathies or something. But now, it looks like you didn't even know?"

I can't process what I am hearing. I can't understand how casually Tariq is talking about this information that I have been seeking so desperately, and I can't make sense of how easily he found out. I've been searching for this knowledge my whole life. Tears accumulate in my eyes. "Why would Hassan tell you and not me?"

"I think your aunt told him to hold off a bit until you've settled in. She didn't want to stress you out and give you more heartbreak after everything. We just spent a lot of time chatting last night and, I don't know, maybe he felt comfortable with me knowing that I was, am, your husband. Maybe he felt like it would be easier if the information came from me."

"Was Tariq. *Was,*" I say, adamantly. "We're not married anymore."

"But we could be again, if you just gave us another chance. I want you back, Yasmine. We can work through this."

My head spins and my heart needs to leap out of my body. "This isn't the time Tariq. Maybe we can talk about our marriage later. What happened to Baba?"

He runs his hand over his face and lets out a long breath. "Yasmine, I want to be there for you. I want to be the husband I should have been. I promise you, I've changed." He puts his hand over mine. "Will you let me take care of you?"

Those words wash over me like a flock of elephants stampeding through a desert. I'm tired of trying to keep it all together. I'm tired of holding it all in for Reem and for Yusuf and for everyone. I'm tired and in pain, both physically and emotionally. I am at a loss for what to do or how to keep moving.

But there's one thing that's become clear through this entire ordeal, and it's that I don't want or need his help. I had moved to Lebanon on my own. I found shelter in Syria when a war broke out. I don't need him, and I don't want him.

I move my hand away from his. "What happened to Baba?" My voice is firm, demanding.

"He died some years ago," he relents. "He's buried at a local cemetery. We can go visit if you want."

The car stops once we arrive at the clinic. I sit for a few moments, unable to move until Tariq gets out, opens my door and grabs my arm to lift me out.

The clinic is in a small white building with trees and a sidewalk lining the front. Inside, I tell them about what happened and then we wait among a row of plastic chairs. It smells of bleach and blood.

Tariq grabs my hand again. "We can just try if you want. Go slow. We can go to therapy. I've been doing a lot of it on my own."

I shake my head. "I can't think about that right now, Tariq. Please, can we just talk about this some other time?"

He nods and we sit in silence.

I'm reeling with the revelation that Baba had been alive for so much of our lives. He was right there. Couldn't he have tried to contact us? My feelings of loss and confusion quickly turn to anger and resentment at his selfishness. He might have not even wanted to be with us. Had he chosen his career over us? Was he alive when Mama died? The war had ended long ago, and people couldn't have still been after him.

Tariq steps out of the waiting room to answer a phone call and the doctor calls me in.

He's tall, with a large pot belly and a seventies moustache. He opens the bandage and eyes the wound critically, making strange sounds as he studies the area, poking it and tugging at the skin slowly healing around it. "Tsk tsk tsk, does it hurt anywhere else?"

"I've been feeling pain around the wound, like an aching, burning sensation."

"There're a few pieces of shrapnel still inside. We need to remove them." He frowns. "You should have had it checked sooner. It's going to leave a big scar." He washes his hands at the sink and calls the nurse to bring in supplies. "The pieces are not lodged deep, so we can do this here and it won't hurt too much. We will make sure the wound is clean."

I wait a few minutes, sitting on the bed under the bright lights alone until the doctor comes back with a nurse and a tray of medical tools that look like they belong in a surgical room. I don't believe him when he says it won't hurt. He sanitizes the area, grabs a large tweezer-looking thing and picks two pieces of metal out of my arm. A hot burning sensation pulses through my chest and a stream of liquid drips across my arm. When it's all over, a fresh bandage is wrapped around the wound.

My head spins and I'm sweating, trying to breathe at a normal pace. "I don't feel well," I say. The doctor asks the nurse something and she comes back shortly with water.

He hands me the water and reassures me. "I checked your blood pressure and it's fine. I think you are probably feeling dizzy from the stress and the injury. Other than the shrapnel, it looks like it's healing fine, but it will take a long time. I'll give you some antibiotics. Take them just in case, and keep changing the bandage every day. It's important. Also, try to keep it away from water." In the nearby sink, my blood streams off his hands and into the drain.

Tariq is waiting in the lobby.

"I want to go to the gravesite. I want to go see Baba."

His smile turns into a frown. "I don't think we'll be able to make it, Yasmine. But I promise we'll come back when the situation is better. I promise, I'll bring you back here soon."

"Bring me back? What's wrong with right now?"

"I was on the phone with my cousin, the one that works for Emirates Airlines. He got us on a flight out to Dubai, tonight. We need to get back, pack our things and go to the airport. There isn't enough time to do anything else. This appointment took longer than I expected."

I take a deep breath. Then, I nod vaguely, following him out the door.

Nawal and her children are not home when we get back, but there's a fresh display of food on the dining table along with a note: she was going to be back in the afternoon and we should make ourselves comfortable. Ziyad is on the balcony, and he either doesn't notice us return or is avoiding us all together.

"We'll leave for the airport at six. That should give us enough time. You should eat something and get some rest before we go."

I turn to him. "Tariq, I'm not going with you."

He scoffs and raises his shoulders. "What do you mean? What else are you going to do, Yasmine?"

"I don't know. I'm not sure if I want to leave Syria right now."

He looks at me dismissively and it reminds me of the way he used to talk to me, like I am an idiot who doesn't understand life and how it works. "Yasmine, that's ridiculous. Don't be ungrateful. A lot of people can't find a way out and I got us tickets for tonight. You can't just say no to something like that. What about Yusuf? Didn't he say he wanted you back in Toronto?"

"I'll talk to Yusuf on my own and he'll understand when I tell him."

He exhales a frustrated breath. "Yasmine." His tone is firm. "You're coming with me."

"I'm not." I plant my feet on the ground. We're both surprised by the tone of my voice.

Ziyad walks in. "Everything okay here?"

"Yes, we're fine. Yasmine is just being unreasonable. She wants to stay!" He raises his arms in the air toward him. "Please, Ziyad, tell her how ridiculous this sounds. It's irrational and she's going to regret this. How hard was it for you to find a ticket?"

"She's an adult. I presume she can make her own decision," Ziyad says.

"It's not that simple. What if something happens to you, Yasmine? Do you think Yusuf will ever forgive me?"

"I'm not your responsibility anymore, remember?"

"You'll always be my responsibility. Especially here and now."

"Tariq. Please."

Tariq curls his fists and anger flits across his face. He's searching for options, wondering if there's a way to force me to go with him. I take a step back.

"Prove to me that you've actually changed, Tariq. Right now, you're reminding me a whole lot of the person I left." I pause. "You don't control me. I make my own decisions. I need to visit Baba and I need to know what happened. Let me have this. I will come back when I'm ready."

All three of us stand in silence, staring at each other and weighing our options. Ziyad walks back out onto the balcony.

"Yasmine, this is so dumb. Please don't be stupid. You'll be stuck here for a long time."

"Tariq, just because this doesn't make sense to you doesn't mean it's dumb. You never understood me. You don't know what I value and I don't expect that to change. I am not yours anymore."

He lowers his shoulders and rubs his face. "Fine. Do what you want. But don't come running back to me if you change your mind."

"I won't. And even if I do change my mind, it will be on me. I'll figure it out."

I turn away from him and he goes into one of the rooms, presumably to gather his things. I hear slamming and thudding behind the closed door as I take a moment to breathe. I pick up a plate, fill it with rice and fattoush and make my way out to the balcony.

"Want some?" I ask Ziyad. "I brought an extra spoon."

"You're not dumb," he whispers.

"Thanks."

"I get why you wouldn't want to leave."

"Thanks." I'm not sure if I believe Ziyad and my mouth can't seem to spew anything else. I wonder if he's only saying this because he wants something from me.

"I also don't want to leave."

I'm taken aback by his admission. Why wouldn't he want to leave? He's got a nice life, he has wealth and freedom, unlike me who's going back to fight a divorce war. "Why?"

"It's like, I found something here. Some sort of grounding, a simplicity. You. And I'm sorry, I don't mean that in a weird way, but you understand what I mean when I say that I found a stillness with you."

My shoulders slump. I wish he would stop saying these things. But I also don't. I sigh. "I know."

"What happens when we leave here?"

"I don't know, but you'll find that same calm somewhere else. If you found it here, then, it's in you. Not me."

"Will you keep in touch?"

I smile, thinking about a future when I am not heartbroken and riddled with problems. "I'd like that. Maybe even meet for coffee at the Colombian in a year, and you can tell me about the book you'll be writing."

"InshAllah," he says.

"If I'm allowed to ask…what was that talk about your Baba back there?"

"My dad is apparently buried here."

He turned his face toward me, eyes wide. "How?"

"Hassan apparently told Tariq last night that my dad was here in

Homs for years after we left. He was alive. And I need to find out what happened. I need to visit him."

"Wow."

"I found some articles from the *Damascus Times* that made me wonder if he'd come here from Lebanon. Elissa had also hinted at it, and she showed me a picture dated from the nineties. But I just don't get it; there's got to be something more. How could he have been here and never tried to find us? I can't leave now that I'm this close."

He rubs his chin. "How does Hassan know anything?"

I finish chewing the chicken and swallow hard. "Apparently Baba had been in touch with Nawal's family. Hassan knew him pretty well. They were all really close for a long time."

"Does that make you upset?"

Upset isn't the right word to describe what I'm feeling. Betrayed. Furious. Indignant. Heartbroken. Those are maybe closer. None of it matters anyway because I can't ask Baba why he never reached out or if he ever loved us.

Nawal comes home a few hours later with bags of groceries and household supplies. Tariq approaches the door with his bags. "Thank you so much, Khalto, for letting me stay here, for welcoming us and all of your hospitality."

"Are you leaving?"

"I got a flight out tonight. My cousin works for the Emirates airline and he pulled some strings."

She nods and looks the other way, to me. "But what about Yasmine? He couldn't get her a ticket too?"

Tariq is quiet for a moment, like he's ashamed. "She wants to stay for a bit. I told her about her dad. Hassan told me last night."

Khalto Nawal looks back at me with a sad stare. "Allah yirḥamo," she says.

"Thanks for getting us out and everything else." I say to Tariq, before he gets the chance to say anything else.

He nods and hesitates for another moment. "Yasmine." He

scratches his beard. "Can you promise me that we'll talk when you get back?"

"Of course. We still need to figure out all the paperwork."

"No, I don't mean that. I mean just talk about what I said earlier, that I'm really trying and I miss you."

I can't be married to him again, but giving him a little hope will buy time. "InshAllah. I'll call you when I am back in town."

He walks out and I dream of an amicable divorce, of sitting in a living room, alone, drinking a can of Sprite and reading one of Ziyad's books.

CHAPTER 28

Yusuf isn't pleased when I tell him I am staying behind in Syria, but he'll come around to accept my decision. On the phone, I promise that I will be back in time for his wedding in November. I assure him that I'll keep in touch and stay safe. He's always been my protector, and this new phase in our relationship is going to take time to adjust to.

I also tell him what I've learned about Baba.

He's quiet. I had told him about the letter when I first received it, but he had shrugged it off as some sort of sick joke. After that, I didn't update him on my findings. I meant to tell him about the pictures and articles, but the war had made it difficult to speak for more than a few minutes. Plus, I didn't think it was something that should be shared over the phone — but here we are.

"Yusuf?" I say to his silence.

"I don't understand. Did Mama know?"

"I have no idea. I'm going to find out more from Khalto, if she'll tell me anything."

"Oh." His voice cracks, and I know he's trying to hold back his anger, for my sake.

"I'm mad too," I say.

"Why were they like this?"

"I don't know."

"Why couldn't they just be normal and stay together?" I wonder if he's thinking about all the sacrifices he's made. "And Mama, she went through cancer all on her own. What an ass." Yusuf doesn't swear so this comes as a bit of shock.

I don't want to continue this conversation over the phone. I want us to be sitting with each other. I want to be able to hug him and I want him to wipe away my tears. "I promise I won't be long Yusuf. I'll find out what I can and will keep you updated."

"Okay," he whispers.

"I love you."

"I love you too. Please be safe."

I hang up and Nawal sits me down at the dining table. She makes a pot of black tea infused with mint and pours me a cup. "How are Reem and Fawzia?"

"They are okay. I don't know. It's been a difficult summer for them."

"Ouf, all the tribulations that have hit them. It's a lot. You know, Ahmad stayed with us for a while when he came to Homs. He was a sweet kid, but tormented."

"Really?"

"Yes, especially after he left prison." She spins a napkin in her hand. "Did he bring you those letters?"

"Wait, Ahmad was the one who brought the letters to me?"

She nods. "Yes, Akram left them with us, just before he died. I never got rid of them — it never felt right — until we heard that you were coming to visit. So I gave them to Ahmad to deliver them to you." She takes a sip of her tea. "Your dad was wanted by a lot of powerful people, you know. We met a long time ago. Anas and I met him and your mom on one of our trips to Lebanon. Actually, we were at their wedding. They were happy then." She taps the table with her index finger.

"Why was he wanted by anyone?"

"Ouf, why was he *not* wanted?!" She chuckles. "Your dad poked a lot of people the wrong way. He was always controversial."

"Like what? How?"

"Well, first, he found out that his older brother-in-law was colluding with the Lebanese Front. The Mossad was also paying him for information." She purses her lips. "By the way, Yasmine, this stays between us. Please. The Syrian government isn't like Lebanon's. People can go to jail for saying the wrong thing. This can't become public;

your family doesn't know the details and it's better if these things are left in the past."

I nod.

"Anyway, there was that, and he fought with his brother. His parents wanted the family to be protected so they didn't want any of these details made public, but Akram wanted to expose everything." She takes another sip of her tea. "And then, he started getting intel somehow on them and started writing articles about the plans and missions of the different militias, especially those that were targeting the PLO." She looks behind me, reminiscing, into the far distance. "He always had a bit of a soft spot for the Palestinian struggle. I don't know if that was because of your mom or if it started before, but she certainly didn't harm his passion."

"So, what, he just wrote a bunch of articles and people came after him? I doubt he was the only controversial figure anywhere."

She shakes her head. "His family found out that he knew and wanted to expose them. You see, your dad wasn't just controversial, he had access to the world because he could speak and write English."

"What, how?"

"When he was younger, your grandfather sent him to London to study. Your Baba was very well educated, you know, and his English was good. That's where I think he realized how much he could do. How much power he could hold because of his skills and his connections. People in London wanted to print some of his articles. You see, Yasmine. He had reach and everyone knew that. So, some of them came after him. He never said this out loud, but I believe they threatened to hurt his family. All of you."

I wrap my fingers around the teacup. The heat is a nice contrast to my cold sweaty hands. "Did he ever talk about us?"

"All of the time, ya Yasmine."

Then why didn't he try reaching out? It would have made sense if he didn't want to be a father. I swallow a lump in my throat, and she puts her hand on top of mine. "Some of us tried to convince him to go to Canada and find you, but your mom didn't keep in touch with a lot of people after she left. We didn't have a way to reach her. Maybe she was scared. I think she didn't want people to know where she was. She knew of all the things your Baba was involved in." She took a deep breath. "Wallahi, I don't know."

"I don't understand."

"He was paranoid. He couldn't have lived with himself if anything happened to you. I think he thought that even if you were all in Canada, you wouldn't be safe. To him, the safest solution was to stay away." She grasps my hand again. "Yasmine, war does things to you psychologically. I've seen it everywhere. Your dad ... he wasn't well. He didn't think he was worthy of anything. The war, his ambition, it sucked everything good from him and his life."

I nod. I had just seen this in Lebanon.

"He died of a heart attack at 38. I think his heart just couldn't handle it anymore, especially after the war ended. It was like he lost his sense of purpose or meaning. He didn't know what to do with himself. He worked odd jobs in construction here and there to make a living, but it was like he was just waiting for death to take him."

"Do you know where he's buried?"

"Of course, we buried him. We were all he had."

"Can you please take me?"

She smiles. "Of course, let me get my things."

We leave ten minutes later.

Baba is buried in a cemetery that's perched on a hill, overlooking Homs. Most of the graves are covered in grass and weeds. Simple tombstones line the pathways, neatly identifying the people who lie beneath. Khalto Nawal waits in the car and I follow her instructions for locating his grave.

I walk along the gravel paths surrounded by grass and trees and stop when I see his name. Akram Hassan 1954–1992. I stand motionless.

I had come to Lebanon with the expectation of exploring life on my own and of connecting with the people who had shaped my life from afar. I never expected to be standing here at Baba's grave, waiting for some sort of closure that I can't grasp because he's gone. Mama is gone. The generational break in our histories is intact, stripping me of ever rectifying the pain created by their absence.

But history cannot be fixed. We can't change what we get — and what I got is two parents buried oceans apart as a consequence of a war, histories buried in their graves.

I try to speak directly to Baba, tell him that I miss him, but the words don't come. They're lodged in my mind, barricaded by a flood of anger and regret, with anger at him for not trying harder, for letting the war get to him and breaking us apart. Instead of talking to him, I picture Mama sitting with me, her head shaking at the truths that I had now uncovered — so many stories that she had kept hidden, hoping to shield us from pain. I see her sitting next to me and I want to tell her that it's okay to be angry, that the circumstances of her life would have made it impossible to truly be happy. I want her to tell me about her grief, see the relief on her face when that crushing burden is shared. She carried not only her trauma but her inability to declare that moments were difficult, that oppression was unjust. Because in that admission, she could have given herself permission to ask for help, in a way that could alleviate her pain. Instead, she was imprisoned by her own sorrow.

How can I find peace if I can't acknowledge that the war lingers in me, too? I'm ready for that war to end.

I close my eyes and submit to the power of my tears. At first, I weep quietly, but this quickly turns into a sob that turns into unstoppable thudding in my chest. I think I might cry until death, just like the others who lie here.

After a while, I turn to the tombstone again. "Baba, I love you and I'm sorry for the way your life turned out." I lift my hands with palms open to the sky and pray that Allah forgives him. I pray that he be reunited with Mama and us in a place and a time where pain and oppression does not exist, for light in his grave. And then, I pray for ease in my own life and the life of my loved ones, especially Reem.

When I'm ready, I stand, dust my pants, and walk back to the car that waits.

Khalto Nawal says, "You ready?"

I'm not, but there is nothing left to do.

I'm sitting on the balcony watching the sunset, reading from Ghazali's book on divine providence when Ziyad walks out and sits on the chair next to me.

"I went to visit my dad's grave," I say.

He turns to face me. "How are you?"

I shrug. "I don't know, I don't feel better. Sometimes I wish I hadn't known anything, other times I feel like this pain, this ache is good for me. Like it's helping me grow. I'm just tired."

"You're the one who told me that god enters the heart through its cracks."

"I did."

"Perhaps it's only uphill from here."

"InshAllah."

"Want to read out loud?"

I smile and begin to read and translate for him one last time. Tomorrow morning, he will be on a plane back to Seoul. When I finish the chapter, he doesn't ask me anything about the text as he normally does. We both stay silent watching cars drive by, honking from below amid a crowd of pedestrians moving about their lives.

"You know, one of the things that drew me to Islam was the thought that we are all travellers on this earth, that none of us are supposed to be fully tied to this place because we're all here temporarily." He pauses for a moment and bites his thumbnail. "Through that I finally felt like I knew how to belong, how to exist, how to be a part of different places, be with different people." He turns to look at me.

"I realized that sometimes those meaningful connections of belonging actually come from our relationships with people and that we benefit from them in different ways. I'm grateful for our time together."

I know instinctively what he is saying.

"Once the war ends, which I hope is soon. I'm going back to Lebanon. I'm going to finish the research that I started."

He brushes his hair back. "Promise me you'll be safe?"

"I'll do my best."

"And you can tell me about it when you get back."

"InshAllah."

We remain silent for the rest of the night, drawing energy from each other's existence.

The next morning over breakfast, Khalto Nawal hands me a notebook with a scribble inside the flap. "Ziyad said this was for you." She reaches out across the table and sets it down.

Yasmine, I hope you can use this to write all the things that make you cry and hurt, and occasionally maybe the things that bring you joy.

Love, Ziyad.

CHAPTER 29

Yasmine leaves and we hope the war ends soon, but it's now late July and there's no end in sight. Mama spends her days in front of the TV when it's working. She shouts obscenities and slurs at George Bush and Condoleezza Rice whenever their faces pop up on the screen. Some politicians at UN meetings declare Israel's aggression an excessive use of force and a violation of humanitarian law. We curse at them equally because they are also useless. People continue to die and buildings continue to be turned to dust. I embrace the anger and let it flow through me in honour of Yasmine.

We spend our days at home, only leaving the premises for necessities like food. Qalimat shuts down once all the students flee. The streets are empty now, the shops closed. Tourists that flocked to our cafés and restaurants have disappeared into the safety of their home countries. Even the Lebanese with foreign passports slowly make their way out. Soon, this country will be filled with only those who understand the power of destruction. Those whose bodies will relive every shake, every explosion, every death.

We wait for the war to gradually progress toward the north. Our family in Beirut eventually joins us in Trablous and our home becomes a sanctuary to twelve people, including Mariam, her sisters, her husband, and his parents. During the second week of the war, 'Ammo Ashraf brings over his elderly parents-in-law who live on a farm with our other uncle. He stays behind to tend to the plants.

There are people in villages across the south that are still stuck, encapsulated by both Israeli military and HizbAllah militia. They don't have food or water, awaiting the timely arrival of death. Those who do try to escape and drive north are murdered on their way out. The Israeli military screams they are terrorists, even the women and children.

People come to bury their dead here, finding sanctuary in the eerie quiet. There's more time, more space for funerals in the north. Though our days aren't filled with the same consistency of bombs and shelling, we aren't completely immune. On a few occasions, a bridge or a building is destroyed in town and becomes a relic of the time, a reminder that we were not safe.

I begin joining 'Ammo Ashraf at his family farm, helping his brother tend to the land. We bring back food, vegetables, fresh grapes, and ripe figs for the neighbourhood.

One day in the field, a middle-aged woman is feeding the chickens in the open field, near the grapevines. She removes her glove and introduces herself as Dr. Seewan.

"Doctor? And you're here working on a farm? People probably need you back in the villages."

She smiles. "I'm not that kind of doctor. I'm a doctor of philosophy."

I pick up a bucket of seeds and throw them to the chickens, who flock toward me. One of them follows me even after I've finished feeding them and stands at my leg.

"Where do you teach?"

"Oh, not here. I teach at the University of Toronto."

"Why are you here? Everyone is gone. Are you not Canadian? Doesn't the school want you back?"

She angles a ladder under the grapevines and I bring a basket over. "I don't teach in the summer. I'll go back at the end of August, before the term begins."

What the hell was this woman doing here when she could have fled already? "Do you not have farms in Canada?"

She laughs and hands me a string of grapes. "I like your bluntness, Reem. Ashraf didn't exaggerate when he told me about you."

"What did he say?"

"He said you have a fiery character and that nobody can stand in your way. I was kind of like that. Now I'm more tired than anything else."

"So why are you still here?"

"My parents are your uncle's neighbours. They are elderly and I don't want to leave them. I'm all they have."

I know what that's like.

"I hear that you want to apply to graduate programs. I teach international relations at the university. What are you interested in?"

I bite the inside of my lip. "Actually, I was thinking of applying to their architecture program. I'm still working on my applications. They are due in October."

She steps down the ladder. "Come let's go inside. I made some fresh strawberry juice this morning."

I sit on the green flowery floor cushions laid out against the wall in the living room. She's balancing a tray of drinks. I take a sip of the pink liquid. It's thick and sweet, flowery gold. "Did you make this?"

She smiles. "I did."

"Well, if you get sick of teaching, you can always come back and sell this."

"Teta, Allah yirḥama, used to make it for us growing up. There's nothing better than freshly squeezed juice when you know that the person who grew and picked those fruits did it with love, knowing that it is nourishing for the ones we treasure. That love gets transfused, you know? The plants, they know when they're treated well and they bear greater food when they are tended with love. It's the same with the animals. They will provide eggs when they are happy, but lock them up for longer than they want and they won't feed you anything."

"Do you have a farm back in Toronto?"

"Not a farm, but I have a garden. Maybe you can visit sometime."

"Right, maybe, if someone gets me out of this country."

She writes something down on a paper and hands it to me. "This is my email. Send me your application statement. I'll review it."

"I can't ask you to do that."

"Why not? I'm just sitting around here. I could use some intellectual stimulation."

"But Khalto, why?"

"What do you mean, why? What am I if I can't give back to the people of my homeland? The people who need me the most?"

I drink the last sip of strawberry juice, savouring every last lick, chewing on the tiny seeds on the insides of my cheek.

"Um, okay. Why don't I just bring my laptop next time and I can show you?"

She agrees and I return to collecting eggs from the hens as instructed by Ashraf before leaving. That same chicken who stood near my leg is guarding four of them. I move closer and she pecks my hand. "I just need the eggs, chicken." She pecks more.

When I tell 'Ammo Ashraf that I couldn't get the eggs, he laughs. "That's Su'diye. She's a little feisty. First one to eat, last one to leave her eggs."

I return the next day with my statement. First, Dr. Seewan and I pick ripe tomatoes and eggplant and fill the boxes that I had in the car. When we're done, she invites me next door and greets me with another jug of strawberry juice. Our conversation is halted every few minutes to help her mother, ill with dementia. She shouts obscenities at her daughter. I sit in the kitchen staring at the yellow cabinets while I wait for her to return. Her mother eventually falls asleep while her father drinks his coffee on the steps of the garden, and we get an undisturbed hour.

Dr. Seewan becomes the mentor I didn't know I needed. She rips my statement of interest apart multiple times and I come back each time with an updated version. It takes about ten versions to finally become acceptable to her and although her feedback feels harsh at first, she always pairs it with a cup of fresh strawberry juice and ends her criticism with a reminder that she wants to see me succeed.

She's reading the last version while I study her facial expressions, bracing myself for what's to come. After a few moments of her humming and nodding, she sets the paper down and places her hand on top. "I'm proud of you, ya Reem."

My leg shakes under the table. "What?"

"This is excellent. It's perfect."

And that's it. I'm done. Ready to send it off into the world.

"With your grades, your letters of reference and this, I think you'll make it."

She leans in and cups my face, staring at me intently. I begin to cry and she pulls me forward into a hug.

"I'll put in a good word for you with the admissions committee."

As the moon sets and the sun rises, day after day, I begin to feel hope again. Yasmine calls me and I tell her about my interactions with Dr. Seewan. My cousin tells me that she's made plans to stay in Syria, despite the warnings. She promises to return when the war ends, and I wait for the time to come. I wait for our reunion, not only here, but in Toronto too.

As time goes on, destruction across the country gets worse. On the worst day, eleven buildings in Beirut are obliterated. Civilian buildings, some of them schools, people's homes — contrary to what the lying pelicans of the West claim.

For a month, Israel bombs the country with intensity. And then a ceasefire is announced on August 11. HizbAllah declares victory. But what a selfish victory it is. They survived yes, but at the cost of over a thousand people. Nothing changed. They still hold hostages and now our country is destroyed beyond measure. The lives of so many are altered forever. This is inevitably the outcome of war. There's nothing to be gained except for a growth in evil and egotism among the political elites.

Sometime in mid-August, Dr. Seewan prepares to leave the country. She hires a nurse to care for her mother while her other sister make her way back from Dubai. When she tells me this, I blurt out, "Wait, you have another sister who could have helped her?"

She nods. "She was really scared by the situation. It's not her fault."

"Doctora, you're a saint!"

She hands me a package.

"What is this?"

"It's for you. For when you begin your studies so that you never forget where you came from. So that you enjoy every single moment of the future."

"But what if my future is filled with nothing but crap?"

She laughs. "Then embrace it and keep fighting against the pile of garbage. That's the only way to live."

I open it and it's a large notebook with jasmine flowers on the cover. It the type that comes with a matching pen. A fine, heavy, expensive looking thing. "Is this an actual pen?"

"It is, and it's expensive, so take care of it. A pen is one of the greatest weapons you can wield, Ramroum. Use it well."

We hug for an eternity. "I'll see you again soon, inshAllah, okay?"

"Okay." I repeat her words in my head, imagining a future filled with possibilities. When she leaves, Su'diya comes to peck at my leg.

GLOSSARY

'azā: lit. "funeral wake," sometimes used to express extreme displeasure (with an action or situation)

ahlan: hello or welcome

Ākhira: the afterlife

al zamman: time (typically not used in colloquial speech)

Al-Khalişa: Palestinian village ethnically cleansed by the Haganah militia. Kiryat Shemona was later built on the village's ruins

alḥamdulillah: thank God

Allah yirḥamon: may they rest in peace

Allah yirḥama: may she rest in peace

Allah yirḥamo: may he rest in peace

'araf: lit. "disgusting," often used to mean "miserable" or "boring" to describe a situation or a place

arguileh: hookah pipe

arz: cedars

assalamu 'alaykum: common greeting meaning "peace be upon you"

'Ammo: paternal uncle; commonly used to address an older male adult as a sign of respect

Āyat al-Kursi: The Throne Verse (in Quran)

banadoura to bandora: two different pronunciations of the word "tomatoes" but each indicates a different accent and thus national origin. The first is Lebanese, the second Palestinian

bint: girl or daughter depending on context

Daḥieh: suburb; refers to the southern suburb of Beirut

doctora: female PhD holder or female MD

druze: a religious community

du'a: supplication

Dhuhr: midday prayer; sometimes used to mean "midday"

dukani: small shop (in Lebanese accent)

Fajr: dawn prayer; it could also mean "dawn" depending on context

Fatiḥah: first surah in the Quran

fattoush: Levantine salad

knafeh: dessert, popular in the Levantine region

habibi: my love, my friend, or sweetie (when addressing a child); used when addressing a male

habibti, habibte, or habibty: my love, my friend, or sweetheart/sweetie; used when addressing a female

haramiyeh: thieves

hasbunallahu wa ni'malwakil: God is my only solace

Hezbollah or HizbAllah: Lebanese resistance group; first represents the way non-Arabic speakers pronounce it and second represents the way Arabic speakers pronounce it

'iddah: a period of three lunar months during which a woman cannot marry after divorce or the death of a husband

ihya': revival

inshAllah: God willing

Isha': evening prayer; last prayer of the day

Jeddo: grandfather

kibbeh: a dish made with bulgur wheat and minced meat

khalas: enough/stop it

Khalto: maternal aunt; commonly used to address an older female adult as a sign of respect

khara: shit

laban: yogourt

labneh: strained yogourt

ma'lubi: in Lebanese accent; lit. "flipped over." A Levantine dish made with chicken/meat, rice, and vegetables

mana'ish or manaqish: dough topped with various ingredients and baked together

maramiyeh: sage

marhaba: hello

mashAllah: lit. "praise be to God"; used to express excitement and/or appreciation

mashi: okay; all right

mlokhiah: a dish made of jute leaves soup with chicken or meat

mukhabarat: intelligence agency; someone who works for an intelligence agency

na'am: yes

'omri: my life; used to signify affection

ouf: speech particle used to express frustration or shock

qusa: zucchini (also describes a dish of zucchini stuffed with rise and minced meat)

salam: lit. "peace"; used to say "hello"

salams: plural of "salam" used to add emphasis

shukran: thanks

Soor (city): Tyre, city in south Lebanon

souq: market

subḥanAllah: lit. "glory be to God"; used to express praise and appreciation

tajweed: a set of rules governing correct recitation of Quran

tarnib: card game

tayyeb: all right

Teta: Grandmother

tfaḍali: welcome (when addressing a female); also used as "there you go"

turmus: lupine beans

Trablous (city): Tripoli, north Lebanon

wallah or wallahi: I swear to God

wallaw: used to express shock; used as "don't mention it" in response to someone's thanks

ya ibn il kalb: lit. "you, son of a dog!"; a phrase used as an insult

kiss ikhtak sharmouta: a vulgar phrase used as an insult

ya: a speech particle used to address a person or get their attention

yallah: come on; let's go

za'atar: dried thyme

zaffeh: wedding procession

AUTHOR'S NOTE

I was in my grandparent's apartment in the Daḥieh when the airport runway was bombed in July of 2006. We subsequently fled to a nearby neighbourhood before finally fleeing to Syria several days later. Many of the events that occur in this book happened in real life. This includes the story of the family car targeted as it fled the south, the bombings, the fact that there's a mass grave under the sports stadium in Beirut, and that one of the oldest synagogues in the country was destroyed by an Israeli bombing in 1982, after which many of the Jewish families fled the area. The synagogue was restored in 2010. That being said, I did take a few creative liberties with some of the descriptions. Specifically, the Burj Al Barajni camp was not directly targeted in 2006, but the nearby neighbourhood of the Daḥieh was carpet-bombed. In fact, since then the Israeli military has named their strategy of carpet-bombing neighbourhoods and using disproportionate force as the Daḥieh Directive.

The characters, the Athar hotel, and Qalimat school are all fictional.

RECOMMENDED RESOURCES

For more information on the history of Lebanon and Palestinians, consult this list of recommended resources:

- Fawwaz Traboulsi (2012). *A History of Modern Lebanon*. Pluto Press
- Khalid Rashidi (2020). *The Hundred Years' War on Palestine*. Macmillan Publishers
- Robert Fisk (1990). *Pity the Nation*. University of Toronto Press
- Ghada Karmi (2015). *Return: A Palestinian Memoir*. Verso Books
- Illan Pape (2006). *The Ethnic Cleansing of Palestine*. Simon and Schuster

ACKNOWLEDGEMENTS

Those who are close to me know that I've been wanting to write a novel for a long time. It wasn't until the start of the pandemic that the idea for this book came to me, out of a desire to be around my extended family and my deep sense of nostalgia for Lebanon, to taste fresh oranges from my aunt's garden overlooking the Mediterranean. That being said, I could not have written this book without the love and support of my family. My parents, who poured all that they could into raising and supporting me. I am always grateful for their love and sacrifices.

Thank you to some of my friends who read very early versions of this novel and spent countless hours discussing it during our writing sessions: Tendisai Cromwell, Abbeir Hussein, and Fatima Andad. Thank you to Aeman Ansari for editing the original manuscript and Danny Ramadan for the mentoring session at the BIPOC Writers Connect Program.

I am also eternally grateful for my editor Fazeela Jiwa and the team at Fernwood for seeing and understanding what this book is meant to be. Like many Palestinians, we have learned to guard our pain and history, but I'm happy to have found a publishing team that crafted the safe space to hold my story and allow me to tell it the way that I wanted to tell it.

Last, but certainly not least, thank you to my love and number one supporter Ibrahim Long for reading the novel, suggesting story ideas, and making sure I get the time and space to do the things that bring me joy and healing.